Rome's Tribune

Clay Warrior Stories
Book #14

J. Clifton Slater

Rome's Tribune is a work of fiction. Any resemblance to persons living or dead is purely coincidental. I am not an historian although, I do extensive research. This book is about the levied, seasonal Legion of the mid-Republic and not the fulltime Imperial Legion. There are huge differences.

The large events in this tale are taken from history, but the dialogue and close action sequences are my inventions. Some of the elements in the story are from reverse engineering mid-Republic era techniques and procedures. No matter how many sources I consult, history always has holes between events. Hopefully, you will see the logic in my methods of filling in the blanks.

The manuscript for **Rome's Tribune** has been assaulted, in a good way, by Hollis Jones multiple times. With each advance, she and her red pen tightened and adjusted the story. Her editing notes are the reason the story makes sense and flows. For her work, and sometimes not so gentle insistence on changes, I am grateful.

If you have comments, please e-mail me.

E-mail: GalacticCouncilRealm@gmail.com

To get the latest information about my books, visit my website. There you can sign up for the newsletter and read blogs about ancient history.

Website: www.JCliftonSlater.com

Thank you for making Alerio's books a success.

Euge! Bravo!

Rome's Tribune

Act 1

Rome's influence in the western Mediterranean stretched to a disputed Sicily in the south, north to Tuscany, and the western shore of the Ionian Sea. There was commerce and armed sorties beyond those boundaries but no conclusive victories. Yet, when the Republic flexed its military muscles, the Qart Hadasht Empire and neighboring nation-states felt the potential of a future conqueror.

A thousand miles to the east, the name of Rome was barely in the consciousness of the Kings, Aristocrats, and Democratic managers of the region. They had their own troubles which kept them out of the west. The eastern Mediterranean and the Aegean Sea had experienced so much upheaval, the power vortexes created opportunities for conflicts. These gave rise to lesser states seeking to protect what little they controlled.

Once mighty dynasties were on the wane but still active. Macedonia struggled to reclaim past glory. Sparta withdrew to Peloponnese. Egypt held authority only because it was the breadbasket of the region. And Athens' vaulted navy and Hoplite corps were weakened from decades of war. None could not control vast areas.

The vacuum required smaller city-states to take up swords and launch navies to guard their territories. Only a few, such as the Isle of Rhodes and the disjointed islands and coastal cities of Cilicia, managed to gain notoriety.

In the previous campaign season, General Barca Hamilcar attacked down the center of Sicily without sufficient forces to conquer the entire island. It was a deception by the Qart Hadasht

1

military leader, and it worked. The Roman Senate failed to respond with force because the legislative body was focused on their new navy.

But the Republic's indecisive response to General Hamilcar ended. They voted former Consul Aquillius Florus as Proconsul for Sicilia and funded a half-Legion to implement Florus' judgements. Then the Senate launched an entire Legion at Barca Hamilcar's southern flank.

Welcome to Summer, 258 B.C.

Chapter 1 – Five Elements of a Shield Wall

The gladius flipped in the air. Remaining at hip level, the blade spun before the hilt slapped into the calloused palm. Then the wrist snapped, and the sword rotated again, almost as if fixed on an axle.

"Tribune," a Centurion inquired, "throw javelins?"

"Hold them," Alerio directed. He flipped the blade again. Whereas some people tossed a coin nervously while waiting, Tribune Sisera flipped his gladius. "Hold."

It was not the situation making him anxious. Although with two thousand Qart Hadasht mercenaries coming over a low hill, he had good reason to be apprehensive. The idea of fighting blade against blade and shield against shield did not bother the Tribune. It was not participating in the violence of the shield wall that ate at his soul.

"Stand by two javelins," he instructed.

"Stand by two javelins," his six Centurions repeated.

The ready-order filtered through the ranks of infantrymen as NCOs, squad leaders, and pivot men echoed the instruction.

"Stand by two javelins," a voice commanded from Alerio's right.

The speaker was Marcus Flamma, Tribune of Second Maniple's right side. Like the path traveled by Alerio's directive, Tribune Flamma's order shot through the other half of the Maniple formation. Then Flamma raised his left arm, stared around the limb, and gazed across the distance at Alerio.

Marcus Flamma appeared to be a model of nobility and an example of a fine staff officer. He was both and no one could argue the statue worthy imagery unless they noticed his hand. It floated beside the red horsehair combed helmet trembling from fright.

Alerio bowed to his counterpart, sheathed his gladius, and reached for the sky with his right hand. With arms held high, the two staff officers from Second Maniple watched and waited.

A mounted Junior Tribune rode up and reined in his horse.

"Tribune Sisera, Senior Tribune Iterum sends his compliments," announced the youthful staff officer. "He would like you to stop holding and throw the cursed javelins. Right now. As in, this very instant."

Alerio jutted his chin forward and studied the horde prancing across the field and the empty hills behind them. Then he glanced over his arm at the young officer.

"Please inform Senior Tribune Iterum that his Second Maniple will throw our javelins when the enemy is within range," Alerio told him. "Please. Return to the headquarters staff and let me concentrate."

The teen nobleman jerked his horse around and trotted for a break in the ranks of Third Maniple. Flamma bobbed his head in Alerio's direction soliciting permission for his half of the Maniple to throw their javelins. Indicating no, Alerio responded with one abrupt shake of his head.

From the other side of Second Maniple, the inexperienced infantrymen and officers of First Maniple had already tossed three flights of javelins. Each man carried three, but the first rank had not thrown. That meant, they had maybe nine hundred of the almost three thousand javelins they brought to the fight. But a battle count was never accurate. Some infantrymen were fond of chucking javelins in excess of those ordered. As a result, used javelins, having caused few casualties, peppered the ground in front of First Maniple. They resembled stalks planted by a drunken farmer.

There were plenty more stored with the Legion supply wagons. Unfortunately, the wagons and the additional javelins were behind Battle Commander Bonum Digessi and his staff.

The main body of the mercenaries halted at the edge of the used javelin garden. Tribune Sisera swore at the First Maniple's mistake of showing the Qart Hadasht soldiers the range of Legion javelins.

"Arrows," Alerio warned.

The notice was passed through the Second and over to the First Maniple. Both raised shields overhead. Down the line, Marcus Flamma eased up until he and the combat officers stood in the shelter of the heavy infantry shields. All the officers of Second Maniple sought sanctuary, except Alerio Carvilius Sisera.

Flights of arrows arched over and dug into the faces of the shields and the soil around the formation. Tribune Flamma and the twelve Centurions peered at Tribune Sisera from under the protection.

By standing in the rain of arrowheads, Alerio was not trying to prove how brave he was, or that he had an excess of courage or a death wish. The most experienced combat officers understood. Tribune Sisera remained in the open to maintain a clear view of the battlefield, the enemy, and the hills. Moments after the arrows began falling, his daring paid off.

***

"Cavalry," Alerio alerted the combat line. To demonstrate his next order, he stacked the flat of his hands up, placing the palm of his right hand on the fingertips of his left. Then he instructed. "Assemble a barrier. Third rank, throw on my command."

The front line of shields remained grounded. But the second row crowded forward and put their shields on top of the front row. Behind the six-foot-high wall, the third rank of Legionaries fell back with javelins in their hands.

Stacked and braced using only the extended arms of Legionaries, the top of the wall was weak. But to a horse, the shields might as well have been the side of a brick building.

Alerio waited until he could hear horses and mercenaries yelling as they jumped out of the way of the charging enemy cavalry.

"Throw two," Alerio shouted while dropping his arm.

Tribune Flamma aped the signal, releasing his section of the Maniple's third rank.

Three hundred javelins almost clipped the top of the Legion shields. As intended, the low trajectory gave the barbed iron tips range. Men cried out and horses screamed. When the second flight of Legion javelins impacted flesh, panic replaced the cavalry assault.

"Unstack them," Alerio directed.

Along the seven-hundred-and-twenty-foot wall of shields, the second rank stepped back, drew their gladii, and braced against the front rank.

"Throw two," Alerio instructed. "Centurions, take command and prepare for contact."

While the staff officers remained back and on vigil, the combat officers directed the fighting and rotations along the shield wall. Keeping alert for changes in the enemy formation, Alerio and Marcus scanned the battlefield.

In the face of chaos, Tribune Marcus Flamma shivered. On his left, Alerio Sisera fought the urge to begin flipping his gladius.

The Qart Hadasht cavalry, after the broken charge, remained behind the attacking mercenary Companies. Always threatening, the mounted soldiers feigned attacks but then wheeled about and retreated to beyond javelin range. Their shallow ventures were not deep enough to elicit a warning from either Alerio or Marcus. Yet, the cavalry movement required monitoring.

Along the combat line, Legionaries stood shoulder-to-shoulder holding their positions but fighting individually or in pairs. The disjointed chops and blocks gave no hint of superior training.

Evenly matched on both sides, attrition would be the deciding factor of the battle, unless acted upon by five elements.

A Legion combat line was susceptible to three types of assaults. One being a specialized unit designed to spearhead a breach. Another was a skilled warrior using brutal techniques to cut up a carousel of Legionaries. And the third, a powerful giant with enough strength to cleave an opposing Legionary to his knees while splitting his shield and possibly his head. And then injuring the next Legionary to step up and fill the gap. Those three elements had the most impact on the Maniple in a stationary combat line.

The fourth element shifted to the Legion's response to the assaults. At every potential breach, the cohesion of the squads allowed them to swarm the attacking force. When a separation occurred, infantrymen did not waver, the second line doubled their effort to neutralize the threat, while the front rank fought to seal the gap. Repeatedly, the enemy opened, and the Legionaries closed breaches.

And yet, the Legion combat line remained stationary and vulnerable. His patience at an end, Alerio decided to employ the fifth element of line combat.

***

"Centurions, stand by," he shouted to his six combat officers.

"What's doing, Tribune?" his most senior Centurion asked.

"They look hungry," Alerio informed the officer. "Let's feed them."

"Steel and wood, sir?" the Centurion inquired with a grin.

"I am fresh out of grain rations and patience," Alerio replied. "On my command."

Heeding the coming warning-order, the Centurions and NCOs rotated the front rank off the line and inserted fresh arms and legs into the fight.

"Ready, sir," the senior Centurion reported when the rotations were completed.

"Stand by," Tribune Sisera shouted.

"Standing by, Tribune," the infantrymen of his six Centuries answered.

After issuing the alert, Alerio aimed a finger at his chest before pointing at Tribune Flamma to indicate 'me first, then you'.

"Centurions, stand by," Marcus Flamma said giving his own warning-order.

As the right side rotated fresh Legionaries to the front, Alerio sent his infantrymen into action.

"Advance, advance," he commanded.

The front line of Tribune Sisera's section of the Maniple repeated the instructions. Then momentarily, they braced and together took in a deep breath. The time for fighting individually had ended.

***

On the forward rank of the Qart Hadasht line, the soldiers sneered. After dodging the javelins, which they found deadly but avoidable, they went blade and shield against Rome's military. Nothing in the fighting showed them the fearful reputation of the Legionaries. Many warriors elbowed their way forward to get a chance to fight the Latians of the Republic.

Individually, the soldiers realized the Legion was composed of fit men. But nothing special, just men with big shields and short blades. Before midday, they expected to pierce the Legion line and make it a proper free-for-all fight.

Then, unexpectedly, the flow of shields smacking together and swords beating on the wooden surfaces ended. For heartbeats, as if the battle had paused to take a breath, resistance stopped. Puzzled, the mercenaries glanced from side to side to see if any of the other warriors were experiencing the same inactivity.

***

"Advance!"

Constant hard training gave Legionaries muscles of coiled steel and explosive power. The big infantry shields went from idle to shooting forward as if shot from a bolt thrower.

Hammered by the Legion scuta, the shields of the soldiers rocked back and violently smacked them in the face. Dazed by their own shields, they were unprepared when the Legionaries stepped forward as if a single monster.

And thus, the fifth thing that made a difference in a shield wall battle was introduced, the Legion attack line.

The Legionaries took one pace into the newly formed gap while stabbing with their short blades. Two hundred and eighty gladii, as if fixed spikes on a rail, stabbed into the Qart Hadasht front rank.

Many warriors fell wounded and, yet, felt lucky to survive the attack.

"Advance!"

Again, the shields powered forward launching anyone upright into the second rank of Empire soldiers. Following the bash, the solid row of shields retreated. They were replaced with two Legion lines stepping forward.

The wounded Qart Hadasht soldiers, thinking themselves lucky, died under stomping hobnailed boots. And then the two hundred and eighty gladii stabbed from behind their shields, seeking more flesh and blood.

***

Bedlam engulfed the front ranks of the Empire forces. No longer did soldiers attempt to shove forward to have a go at the Legion. Now they scrambled, backing away from the united front of big infantry shields.

"Step back, step back!" the Centurions and NCOs ordered.

The Qart Hadasht Captains breathed sighs of relief when the Legion lines withdrew. Only a section of their front was in disarray. Soon they would have the affected Companies sorted and…

"Advance, advance," Tribune Marcus Flamma instructed.

A wave of devastation rolled up another section of the Empire forces. This time, it was courtesy of the right side, Second Maniple, Calatinus Legion South.

Chapter 2 – Follow Orders

Without observing the cavalry, one might assume the advances by the Second Maniple had broken the Empire's attack. But Alerio knew better.

"Tribune Sisera, let me be the first to congratulate you," Marcus Flamma exclaimed as he jogged up to Alerio, "on a masterfully executed counterattack."

"Marcus, I don't think it was us," Alerio informed the excited Tribune. "Their cavalry left the field of battle before we moved on them."

"Did you think they were going to retreat anyway?" Marcus questioned. A little of his enthusiasm faded but not much. "Still, we royally bloodied them."

Both staff officers regarded the hills where the last of the mercenary soldiers were carrying their wounded to the crest. The slow retreat seemed to offer an opportunity to pursue the fleeing enemy forces.

"Do you think Battle Commander Digessi would allow us the privilege of pursuit?" Marcus inquired.

"I hope not," Alerio said surprising the other Tribune.

"Remember. Upon the conduct of each, depends the fate of all," Marcus mumbled.

"Excuse me," Alerio remarked, "I didn't catch that."

"It's from General Alexander the Third of Macedonia," Marcus told Alerio. "He said, remember, upon the conduct of each, depends the fate of all."

"What does a General from ninety-two years ago know about our situation?" Alerio asked.

"I, or rather we, could end this war right now by annihilating General Hamilcar's army," Marcus explained.

He indicated the remnants of the mercenaries still visible on the slope.

"Do you think that mob was 'Elephant Trunk's' army?" Alerio inquired while pointing at the retreating units.

"Well, yes. Intelligence reports that he is spread thin with no reserve Companies," Marcus commented. Then he paused and thought before saying. "I see. You don't believe we just fought the Empire's Sicilia army?"

"Two observations, Tribune Flamma," Alerio offered. "I did not see a General and his staff come over that hill. And I have seen unopposed withdrawals before. Never have I witnessed wounded left trailing behind like bait for wolves."

"You think they wanted us to give chase?" Marcus guessed.

A galloping horse interrupted their conversation. It stopped and the Legion's senior staff officer, Lacrimari, glared down at them.

"You two report to Colonel Digessi, this instant," Lacrimari ordered.

"Are we to be commended, Senior Tribune?" Marcus inquired.

The ground trembled. A moment later, the Legion's cavalry closed in from the flanks. They met in front of Second Maniple and came abreast. Then on a line, the horsemen charged up the hill.

"Useless," Alerio uttered.

The last of the Qart Hadasht forces had topped the rise and vanished down the far side.

"You will be lucky not to be demoted to Centurions after that stunt," Lacrimari informed them. "Get going before the Colonel sends the First Century to collect you."

Lacrimari kneed his horse and moved off in the direction of First Maniple.

"Maybe we should have thrown the javelins earlier," Marcus offered as he walked to his section.

"I don't believe the javelins are the problem," Alerio called after him. Then to his half Maniple, he announced. "You took the fight to the enemy and won. Thank you for the honor of allowing me to serve with Second Maniple."

The six Centuries, including the wounded Legionaries, responded with a boisterous, "Rah!"

Alerio was part way to the gap in the Third Maniple's line when the other half of the Second replied to Tribune Flamma longer speech, "Rah!"

***

"I don't care about the javelins," Battle Commander Digessi thundered at Senior Tribune Iterum. His words and some spittle from the angry Colonel shot across the space between the mounted officers.

"You were right," Marcus whispered as he came up behind Alerio, "it wasn't about the javelins."

He eased to Alerio's side and braced. Together, the Tribunes for Second Maniple waited for the Battle Commander to turn his rage on them.

"Iterum, when I give an order, I expect it to be carried out by my senior staff officers all the way down to my greenest infantrymen," Digessi bellowed. "And if I wanted any of my units to advance, I would have given the order. Your rogue Tribunes tipped the enemy off to our true capabilities and crushed my chance to end the Qart Hadasht army. And to win victory and glory for General Calatinus."

Without realizing it, Alerio rocked his head. The horsehair comb on his helmet magnified the nod of disagreement. Colonel Digessi and Second Maniple's Senior Tribune Iterum caught sight of the contrary motion. Iterum slid off his horse.

"Do you have a problem with the Battle Commander's analysis, Tribune Sisera? Or is it you don't want the Consul/General to win glory?" the Senior Tribune for the Second growled as he stomped across the distance. Once his face was pressed into the opening of Alerio's helmet, Iterum clarified. "Because if you do, maybe you should petition the Consul for your own Maniple command. Or maybe you are holding out for someone to hand you a Legion of your own. Is that what you want?"

"No sir," Alerio responded. "It's just..."

The Senior Tribune pulled back and spun in a circle.

"Everyone, pay attention. After consulting with the Goddess Veritas," Iterum mocked, "Tribune Sisera is about to give us the facts from the Goddess of Truth."

The time to negotiate was always before a duel started. Once blades crossed or concepts collided, only the hostility remained. Even caught up in a mismatch against an unbeatable opponent, Alerio did what had served him for years, he attacked. But first he wanted to know if he would be allowed to fight.

"Permission to speak freely, sir," Alerio requested.

"You seem to have no problem communicating your views silently," Digessi pointed out. "Go ahead, try it with words."

Before Alerio could begin, his boss spoke up.

"You heard the Colonel," Iterum ordered. "Speak up, Tribune Sisera."

The prompt from the Senior Tribune was unnecessary as the Battle Commander had already given permission. Then, it occurred to Alerio. Iterum's blustering was an attempt to deflect the Colonel's anger away from him and transfer it to Alerio.

***

Alerio's proposed argument had an elusive danger running through the heart of the reasoning. The young Junior Tribunes and veteran bodyguards of the First Century presented no issues. And the opinions of Marcus Flamma and the other Tribunes did not carry weight.

In a Legion, there were just seven officers with the power to ruin the career of a staff officer who spoke against authority. And while the protection afforded by his adopted father softened the punishment from most, Alerio still had to be careful of his words. With General Calatinus in Messina, the Battle Commander reigned as the ruling authority. After acknowledging Colonel Digessi, Senior Centurion Sanctoris, the Legion's senior combat officer, Senior Tribune Iterum and the other two Maniple commanders, plus the head of Planning and Strategies, Alerio stepped to the center of the command staff.

"I really have no remarks," he stated to a round of groans. Their outburst intended nothing personal, it had more to do with wanting a good drama than with malice. Alerio allowed the sounds of disappointment to fade before continuing. "I do sir, have questions."

"Ask your questions, Sisera," Digessi directed.

With the Colonel's permission, Alerio felt safer in rattling off his list of defensive queries.

"Did you see a General and a command staff on the far side of the battlefield?" Alerio inquired while indicating the large staff around the Colonel. Then he waved a hand at the

15

Legionaries from First Century. "Or a ring of men sworn to die to protect a General or a Battle Commander?"

Most of the command staff perked up at the hint of theater in the Tribune's presentation.

"Was there a triple line of hardened veterans waiting to engage the enemy standing between the fighting and a General? And why did the cavalry withdraw before your Maniple advanced and decimated the enemy?" he continued working outward from the Battle Commander. "And at the shield wall, did they have two brave and inventive staff officers going above and beyond their duty to save the lives of their Legionaries?"

For a moment, the staff was silent when Alerio stopped. Then one by one, they chuckled, realizing that Tribune Sisera had turned the questions into a defense of his actions.

"I ask you, Battle Commander, was that a battle with an army? Or was it a skirmish with regional units?" Alerio inquired. "And finally, sir, I ask. When do you plan to give a medal to Tribune Marcus Flamma for his courage and intuition?"

Colonel Digessi peered across the battlefield to where the horses of his cavalry picked their way down the slope. Returning, it seemed, from a fruitless pursuit over the hills.

"Your argument has merit," Digessi conceded. "And to answer one of your questions, I will gladly award a medal to Tribune Flamma, when he has done something to earn it."

Having dodged the punishment for not getting permission to engage off the Legion line, Alerio felt cocky.

"Thank you, sir," he beamed up at the Battle Commander. "Is that your final thought on the subject?"

Then in a feat of self-restraint, Alerio resisted the urge to mention that he looked forward to drinking vino at Flamma's fictitious award ceremony. But only because, he could not think of how to phrase it in the form of a question.

***

Late in the evening of the next day, Alerio ducked out of the brightly lit interior of the staff officers' mess. Three dark rows of Legion tents over, he pushed aside another flap and walked into the muted interior of a big tent.

"Tribune. Is it that bad?" a heavily bandaged Legionary inquired.

"You are too mean to die," Alerio said to the wounded infantryman.

"He is more like, too ugly," a patient on the other side of the tent added.

"You are both too feisty to be in the hospital," Alerio teased. "I have latrines that need tending. Maybe in the morning…"

Fake outrage and laughter came from the ten men in the hospital tent. The room stunk of vinegar, blood, and sweat. It was unpleasant and most staff officers avoided the environment.

"You know, sir," an older Legionary admitted. "The first time you came in, we were afraid you would pray for us."

"None of you seem to be candidates for the Goddess Nenia. Your bodies are intact, more, or less," Alerio replied. He peered around with a serious expression. "Although you all seem to embrace the gift from the Goddess Algea."

"Pain is our friend," an infantryman declared while raising up on an elbow.

"How is that?" Alerio questioned.

17

"Algea's pain lets us know we are alive," the young man responded. Then with a moan he dropped back on his pallet.

"And so, it does," Alerio agreed. "Now. Do you need anything? Vinegar, food, or…"

"We could use more vino, sir," another patient said.

"Odd that," Alerio admitted while pulling a wineskin from under his cloak. "I seem to have an extra."

Alerio handed the man the vino and walked down the bedrolls. He stopped and talked with each injured man. The wineskin followed as men took streams of vino before passing it forward. At the last patient, he handed Alerio the wineskin.

"Delicious," Alerio pronounced after taking a drink. "And much too good a vintage for a lot of malingering infantryman."

With a disapproving shake of his head, Alerio dropped the wineskin into the hands of the patient next the exit as he left.

Outside, Alerio inhaled the clean night air.

"You know Tribune Sisera," a voice mentioned from the dark. "Stealing from the Tribune's mess is a punishable offense."

"What do you expect me to do, Senior Centurion?" Alerio commented. "They will not let me into the Centurion's mess. Who else am I supposed to steal from?"

"Command thinks you are a lush, sir," Sanctoris added.

"Maybe I am," Alerio offered.

From the hospital tent, a few rough, moderately drunk voices sang.

"Tullia Major, Tullia Major
Leave the mug be

Open your eyes and see
The vino is tainted
By jealousy."

"Tullia Major, Tullia Major
Beware your spouse
He is an unfaithful louse
Guard your position
from abuse."

"Tullia via your birth order
Your last sip brings death
Your last kiss becomes your last breath
All for naked ambition
All to drive your sister's ascension."

Although a few gasped for air between words, most of
the wounded in the tent joined in the singing.

"Tullia Major, Tullia Major
Rush now and flee
You are your sister's trophy
A way to the crown
She foresees."

"Tullia Major, Tullia Major
Driven by need
Your death by others' greed
Is as gruesome
As the deed."

19

"Tullia via your birth order
Your last sip brings death
Your last kiss becomes your last breath
All for naked ambition
All to drive your sister's ascension."

Sanctoris allowed a knowing smile to light up his face. It was clear the Senior Centurion understood and appreciated Tribune Sisera's attention to the wounded.

"Tullia Minor, Tullia Minor
Evil you embrace
Sitting in your sister's place
Ruled by her husband
In disgrace."

"Tullia Minor, Tullia Minor
What a legacy
Open your eyes and see
The present is tainted
By jealousy."

"Tullia via your birth order
Your last sip brings death
Your last kiss becomes your last breath
All for naked ambition
All to claim your sister's ascension."

"It takes good vino to grease an injured man's throat for song," Sanctoris explained. "Good night, sir."

"Good evening, Senior Centurion," Alerio acknowledged.

As he walked away, Alerio pondered just what the Senior Centurion wanted to speak about. Figuring the Legion's senior combat officer would get around to it eventually, Alerio headed for his quarters.

Chapter 3 – Thermopyl

In the tent he shared with Marcus Flamma, Alerio found his fellow Tribune in his usual position. Sitting at a camp desk with his nose stuck in an old scroll.

"What are you reading tonight?" Alerio questioned.

Marcus lowered the paper and fixed his eyes on Alerio.

"You don't seem to be as inebriated as they suggested," Marcus observed.

"Yet, you are exactly as they described," Alerio retorted. "Brain somewhere else and a piece of literature in your hand."

"Aren't you curious?" Marcus mused.

"I read enough to be educated," Alerio said in his defense. "Just not as deeply as a scholar, or a certain Tribune that I know. I might be interested, unless you have changed to bawdy texts. In that case, I am definitely not interested in what you are reading."

"I meant what people around the camp say about you," Marcus corrected. "The opinions range from holy man to talented tactician and extend all the way to brutal killer or a full on drunk."

"If it pleases you, I am all of those," Alerio replied. "Usually, one at a time but often I combine them."

"See, you don't care what other's think about you," Marcus summed up. "How can you do that?"

"Pray and think?" Alerio asked. "Or fight and drink?"

"No, no. Care about their opinions," Marcus admitted. "I care so much I am afraid to take a chance. I fear disappointing my superiors and letting down my family."

"Wait. You weren't afraid of dying during the battle?" Alerio asked while sliding his chair over.

"Only of failing the Goddess Pietas and dishonoring her gift of duty," Marcus answered. "Of dying, I expect the Goddess Nenia to be swift."

"Sometimes she takes the soul quickly," Alerio confirmed. "Other times, Nenia is painfully slow."

"I am petrified of failing, not death," Marcus assured him. "How can I win medals and glory if I fear taking a chance? Unlike you, or King Leonidas the First of Sparta, I haven't the courage of my convictions."

"King Leonidas?" Alerio inquired. "What are you reading?"

"It's an account of a battle from two hundred and twenty-two years ago," Marcus responded by offering the paper rolls to Alerio. "It happened at Thermopylae a place off the Malian Gulf. That is in the heart of the Greek city states."

"Tell me about it," Alerio requested while waving off the scroll. "But hold on, I want to get a beverage to sip while I enjoy the story."

"You expect me to read it to you?" Marcus asked as his head turned to follow Alerio.

"Read to me," Alerio instructed. "or be bothered by my questions about translating from Greek. I'll leave it up to you."

Alerio poured a dash of vino into a mug than topped it off with a healthy filling of water.

"That is not the drink of a lush," Marcus commented.

"Don't believe everything you hear," Alerio suggested as he leaned back in a chair. "Now tell me about the battle at Thermopylae."

Marcus Flamma rolled to the beginning of the scroll and began to read.

***

I, Erechtheus of Thespiae, declare this account to be as accurate as I can recall. You see it's the headaches and the insistent itching of the scar on my scalp that distracts me. Although the scar is why the scribe paid me for this accounting of how I earned the wound.

Earned you ask? Yes, the mutilation that leaves me confused at times, in pain often, and clawing at my head with my fingernails was surely earned.

Where? At a hot spring near the Gulf of Malian.

Who caused the injury? I don't rightly know. It could have been an Aramean, a Babylonian, a Medes, or one of Xerxes' Immortals. They were everywhere at the…sorry, my mind wanders. Let me get back on track.

At the beginning of September, we marched from Thespiae. On the second day of the trek, we came across a unit from Thebes. My squad and I were ready to fight them, but my file leader and the Phalanx's Sergeant ordered us to stand down.

My file and I knew we could not trust those arrogant, thieving, traitorous Thebans. But when the NCO for the entire Phalanx orders you to standdown, you do. It was one of Commander Demophilus' rules.

Rule one, if you want to fight the invasion, you follow orders. Well, my file wanted to fight, so we kept the shields on our backs, our spears covered, and our swords sheathed. But it didn't stop us from letting the Thebans know our opinion of them for siding with the Persians in the past.

Days later, at a mountain town called Gravia, we met up with fighters from other cities. We camped on one side of the village and the Thebans on the far side. The separation barely helped.

In the next two days, other fighters began arriving. Men and equipment from Arcadias, Tegeans, Mantineans, Orchomenians, and Hoplites from Corinth, Phlius, Mycenae, plus, warriors from Peloponnese and bowmen from Crete. I lost count, but Commander Demophilus told us we numbered over seven thousand. And with each arrival, ancient rivalries flared as men from city states with contentious histories camped close together. I thought we would have a battle right there on the mountain. Somehow, the Commanders kept a lid on the boiling pot.

A few of us asked our officers why we were not marching to the Gulf of Molian. My Lieutenant explained we were waiting for representatives from one more city.

"We have seven thousand heavy infantrymen," a Hoplite pointed out. "Sir, why wait?"

"The Commander of the expedition has yet to arrive," he offered.

"Who is that sir?" another infantryman asked.

"I don't know," our officer answered. "Once he gets here, I expect the various Commanders will spend a few days holding meetings and sorting out the order of march."

With a few days of idle time ahead, I joined a group of archers from Crete for an early morning hunt. I am, or rather, I was good with a bow when my vision didn't blur. Let me tell you, those Cretans were dead accurate with their arrows. And pretty good guys. They let me trade a few winter furs for fresh meat. As I said, they were excellent bowmen.

Around midday, the hunting party and I began the hiked back to Gravia. Then boots scuffing on the trail behind us caused us to turn. And we just about jumped out of our skins. Coming up the trail were Spartans.

Scarlet capes streaming behind them, they moved fast up the steep slope. We didn't hurry when the three hundred Lacedaemons were by us. As my Lieutenant had discussed, once the overall commander arrived, and I had no doubt a Spartan would command our unified force, he would hold meetings. To reinforce the thought, armed Helots and other Spartan slaves followed with supply wagons.

When we arrived at Gravia, rather than settled military camps, we discovered mayhem.

"Pack up. We are marching out," my file leader instructed.

"I thought we had a few days of waiting," I remarked.

"The Spartan Commander stopped on the trail and called for any Commanders in hailing distance," my file leader explained. "Demophilus and a few others walked over to tell the Spartans where they could camp."

"So, where are they?" I asked while shoving my gear into pouches.

"They aren't. The Lacedaemons marched away," the file leader replied. "King Leonidas said he will meet with everyone at Thermopyl."

"The Spartans sent a King?" I questioned before remarking. "This is going to be a serious fight."

"Demophilus' rule number two," the file leader reminded me.

"I know," I acknowledged while tying the flaps on my gear. "Rule two, if you don't want to fight stay home."

***

Marcus Flamma put the scroll on the desk and picked up Alerio's drink.

"Reading is thirsty work," he announced before taking a gulp. Then he complained. "This beverage is as weak as my little sister."

"I never thought about the Greeks doing forced marches like the Legion," Alerio commented. "Or so many of them being heavy infantrymen. I only knew the Spartans are almost as tough as Legionaries. Please, read more."

"So that I can entertain you?" Marcus asked.

"No. It's so I can learn how your mind works," Alerio informed him. "Maybe I can find a way to push you out of your fear of making mistakes."

"Really?" Marcus inquired while picking up the scroll.

"No," Alerio admitted. "It's so you can entertain me."

Marcus Flamma glared at Alerio before turning his eyes to the scroll.

***

The Spartans marched away as if they had no use for us or their own supplies. A few times as we marched through the mountains, I caught glimpses of scarlet on the trail ahead.

26

Then the colors were swallowed by the trees, curves, and distance. It wasn't until we neared the end of our journey that I next saw the Spartans.

The long caravan of soldiers, slaves, and wagons reached the summit overlooking the Gulf of Malian. Blue waters jutted inland to where they touched either low, soft beaches or high, hard cliffs. At the base of the thirty-five-hundred-foot mountain, a narrow strip of empty land weaved along the water's edge.

Did I say empty? Empty of structures but not of three hundred scarlet cloaks. The Lacedaemons were paired off and inspecting every foot of flat land.

My attention was pulled from the view below when the convoy started down the winding path. Bordering the trail, warriors in full armor called to us.

"We have your backs. Give us wine," they proclaimed in drunken revelry. "No enemy will pass behind you while a Phocian warrior remains alive."

As men marched by, they handed wineskins to the Phocian force. It was our way of thanking them for protecting our flank. We knew mountains and the existence of animal trails. But like the Achaemenid army, we did not know the goat herding paths that cut across the face of the mountains. The local Phocians did, and they would stand watch at the trailheads to prevent units from King Xerxes' army from using the shortcuts.

Thermopylae, I spit on the blood-soaked earth and the stinking waters of the hot gates. Oh, sorry, I was overtaken by emotion as I remembered arriving at Thermopyl.

We had no sooner reached the base of the slope when a pair of Spartans stopped Commander Demophilus. The next thing I know, half my Phalanx are digging at the hot gates. By early afternoon, we had trenches spreading sulfur water across the land as neatly as irrigation trenches. By evening, the ground was sloppy mud and the waters of the thermopylae were soaking the soil and draining into the Gulf of Malian. It wasn't until two days later when I realized the reason for creating the treacherous footing.

From north of the bay, riders in ceremonial dress appeared. They rounded the Malian Gulf and rode straight for our swamp. By the time they reached the Phocian Wall, they were covered in mud and not looking so snobbish.

What wall? I apologize. Besides draining the sulfur water from the hot springs, King Leonidas ordered the construction of a battlement. It was rushed and rough but long enough to block most of the pass. Around the end of the Phocian Wall, you could march three columns or drive a chariot through the gap. We cut trees and stacked two walls of logs then filled in between the stacks with dirt and rocks. It was a good barrier.

Where was I? Oh, when Xerxes' honor guard reached the end of the mushy ground, they encountered a Spartan circus.

Fifty naked Lacedaemons were doing handstands, cartwheels, and other general gymnastics. Behind them, fifty more sat in the dirt oiling and combing their hair or trimming their fingernails and toenails. Behind them, another fifty were braiding each other's hair. All one hundred and fifty Spartans ignored the arrival of Xerxes' cavalry.

"Who is in charge?" a Captain of Horse shouted.

None of the Spartans gave him so much as a glance.

"I demand to speak with someone in authority," he said raising his voice.

It carried easily to the wall. I know because I was sitting on the logs with my legs dangling over the side. Behind me and hidden, the other half of the Spartan detachment waited. If the cavalry moved to engage with the circus, they would quickly encounter ready shields and spears.

When enough time had passed to make the Achaemenid Captain squirm out of frustration, King Leonidas strolled from behind the wall. As he crossed the distance, he paused to speak to some of his lounging men further irritating the representative.

"The great King Xerxes offers you friendship," the Captain announced. He was good at hiding his irritation and speaking courteously.

Several Spartans moved to shield Leonidas' sides when the King removed his helmet.

"You and your men will have freedom. All that is required is to embrace the title Friends of the Persian People," the Captain continued. "Take King Xerxes' offer, and he will grant you lands that are far more fertile than what you possess."

I rocked back in surprise and almost fell from the wall. It seemed Xerxes did not want a fight. The terms sounded good, but what did I know of diplomacy?

The naked Lacedaemons stopped tumbling and stepped back. While they moved to the rear, the ones tending their hair and nails marched forward and assumed positions behind their King. Still stepping back, the naked men reached their armor and shields and quickly dressed. In a few heartbeats, the Achaemenid cavalry faced three hundred armed Spartans in a narrow space.

"If you will not accept friendship. Save your life and the lives of your men," the Captain suggested allowing the diplomatic demeanor to slip away. "Lay down your arms."

Leonidas lifted his head gear and slid the bronze helmet down over his ears. Then he raised his spear and pointed the iron tip at the Captain.

"Tell Xerxes," Leonidas challenged, "to come and take them."

The horsemen wheeled sharply about. I believe they would have galloped gallantly away except for the deep slop. The final insult to Xerxes' honor guard was a mud bath courtesy of King Leonidas.

From the north, additional cavalry, columns of marching soldiers, and a multitude of wagons circled the waters of the bay and began setting up bivouacs. By nightfall, the shoreline of Malian Gulf glittered with campfires as if a million stars had fallen from the sky.

***

Alerio slapped his hand down on the desktop.

"Now that Leonidas was a leader," he exclaimed. "He reminds me of Colonel Claudius when he was demanding the surrender of Admiral Hanno."

"When was that?" Marcus inquired.

"About eight years ago," Alerio replied. "When we were taking Messina from the Qart Hadasht Empire."

"You were there at the beginning of hostilities?" Marcus asked. "But you are the same age as me."

"I was a very young Legionary," Alerio responded. "Read, Tribune Flamma. We can't leave the story there."

Marcus adjusted the scroll and smoothed the pages on the wooden rollers. Then, he continued.

Chapter 4 - A King Fallen by a Herder

The Achaemenid Empire sent their Medes archers forward first.

"There are enough of them to darken the sky with their arrows," someone mentioned.

"Friend, you bring us excellent tidings," Dieneces the Spartan observed. "If the Medes darken the sun, we shall have our fight in the shade."

I wasn't keen on being down range of a thousand arrows. But eight of our files had been selected to hold the Spartans' flank. With my spear and long stick, I had marched to a position deep in the Thespian ranks. It placed me next to the Lacedaemons.

"Don't fail me, Thespian," Dieneces warned.

"If you run, Spartan, you can depend on me to protect your back," I responded, "because I'll be standing my ground."

They weren't given to levity, but he rewarded my boast with a gapped tooth grin. Most of the Spartans had missing teeth. It wasn't like the Thebans whose teeth rotted because of their vile souls. The teeth missing from the mouths of the Spartans appeared to be from fighting.

"Medes' arrows are in the air," Commander Demophilus announced. "Get them up."

I leaned my spear against my shoulder and raised my left arm. The fourteen-pound wood and bronze shield covered me and by overlapping with my neighbors, we created a roof. But the awkward angle of our shoulders and the weight made the cover unstable. To help support the shields, we each carried a stick. Shorter than our spears, the rods were just long enough to help support the overhead shields. Comfortable and unharmed, we weathered the storm of arrows.

When the Medes stopped, possibly because their Captains realized they were wasting arrows, a wave of disturbance came from behind our ranks and files.

"Excuse me," voices apologized as they shoved between armored Hoplites.

When they reached my position, I identified them as our Cretan archers. Each carried a basket and harvested the spent arrows that fell into the formation. Outside our Phalanx like structure, other archers happily picked up arrows.

"Can you get them to send over a few more flights?" the Captain of the bowman asked.

"Not without wounding several men," Demophilus told him.

"That's too bad," the Cretan officer offered. He held up an intact arrow. "Some of these are works of art. Beautifully balanced and ready to be returned at the next opportunity."

"Are you ready?" my Commander asked him.

"Yes. Why do you ask?" the Captain inquired.

"Because the Medes are done," Demophilus explained.

I peered between bodies and helmets to see Achaemenid infantry slogging and splashing through Leonidas' swamp. Their full-throated war cries did not match the mud encased movement of their feet. By the time they approached our front ranks, they were still yelling, but they walked while shaking mud from their sandals and legs. It was hardly an imposing charge.

***

My shield might have been heavy and my chest piece and helmet weighty, but they stopped spears and swords. I can't say the same for the wicker armor and shields used by the attacking company. We shredded them as if we were harvesting grain.

Soon bodies and shields stacked up in front of our lines. When the pile reached a good level, it forced the attackers to lean over the bodies to strike at us. The wicker man lasted for two of my file's rotation to the front. On our third cycle to the attack line, we encountered sturdy wooden shields and steel swords.

"Arameans from Damascus," a Spartan named Eurytus reported.

"How can you tell?" I asked between blocking and deflecting sword thrusts.

"The blades of their swords have swirls in the metal," he replied before turning his back on the Arameans he was fighting. Then as he strolled by me, he added. "Patterns in their steel are reminiscent of flowing water."

I had watched Spartans do this all morning. They would lower their swords, turn around, and walk off the line. Seeing an opening, a couple of Arameans would leap the barrier and charge at the Lacedaemon's unguarded back. Although several had suffered injuries, the instances did not stop them from performing the trick. After a couple of paces, the Spartans would suddenly spin around and cut the legs out from under their pursuers.

Eurytus walked back to resume his place on the front ranks. During the deadly prank, his place was held by a neighboring Spartan.

33

"They never learn," Eurytus bragged to me as he braced for another set of attackers.

The day did not go well for the soldiers of the Achaemenid Empire.

When my tour of fighting ended for the day, I watched Corinth and Mycenae Hoplites handle the last skirmishes. Before nightfall, Xerxes' soldiers broke contact. They limped away passing workers coming from the camps. Leonidas allowed them to carry away the wounded and the dead.

While they cleaned up the battlefield, another group filled in the swamp. The dry approach would allow for faster assaults on our lines. This meant the next day would be more challenging than the first day of combat. At the time, I had no idea how demanding and life altering.

***

My file mates and I had a leisurely breakfast. Around our campsites, soldiers from other cities dressed in their armor and moved to the front. Commander Demophilus stopped by and told us we wouldn't be needed until the afternoon. With almost a full day to idle away, I strolled in the direction of the Wall after sharpening my sword.

Unlike the day before, there was a steady flow of wounded and dead returning through the gap. I glanced up to the mountain and said a silent prayer to Aniketos and Alexiares. Hopefully, the twin Gods who guard the gates of Olympus would assist the Phocians in guarding our flank and the mountain passes.

There was little room at the top of the wall. King Leonidas of the Spartans and my Commander, Demophilus, were crowded into one section. They talked and pointed towards the battlefield. Cretan archers occupied the rest of the wall. They weren't talking. Rather the island bowmen were shooting arrow after arrow at the enemy.

"Erechtheus," my Commander called from his high position. In all the activity, I was amazed to be singled out.

"Sir?" I shouted.

"Get back to camp and bring up the Thespians Phalanxes," Demophilus ordered.

I turned about and ran for our camps. A line of Spartans passed me going towards the fighting. Something had changed but I didn't know what.

***

It took a while for our Captains, Lieutenants, and NCOs to collect our men from the other camps. Rather than wait for an entire Phalanx, they sent files forward once ready. My file of sixteen Hoplites was the second to dress and head off.

As we jogged, we weaved around wounded soldiers and stacks of dead from various cities. Whatever was happening beyond the wall was taking a terrible toll on the less trained of our soldiers.

We stopped far enough from the gap to allow porters carrying the injured to get by. But close enough to our other file to react in concert to defend a breach.

"Men of Thespiae, lift your heads high," Demophilus announced from the top of the wall. One of his servants helped strap on the Commander's armor while he addressed us. "Today we fight under the watchful eye of a King."

Our eyes shifted to Leonidas. A Helot helped the Lacedaemon put on his armor. Before the Spartan donned his helmet, he noticed our focus.

"Don't look at me, brave Thespians," the Spartan King declared. "I don't watch. I prefer to fight alongside of you."

35

At the notice that a Spartan King had acknowledged Thespiae as a worthy companion, we cheered. Then groups of blood splattered Spartans came through the gap. From the rounding of their shoulders and shuffling of their feet, we could tell they were exhausted.

"Thespians do not keep the King waiting," Demophilus exclaimed. "El-el-el-el-Eu! El-el-el-el-Eu!"

Picking up the war cry, we roared it as we marched to the wall and through the gap.

"El-el-el-el-Eu! El-el-el-el-Eu!"

***

Just as we did the day before, our files were ordered to abut the Lacedaemon formation to prevent the Achaemenid's from flanking the Spartans. But unlike before, the attackers were not a mixture of tribes with inferior equipment. Those attacking and hacking down our Arcadias, Tegeans, and Mantineans were uniformly armored. And to the horror of the soldiers from our sister cities, they fought as well as a Thespian.

"Pull them out and show the Immortals your iron," Demophilus instructed.

As we shoved into the back of the Greek formation, we saw the problem for the Spartans. Because their flank protection kept collapsing, they were fighting on two fronts.

I reached the forward rank, anchored one end, and paused as my file caught up.

"Take the front," my file leader ordered us.

We used our shields to hook the men in front, and as we pulled them off the defensive line, we slashed and stepped into the forward row.

"Trouble, Spartan?" I asked Eurytus.

36

He looked at me while defending against two Immortals.

"Took you long enough to get here," he reprimanded me before spitting a glob of blood onto the ground between us.

By then, I had come to recognize the comment as high praise from one of Sparta's stoic warriors.

And stoic, plus a fistful of honorable terms, could have described Eurytus the Spartan at that moment. One eye was swollen and leaking a clear fluid. The gash that took his eye flowed red down his face. And what he spit on the ground wasn't blood from a cut in his mouth, but from the bleeding he inhaled while fighting in two directions.

"You might want to take a moment and get that treated," I suggested to Eurytus.

Bashing aside an Immortal's shield, I stabbed under the enemy's armor. The man folded forward and I ran my blade down his neck. Unlike yesterday when their dead piled up, the man was pulled away as soon as he fell. Another took his place.

A scarf over his face and identical armor made it seem as if I was fighting the same man and not a replacement. In that respect, battling Xerxes' Immortals was unnerving.

"Good stabbing combination," Eurytus complimented me. Then he responded to my recommendation. "I'll not leave as long as he is watching."

Eurytus fended off two Immortals with his shield, so his sword was free to indicate an area behind the enemy formation. I followed the direction of his blade, and my eyes beheld a wonder.

A bone white throne on a raised platform of polished wood supported King Xerxes. He was standing and screaming something. I assumed it was his anger at the failure of the Immortals to penetrate our lines.

The throne gave credence to Commander Demophilus' remark about being watched by a King as we fought.

Our second Phalanx shoved us back and took our place in the fight. Another unit of Spartans did the same on our flank. At the gap, I looked back to witness a sea of sameness on the other side of the combat line. The Immortals did seem to be never-ending.

"Don't let them fool you," Eurytus informed me. His arm landed on my shoulder as if he were a brother greeting a sibling. Except, the Spartan sagged against me. Using my shoulder to stay upright, he twisted back and made a crude gesture towards the Immortals. "They bleed and die just like any normal man."

The other Spartans coming off the line swaggered as if not tired at all. And they also added insults and dismissive motions in the directions of the Immortals.

The Spartan's insolence drew raised swords and spears shaken in anger from the Immortals. Following the display, they broke ranks and surged forward. Many died on the fresh blades and rested muscles of the Thespians and the Spartans.

Suddenly, I understood the Lacedaemons use of show. It was more than intimidation. An irritated enemy made emotional and unwise choices.

Then Eurytus collapsed but I caught his armor and held him upright. We strolled around the wall as if nothing were wrong. Far be it from me to spoil the illusion of a Spartan circus.

***

My sword suffered the three harlots of a battle. It was nicked, notched, and dull. As I sat with my rasping tool honing the blade, a Helot wheeled a cart to my side.

"Any man who stands with Eurytus the Spartan in battle," the Spartan slave exclaimed, "deserves as much wine as he can handle. Be careful, Thespian, that you don't drown."

He placed a cask at my elbow and rolled the cart away. We boasted two hundred and fifty-six Hoplites in our Phalanx. After everyone had a couple of mugs, there was little wine left for drowning or carousing. Yet, we all saluted the half blind Spartan's generosity.

***

Imagine my surprise when we rotated back to the fight. I found Eurytus standing to my right.

"I can't see out of my left eye," he informed me. Under his helmet, a bloody bandage covered half his face. "I'm depending on you to guard my flank. Don't fail me, Thespian."

Unaware of my fate, I replied, "As long as the Gods allow me to stand, your left side will be as strong as if you had both eyes and four arms."

"You can't ask the Gods for more than that," he added before we both got busy defending ourselves.

The day passed in flashes of moving up to fight and standing exhausted while chewing bread I could not taste and drinking wine I could not enjoy. Then it was back to the front and the fighting.

I remember the Thespian on my left absorbing a spearhead. He wasn't from my file and that puzzled me. Of course, we had lost a lot of men and the Lieutenants were shuffling Hoplites to maintain our files.

An Immortal came in with a low slash and I checked the blade. But I was slightly off balance when the injured Hoplite tumbled into me. I locked my knees and caught his weight on my shield arm. Rolling away from his mass to keep the shield forward, I stepped back and…

I do not recall anything of the battle beyond that point.

***

Lightning flashed in front of my eyes and my neck protested. Someone was wrenching my head and twisting my neck.

"Hold still," a Lieutenant ordered.

He grunted and jerked while leaning his chest into my face. Then a blinding headache blocked my vision and I screamed. When my vision cleared, he was holding my helmet by a flap of bronze.

"Am I still pretty?" I asked.

My joke was supposed to lighten the mood of the Thespians around me. It did nothing except deepen the frowns on their faces.

"He is addled," the Lieutenant declared.

"It was a joke," I protested. Then the sound of my voice registered with my ears. I thought the words, but they hadn't traveled to my tongue and out of my mouth in any coherent manner.

With one man supporting my head and two more carrying my body on a shield, they took me to a campsite with other injured. I slept and awoken when the campfires were low and mostly cold embers. It was either late at night or just before dawn.

"King Leonidas, the Phocians have fled," a man reported.

I struggled and managed to lift my head and then my chest. Balanced on an elbow, I looked around. We injured had been placed at a fire next to Commander Demophilus' camp.

In the dark, Leonidas and my Commander sat at a dying flame. Neither man had the strength to lift an arm to rebuild the fire.

"What happened?" the Spartan King inquired.

"A goat herder showed ten thousand of Xerxes' soldiers a trail through the mountains," the man answered. "Sir, we should flee before they arrive."

"We are here to give the coalition a chance to gather a proper army," Leonidas proclaimed. "The Spartans will stay to delay Xerxes."

"The Thespians will also," my Commander declared.

"Your Hoplites have done enough, Demophilus," Leonidas remarked.

"The men of Thespiae have held your flank for two days, Spartan," my Commander reminded the King. "We will not abandon you now."

"At lease put your wounded on wagons and get them to safety," Leonidas instructed. "And warn the rest, we stand here at Thermopyl for eternity."

I collapsed to the ground. Then, in the center of a storm raging in my head, I passed into oblivion.

***

When I awoke, I was sitting in the bed of a wagon. Beside me was Eurytus with both eyes bandaged. His head lulled to the side.

"Are you alive, Spartan?" I said slowly testing my ability to speak.

"Thespian? Is that you?" he asked. "I thought you dead from the looks of your smashed helmet."

"How did you see my helmet with both eyes bandaged?" I inquired.

"My Helot described the wreckage of your head gear," Eurytus admitted. "It sounds ugly. How are you?"

"Bad enough that I'll hinder my Phalanx during the final battle," I told him.

"What final battle?" he demanded. "They put me in this wagon last night and I've been asleep since."

"The Phocians fled and left our flanks unguarded," I informed him. "Our positioned is compromised."

Eurytus felt around until he located the tail gate of the wagon. Once there, he crawled over and fell to the ground. Steading himself with his hands, he stood, raised his face to the sky, and shouted for his slave and his armor.

In a matter of moments, the Helot had him dressed for war. Then he guided Eurytus to the gap. The last time I saw the Spartan and my Phalanx mates, they were marching around the wall as my wagon drove away.

You might wonder why I didn't follow the blind Spartan to the battle. In truth, I had such a headache that my legs wouldn't support my weight.

My name is Erechtheus, and I was at Thermopylae with the three hundred Spartans and the seven hundred Thespians. So, swear I, on what life the Gods grant me.

***

Marcus rolled the scroll and tucked it into a pouch.

"Heroes all," he said.

"They all died," Alerio pointed out. "And for only three days delay. If I had been in charge, I would have used a fighting retreat to slow Xerxes down."

"And once you reached wider ground, the end would have been the same," Marcus suggested. "With a static defense, Leonidas was able to deliver more damage."

Alerio fell silent before announcing, "Tribune Flamma. If the opportunity ever presents itself to lead a blocking force, I elect you to be the hero."

"Thank you, Tribune Sisera," Marcus acknowledged. "But glory like that is rare."

"It is," Alerio agreed.

Act 2

Chapter 5 – Boar Hunt

Legionaries hated, then loved, and in the end hated again the building of the nightly marching camp. After a long day of hiking and searching for the enemy, they became construction crews. Then, during the night, they slept knowing the ditches they labored to dig, the stockade walls they constructed, and the spikes they planted in the ground stood between their tents and the enemy. But in the early morning as the sun rose, they were required to dismantle the marching camp.

"Stack those posts carefully," the Optio at the supply wagons directed. "If any get damaged, I'll be sure you are on the detail to cut and trim the replacement logs."

In reverse order of how they came out, the salvageable sections of the Legion marching camp were stowed and readied for another day of traveling.

"What is the order of march?" Marcus Flamma asked.

"We are walking rear security," Iterum answered. "Keep the men sharp."

The Senior Tribune rode away and Alerio Sisera strolled up behind Flamma.

"Dust detail he means. And there is no we," Alerio teased. "He'll be riding with General Calatinus. Not eating trail dust and dodging cow paddies with us."

"I believe as the commander for Second Maniple," Marcus corrected. "the Senior Tribune will be with Colonel Digessi's staff."

"As you wish," Alerio bowed to his fellow staff officer. "But Iterum is a political beast, and his red meat is power. And there is nothing as enticing to his ilk as the ear of a bored Consul/General on a long march."

"You are too cynical, Sisera," Marcus observed. Then he waved at a Centurion. "Keep them moving. We are last out but that doesn't mean we can delay the supply wagons."

"Yes, sir," the combat officer responded.

***

The Veles skirmishers stepped off when the orange ball of the sun touched the horizon. Hourglasses might be at different stages of a turn, but the appearance of the sun let everyone know it was time to go. Resembling a fan, the four Centuries of light infantrymen spread to the sides and front of the line of march.

Shortly after the Velites jogged away, the First Maniple marched forward as if a shaft to the skirmishers' arrowhead. Accompanying them were the contubernium mules with a servant for each eight-man squad. Behind the inexperienced infantrymen, the Battle Commander's staff rode walking horses while surrounded by squads from First Century. Along with Colonel Digessi were Senior Tribune Lacrimari, Senior Centurion Sanctoris, and the Senior Tribunes for the First and Third Maniples, the Veles, and the cavalry. Rushing back and forth along the three quarters length of a marching Legion were a gaggle of Junior Tribunes delivering orders or reporting on the position of each Century.

Six Centuries of the Third Maniple marched behind the Battle Commander's staff. Following the infantry were the General's organization and the Tribunes and Optios of Planning and Strategies. Visitors who came from the Capital to elicit favors from the Consul, staff specialists, and Senior Tribune Lacrimari, all shuffled around the Centurion of First Century and his veteran bodyguards to get close to General Aulus Calatinus.

The remaining six Centuries of veteran Legionaries from the Third followed the General's staff. Behind them came their one hundred and twenty mules.

Cavalrymen assigned to the march walked behind the infantry while the rest of the mounted Legionaries ranged near and far from the sides of the columns.

Controlling the rear were Alerio and Marcus. Between the horses and their droppings, the leavings of the mule, the merda from the extra cavalry mounts, and the manure from the cattle, the center of the marching columns got smelly and sloppy. Only a few Centuries from the Second had to walk directly behind the columns. Thankfully for most of Second Maniple, the Centuries at the very back spread out to guard against a rear ambush.

"Any word?" Alerio inquired while riding across the trail.

"Nothing from the head," Marcus told him. "Let me know when you get tired of your perpendicular route."

"I am fine. You stay there and let me know if any Junior Tribunes bring good news," Alerio replied as he reached the other side of the trail. "Until then, I'll keep in contact with our outlaying Centuries."

"You are still a combat officer at heart," Marcus accused.

"No, I am not," Alerio countered. "Don't let the horse fool you. At my core, I am still an infantryman. But don't tell our Senior Tribune. By the way, where is he?"

"Don't you have a flank to inspect," Marcus said brushing off Alerio's comment.

They both knew Iterum was riding with the General and his staff.

***

A mile and a half ahead of where Marcus and Alerio guarded the rear, the forty-fifth Century patrolled ahead of the Legion. Centurion Farciminis noticed a cluster of his Velites and rode to the squad. The skirmishers seemed interested in something on the ground.

"Are we taking a rest?" Farciminis inquired.

"No sir," the squad leader assured him. "This is the third campfire we've discovered. But the first with discarded bandages."

"Show me," the light infantry officer instructed.

The squad split and men went to stand by tiny dirt mounds. From horseback or even while hiking, the covered campfires would not be obvious. The discovery came from the curiosity of a few Skirmishers who kicked the mounds.

"How many more?" the Centurion questioned.

The squad leader sent three men ahead. One located another mound. With four identified, the Lance Corporal guessed and indicated another direction.

"Try over there," he told two other skirmishers.

Two more mounds, then two more, became apparent once the topcoat of dirt had been kicked away.

"Think this is the bivouac for the mercenaries we tangled with the other day, sir?" the squad leader asked.

"I do," the combat officer told him. Waving his arms, he signaled for two more of his squads to come to him. When they arrived, he sent them off in different tracks. "Spread out. Find me the Qart Hadasht direction of march."

***

Frustration nagged at Battle Commander Bonum Digessi. For a week, the Legion had captured small towns along the southwestern coast of Sicilia. Captured was an exaggeration. None of the garrisons were prepared to stand against his heavy infantry. They surrendered, signed trade agreements, and showered General Calatinus with praise and gifts. None of that pomp and ceremony helped a Colonel win glory and build a reputation.

Shortly after the General left for Messina, they made contact with a large mercenary force. But his orders were to wait in place until General Aulus Calatinus returned. Having missed an opportunity to pursue and reengage the enemy, Digessi's annoyance grew with each passing mile.

Then a messenger arrived from a light infantry officer.

"Sir, compliments from forty-fourth Velites," the skirmisher announced with a grin.

The messenger stood on the balls of his feet, speaking over the shoulders of First Century infantrymen. They refused to allow a stranger to pass through and get close to the Colonel.

"You are a happy fellow," Digessi remarked. "Would you care to share the reason for your festive mood?"

"Sir, the forty-fourth Century has found the trail of the mercenaries," bragged the messenger. "It's to the west. We uncovered their campsites and their route beyond there."

"Senior Tribune of Horse. Get a troop out there," Digessi directed. "If it is truly the Qart Hadasht, then we will march them down and destroy the last vestige of the Empire in southern Sicilia."

Junior Tribunes galloped to the cavalry positioned and returned with ten riders.

"This worthy Veles will guide you to the trail," Digessi informed the cavalrymen. "Confirm the enemy's direction of march and get word back to me."

The skirmisher braced, turned, and loped off to the west. As if a two-legged wolf, he covered ground quickly. Behind him, the horses trotted, heading for what Battle Commander Digessi hoped was an opportunity for him to collect a major victory.

***

Until the sighting, Calatinus Legion South followed the Torrente Grassullo River northward. When the cavalry scouts returned with a positive report, Digessi ordered the Legion to veer away from the river on a westerly heading.

A small caravan might have curved into the new path. But an almost mile long parade of men, animals, and wagons, needed to stick to the hard ground on a single route. As such, the advanced units turned and marched west while the tail continued to travel north until reaching the turning posts.

"It seems we are moving away from the river," Marcus Flamma told Alerio when they reached the posts.

"We are," Alerio acknowledged. "I'll check our left flank to be sure they make the turn."

Centuries could get separated from the main body of a Legion in several ways. They could be ordered to patrol a distant feature and lose sight of the columns. Or be told to take a short cut that took them far from the line of march. Or by getting lost in the terrain during a maneuver or in bad weather.

Tribune Sisera did not want to face the Senior Tribune if they lost a Century because a Centurion failed to order a turn.

A mile and a quarter later, they passed the town of Camemi. Another mile and a half along the trek, the Second Maniple and the wagon trains separated from the main body of the Legion. By design, the scouts marked off a southwestern route for the heavy wagons. Marching Legionaries and riding officers could travel rough terrain. But the wagons required, if not level, then at least smooth and firm ground.

The alternate path took the Second Maniple and the supply wagons to a section with a flatter slope. But descending the long grade at a different location stretched the distance between them and the rest of the Legion even more.

In two and a half miles, the wagon route changed again. This time, the grade was steeper, but it lined the wagons up with a fording area at the Irmimio River.

"Can you see the end of the Legion?" Marcus asked Alerio as the two Tribunes walked their horses into the shallow but swiftly flowing river.

"I lost sight of them at the last turn," Alerio admitted.

"Centurion Blatium," Alerio called to the Maniple's senior combat officer. "Can you see the Legion?"

"No, sir," Blatium replied. "Too much distance and too many trees."

"That's what I thought," Alerio said.

They had nine hundred and sixty heavy infantrymen and twelve combat officers. There was no worry about protecting the supply wagons or catching up with the Legion, eventually. Their worry concerned the set up for the marching camp that night. They had the lumber and the food. Being late would draw the anger of the Legionnaires in the other Maniples.

On the far bank, Alerio and Marcus sat on their horses watching the wagons get pulled by mules and pushed by infantrymen. It was slow going getting each transport across the river.

A rider, coming from the direction of the Legion, trotted up to the staff officers.

"Colonel Digessi said when he looked back," the Junior Tribune reported, "he could not see his wagon train."

"Not surprising," Alerio commented, "I can't see him either."

"And Senior Tribune Lacrimari advises that you kick some cūlī," the young staff officer added while ignoring Alerio's remark. "He said if you can't do it, he would replace the both of you with one Junior Tribune."

The threat shook Marcus Flamma and he fidgeted on his horse, but he remained silent. Alerio peered at the river as another wagon moved into the current.

"Kindly tell the Senior Tribune," Alerio instructed, "that we will arrive before dark."

"Maybe we can divide the wagons and send a few ahead," Marcus suggested.

His desperation to please his Commanders had forced him into an unwise action.

"No, we will not," Alerio disputed his counterpart. "Dividing our infantrymen to escort a few wagons is a dangerous tactic."

"Please tell Senior Tribune Lacrimari that we will arrive before dark," Marcus told the young staff officer.

Alerio nodded his approval at their unified decision. Given the answer for the Legion's Senior Tribune, the junior staff officer headed north, riding back to the Legion.

"On this ground, we can make up the distance," Marcus offered. He studied the hills on either side of the river valley and the flat land beside the river. "Once all the wagons are across, we'll push the drivers."

While Marcus focused on the movement of the wagons to please the Colonel and the Senior Tribune, Alerio studied the landscape.

"This place is ugly," Alerio remarked.

"How can you say that?" Marcus questioned. "Look at the green grass, the flowing water, and the trees on the slopes. It is as pretty as a mural."

"Visually, yes," he agreed. "But defensively it is a death trap."

"We have a good view to the north and south," Marcus pointed out.

"But the sides are high and across the river, they get steeper the farther upriver you go," Alerio described. "Put a Century up there, and you might as well have abandoned them."

"I assumed it was us chasing the enemy," Marcus said. "And not the other way around."

"At some point during a pig hunt, a boar will turn," Alerio suggested, "and if you aren't prepared, the beast will gouge you."

"Do you think the Qart Hadasht will come back?" Marcus asked.

"We have the supply wagons," Alerio replied. "An enemy could feed, partially equip, and shelter an army with what we have in those transports."

They had five wagons stacked on their side of the river. And more on the other side, plus two fording across.

"I'm going to move the transports up to make room for those coming over," Marcus told him. "And I am shifting Centuries to provide better security."

"Excellent choices, Tribune Flamma," Alerio praised him. "I guess that leaves me handling the other side."

"If I remember correctly, the water isn't that cold," Marcus teased as he looked at the position of the sun. "They say a noonday dip is good for you."

"Who says that?" Alerio asked as he kneed his horse.

"Most likely someone who didn't have to ride with wet gear," Marcus responded.

Alerio ignored him as his horse picked its way down to the river.

***

As the Second Maniple struggled to bring wagons across the Irmimio River, six miles north the Legion's light infantrymen recrossed the same river. They followed the foot and hoof prints of the fleeing Qart Hadasht forces. The tracks channeled the Legion into a valley with high walls.

"I want to protest our route, Colonel," Senior Centurion Sanctoris advised. He scanned the steep sides and the bend in the river that blocked his view of anything upstream. "This is a place better served by patrols rather than a marching formation."

"Lacrimari, what's your opinion?" Digessi questioned.

"I agree with your primary combat officer," the Legion's Senior Tribune replied.

"But we haven't seen any signs of passage other than the ones we're following," the Battle Commander noted. "Besides, intelligence tells me General Hamilcar is stretched thin. Most of his army is north at Palermo."

"There is one problem, sir," the Senior Centurion pointed out. "We are following maybe fifteen hundred soldiers."

"Yes, the Velites confirm that estimate. Why do you mention it?" Digessi asked.

"In our wake are latrine pits, discarded straps, and assorted gear," Sanctoris explained. "Plus, the hills have scuff marks from our scouts climbing and descending the slopes."

"Yes, and what's your point?" the Colonel inquired.

"Ahead of us the hills are pristine," the Legion's Senior Centurion noted. "I haven't seen so much as a fresh goat track."

"Come to think of it," Senior Tribune Lacrimari began. "I haven't…"

The spear came from a high angle. Falling from such a great height, the spearhead split the Senior Tribune's shoulder armor, crushed his collarbone, and pierced his heart before lodging in his hip bone. Man, and spear shaft, toppled from the horse before anyone understood the ramifications.

In fact, the boar had turned on the hunters.

Chapter 6 – Hot Combat

Consul/General Aulus Calatinus cursed and swore ruination on the infantrymen who snatched him from his horse. Not until he settled under a cocoon of shields did, he realize the danger, and the reason for the rough treatment. Arrows rapped on the heavy plywood shields, but none reached the General. His life had been saved by the quick actions of the Legionaries from the First Century.

At the same time but in a different location in the line of march, Colonel Bonum Digessi kicked away his First Century bodyguards. While he appreciated their dedication to protecting him, he could not fight his Legion by hiding beneath their shields.

"First and Third get to your Centuries and ascertain our position. Then report back to me with the best escape route," Digessi instructed his Maniple commanders. When he searched the worried faces of his staff, he could not find Senior Tribune Iterum. "Good. At least Second Maniple and my baggage train have a levelheaded senior commander in charge."

In a nod to the danger of his high visibility, Digessi slipped off his horse. He allowed just two infantrymen to flank him with their shields as he moved around.

"I need information from our rear and from our front," Colonel Digessi informed his Junior Tribunes. He followed their eyes to Senior Tribune Lacrimari's body. Although the Senior Tribune had fallen from his horse and should be sprawled on the ground, the spear shaft kept Lacrimari's body as straight as a hanging scarecrow. The Battle Commander knew the youths needed reassurance. "I appreciate that you are afraid. But if we are to survive this, it is up to my youngest noblemen. Two of you get to the rear and report on the status of our cavalry. Four of you move forward and let me know the situation with my skirmishers. I can't see around the river's bend. You will need to be my eyes."

The teens dashed off in their assigned directions. While they raced away, the Battle Commander peered up at the heights to the west.

Warriors with spears, arrows, and slings were taking their time aiming before sending down missiles. After the initial volley, the mercenaries were conserving shafts and rocks by picking their targets. Although dangerous and deadly, the bowman, spearmen, and slingers were not his biggest worry. That honor was reserved for the ranks of soldiers appearing on the gentler slope to his east.

"My intelligence was decidedly faulty," the Colonel mumbled at the sight of over a thousand mercenaries. Then he kicked the ground with his boot and offered to no one in particular. "It appears, General Barca Hamilcar's army is not at Palermo."

Adding to his impotence, the riverbank along this stretch of the Irmimio sprouted reeds which signified wet muddy ground. It meant bad footing for his infantry and what cavalry remained in the column.

The Battle Commander was frustrated because he couldn't see around the bend to judge the condition of his light infantry and the strength of the enemy. The only thing worse would be losing his view of this part of the battlefield. Just as Digessi thought it, veteran infantrymen filed in behind him.

Their raised shields facing west protected against the iron heads and rocks launched from the cliff top. But their position left their backs open to missiles launched from the mercenary infantry.

To complete the Colonel's worst-case scenario, the other sections of the Third Maniple shuffled into position to his east. They only had room for a double rank of Legionaries before the start of the slope.

At first, Digessi had a view of the battlefield. But both rows of infantrymen had their backs exposed to the crossfire of enemy incoming. Realizing the danger, the Centurions called out orders and the ranks of infantrymen stepped back closing the space.

Battle Commander Digessi found himself in a tunnel created by shields bringing the nightmare formation he feared into reality. Now he was blind to all the movements of his enemy.

***

Centurion Farciminis of Velites forty-five watched two men of his forward squad disappear below the surface of the river. Not sure if they slipped in the current or if they were cooling off, he followed their shapes downriver. Only when the bodies broke the surface in the turbulence at the bend did he see the arrows.

"Fall back," he ordered. "Optio, find us a defensive position."

Unlike their brothers in the heavy infantry with the big shields, the skirmishers carried medium sized ones. Defense for light infantrymen depended on them working in unison to block arrows and rocks. Spears, however, presented a unique problem.

Farciminis' Tesserarius tossed up his left arm, but the spearhead ripped through the wood and into the Corporal's skull. The Century splashed back across as the river as the flow took their NCO's body downstream.

The gap was a choke point where the river doubled back on itself. On either side of the narrow opening, the walls rose fifty to sixty feet above the riverbanks. Thanks to erosion, the east side offered shelter from above even though it was in range of the opposite bank.

"Interlock shields," the Optio instructed.

With a wall of wood taking the brunt of the enemy missiles, the forty-fifth Century of skirmishers moved along the cliff face and under the overhang. Once set, they provided an anchor at the rear of the Legion's advance units. The other three Centuries began running back to them. Their motivation was more than the assault of shafts and rocks from above. Ahead of them, ranks of Empire heavy infantry marched from upstream.

To the surprise of the forty-fifth's officer, a Junior Tribune sprinted around the bend and dove into the protection of the shields.

"Colonel Digessi wants to know your status, Centurion," the young staff officer said while standing and brushing dirt off his blood splattered armor. His cheeks were flushed, and beads of sweat dotted his forehead.

"Thirsty?" the light infantry officer inquired while offering the teen a wineskin. The boy's hands shook as he reached out. "Take your time, Tribune. We won't know our status until the rest of the Centuries get here."

Later, Colonel Digessi would learn his skirmishers were being cut to pieces by the heavy infantry of the Empire.

Adding to his misery, the price of the information were the lives of three of his Junior Tribunes.

***

The inexperienced First Maniple was slower to move. But they ultimately picked up on the Third's maneuvering and dressed in their armor while getting into position. By the time they formed the back-to-back formation, the interior of their shield tunnel had bodies stacked end to end. One Centurion suggested to his Tribune that he take a Century up to support the skirmishers. Before he could get a reply, the Empire infantry came screaming off the slope.

When the Qart Hadasht mercenaries smashed into the Legion, General Hamilcar accomplished two things. He locked the Legionaries into the long formation on the thin strip of land by the river. And he prevented Colonel Digessi from shifting Centuries to support weakened units or even to begin withdrawing his Legion. In the Irmimio River valley of southern Sicilia, attrition meant certain annihilation for the forces of the Republic.

***

The two Junior Tribunes assigned to investigate the state of the cavalry realized early that riding drew missiles. They leaped from their mounts, released the reins, and traveled on foot. Spurred on by the objects falling from the sky, the frightened beasts raced to the southeast. Instead of running directly south on the flat ground, the mounts headed up the slope and skirted a hill. Rushing to complete their task, the teenage staff officers missed the significance of the route.

After weaving between infantrymen, the Junior Tribunes reached the end of the columns, and gasped. The cavalry was gone. Providing a possible reason for the horsemen's flight, a line of Empire soldiers marched towards the Legion from the south.

In their haste to report their findings, the young noblemen missed the bodies lying two hundred feet away and half submerged in the river. If the Junior Tribunes had looked carefully or bothered to question the infantrymen, they would have been directed to the two dead cavalrymen and their mounts facing, not away from the Legion, but towards it.

***

"Riders coming," Marcus Flamma shouted to Alerio.

In case his voice didn't travel across the water, he wiggled his fingers, made traveling motions, and indicated upriver.

"You saw a spider," Alerio called back, "and you are scared."

Marcus waved off his fellow Tribune and waited for the rider. As the horse drew closer, he realized there was more than one.

When Alerio realized a multitude of horses were coming, he nudged his mount down the embankment and started to cross the river. The leading riders reached Marcus while Alerio was mid-stream. By the time his mount climbed the far embankment, there were two hundred Legion cavalrymen reining in their horses.

"Report," Marcus instructed.

"Sir, the Legion is trapped in the river valley," an Optio of Horse described.

"What are you doing here?" Marcus questioned.

"There is no room for us to maneuver, sir," the NCO told him. "We can't ride effectively in the tight space. And with our light armor, we can't fight our way to the Legion."

"What are we supposed to do with you?" Marcus asked.

"Sir, we just thought you could take the Second forward," the Sergeant said. "We'll guard the wagons."

Marcus glanced at the supply transports. Most were on the east bank with only three more on the opposite shore. His last order was to protect the supplies. Yet, he wanted to help the Legion. But if he got his Maniple killed in the process, he wouldn't be doing anyone any good. Yet…

"Help the other wagons across," Alerio ordered the cavalrymen. Then to Flamma, he instructed. "Marcus get our Centuries armored up and headed north."

"And where will you be?" Marcus inquired.

"I have to change," Alerio told him.

"Change how?" Marcus questioned.

"Not how," Alerio corrected. "I'm changing into my armor."

"But you are wearing armor," Marcus pointed out.

"This situation is going to be ugly," Alerio said. "Pretty Tribune' ceremonial armor will not survive the fighting, but I plan to."

As only those on security duty wore their armor during the march, it required a delay for the rest of Second Maniple to strap on their gear. Only then did the heavy infantrymen jog off to the north.

Marcus Flamma and the nine hundred and sixty Legionaries moved quickly upriver towards the fighting. As they departed, Alerio Sisera shouted at one teamster while sorting through the cargo of another transport.

61

Marcus rode at the front of the columns with doubt eating at his heart. If the Qart Hadasht forces had managed to trap over three quarters of a Legion, how could he and the remaining third hope to make a difference. Just before he ordered the columns to turn around, Alerio Sisera thundered up beside him.

"Here is your glory, Tribune Flamma," Alerio exclaimed. "Whoever thought we would have the opportunity to save a Legion?"

"Or die trying," Marcus responded.

"That too," Alerio assured him.

The fatalism in the remarked caused Marcus to glance over at Alerio. Rather than the silver embossed and polished armor of a staff officer, Tribune Sisera wore armor with buffed out scratches and pounded out dents. Heavy and well used, the gear would be more appropriate on an infantryman than on a staff officer.

"You weren't kidding," Marcus stated.

"About glory or dying?" Alerio questioned.

"No. About you being more comfortable as an infantryman, than as an officer," Marcus submitted.

"I am attempting to get more comfortable with command," Alerio reported. "But this is not the time to stand back and lord it over the infantry."

"Is that what you think of me?" Marcus questioned. "That I hide behind my social status and rank?"

"Whatever I thought of you before today has little value," Alerio informed him. "It is what you do this afternoon that will form my opinion. Not that it matters?"

"Why doesn't it matter?" Marcus asked.

Alerio pulled on the reins slowing his mount. Marcus did as well and in several steps, their horses came to a stop.

In front of them a canyon formed as the land followed the river upstream. They could see a section of three ranks of Legionaries before a bend blocked their view of the rest of the Legion. Two ranks faced a hoard attacking from the east. Another rank stood behind them facing west and catching arrows, rocks, and spears with their shields.

"If we move up too much," Marcus observed, "we will be in range of the missiles."

"And if we stay here, the Qart Hadasht will come for us after they murder the Legion," Alerio declared. "I am open to suggestions, Tribune Flamma."

Marcus studied the high cliff before allowing his eyes to sweep back across the river. The most prominent feature of the eastern slope, besides the throng of mercenary warriors battling the Legionaries, was a mound at the top. Behind the hill, two shaking cavalry horses stood as if abandoned by their riders.

"That pair of mounts, whose horses, are they?" Marcus asked. "And why are they just standing there?"

Alerio shifted his eyes from the end of the struggling Legion to the horses on the hill.

"That, Tribune Flamma, is a blind spot," Alerio professed after scrutinizing the area. "The mound blocks the location from the Empire's command staff. A Century could come around it unseen and peel off the attackers from the end of the Legion line."

Marcus wiggled his fingers as if counting before voicing his confirmation.

"With the end cleared of warriors, the Centuries could begin fighting their way to our Maniple," Marcus said expanding on Alerio's idea. "But the infantry will be fighting back-to-back, defending against the arrows. Stretched out and bogged down, the Legion will be lucky to make it a hundred feet."

"Not if I take Centuries to the top of the cliff and remove the archers, spearmen, and slingers," Alerio offered.

"You said it before," Marcus reminded Alerio, "any unit across the river and on the clifftop will be forsaken. They might as well be written off the Legion roster before they set out on the mission."

"Even more reason that I should lead the force," Alerio offered.

"No, Tribune Sisera, I will lead the assault on the high ground," Marcus insisted. "I'll take three hundred infantrymen with me."

"Just three hundred?" Alerio asked. "Who are you, King Leonidas?"

"If you take a Century to circle the mound and attack their rear," Marcus explained. "And I take three hundred across the river, that will leave enough for Second Maniple to form a triple rank shield wall between the river and the top of the slope."

"You do remember, Tribune Flamma, Leonidas and his three hundred died," Alerio mentioned. Then from the saddle, he bowed to the other staff officer. "My apologies."

"For what?" Marcus asked.

"Because you do more then stand behind the infantry," Alerio admitted. "You study the true art of war."

"I am not a warrior," Marcus protested.

"You are something more. You are a Tribune of Rome. Obviously, you know strategy and troop placement," Alerio acknowledged. "If I ever want to emulate a staff officer, I will choose you as a role model."

"I believe you are reading too much into my description," Marcus complained.

Alerio turned to the columns as they arrived.

"Centurion Blatium. Give me a Century that is not afraid of wetting their gladii," Alerio shouted to the Maniple's most senior combat officer. "And find Tribune Flamma three hundred Legionaries who carry no fear of journeying to the Elysium Fields."

"Is it that bad, sirs?" the Centurion inquired.

Marcus pointed to the clifftop and to the end of the legion line. The infantrymen were mostly buried under attacking Empire mercenaries.

"You are holding Second Maniple here and creating a hard point for the retreating Legion," Marcus instructed.

A wagon with a cursing and agitated teamster wheeled to a stop.

"Where do you want me?" he demanded.

The Centurion and Marcus stared at the driver in confusion. But Alerio confidently turned his horse and greeted the supply wagon.

"Take the load of javelins to the center of our lines and uncrate them," Alerio directed. Then to the senior combat officer, he explained. "Centurion Blatium, do not be stingy with the javelins."

"Excellent, sir," Blatium said. "But where will you and Tribune Flamma be?"

"I am taking a Century around that mound and freeing the end of the Legion," Alerio replied. His arm indicated the top of the eastern slope. Then he slowly swung the arm, as if he feared to complete the arc, and pointed at the clifftop. "And Tribune Flamma will be leading three hundred Legionaries into hot combat, up there."

Chapter 7 – From Their Peril

Three ranks of Legionaries formed a solid wall stretching from the swampy edge of the river to the top of the slope. Although out of arrow range from the clifftop, the barrier of Second Maniple represented a challenge to Qart Hadasht command. In response, General Hamilcar shifted soldiers from around the bend and sent them downstream to face the new threat. The repositioning of mercenaries created a reduction in the pressure felt by the Legionaries of the First Maniple.

Just behind the three ranks of the Second, Alerio Sisera and his eighty infantrymen stood waiting. On Alerio's order, they would charge up the slope, move behind the mound and around the newly arriving soldiers, drop down the slope, and attack the mercenaries assaulting the squads at the end of the Legion. But first, Marcus and his three hundred needed to clear the archers, spearmen, and slingers from the clifftop.

Marcus Flamma jumped onto the bed of the wagon hauling the javelins. As soon as the arriving mercenaries saw an elevated Legion officer, they shot arrows in his direction. A few Legionaries moved as if to climb onto the wagon and protect the Tribune. Marcus waved them away. Then ignoring the arrows, he braced, saluted, and addressed his volunteers.

"Let us," Marcus exclaimed, "die, my men. And by our deaths, rescue our blockaded Legionaries from their peril."

Three hundred men replied, "Rah!"

None it seemed were frightened by the journey to Hades. They would follow Marcus Flamma to the Fields of Elysium and back.

He leaped from the wagon and jogged southward. His infantrymen, startled by the suddenness of the staff officer's move, raced to catch up with their Tribune.

***

There were three ways to assault a clifftop. Sling hooks and climb ropes directly into the jaws of the enemy. Or locate the natural foot of the slope and hike the entire unit down to it then march back to the heights on the rising ground. Both allowed for a mass of attackers to gather and wait for the Legionaries. The third method wasn't as fast as scaling ropes or as sure as hiking. It fell somewhere in between. It was fast but would leave the three hundred Legionaries vulnerable to being repelled.

"Centurion Philetus. Give me six good climbers," Marcus said to his most experienced line officer.

The combat officer walked away and strolled between the Legionaries. He signaled out six as he moved. Then he pulled an NCO out of the ranks and shoved him towards Marcus.

"You six look lean, like climbers," Marcus greeted the infantrymen. He focused on the seventh man. "But you don't."

"Sir, I am Optio Feri," the NCO reported. "I am your shield."

"Is there a problem, sir?" Philetus asked. "If Feri is less than satisfactory, I can assign another bodyguard."

"No, Centurion. I am sure the Optio is up to the job. Let's hope he is up to the climb," Marcus reflected. Then he peered into the faces of his climbers. "You are my spearhead, and I am your locking pin to the Centuries. Together, we will pierce the enemy's defense."

"Where do we climb, sir?" one of the six inquired.

He glanced around at the cliff and the fighting upstream.

"There is a wash about a hundred feet from here," Marcus explained. "I didn't want us loitering around the base of the flume."

"How do you know the wash Tribune?" Centurion Iacōbus, his second combat officer, inquired.

"I remember it from the ride up," Marcus told him. The combat officers knew Flamma as a studious staff officer who read a lot. They hadn't realized when not engaged with the written word, he was an astute observer of his surroundings. "The bottom section will require a boost and at the top are Qart Hadasht warriors. We are going to kill them and gain the clifftop. Draw your gladii."

Without waiting for more questions, Marcus Flamma sprinted directly southward. Feri was right on his heels with the six climbers not far behind him. At one hundred feet, Marcus turned sharply to his right and ran to the base of a dry gulch. Flexing his knees, he bent and offered his shoulders to the first climber. Seeing the Tribune's position, Optio Feri mimicked the staff officer.

When the six climbers were up and ascending the gully, the Optio spun, grabbed two Legionaries, and positioned them as new steps.

"Sir," the bodyguard called. "Follow me."

The offer was bold and presumptuous. Most staff officers would wait to see if the Legionaries had secured the top before joining the climb. But from Tribune's Flamma words and his actions, the NCO felt that Flamma wanted to be part of the attack.

"Go," Marcus responded.

Feri placed a foot on a shoulder of an infantryman and jumped. Where the climbers had landed on their feet, the Optio landed on his knees. With his shield on one arm and his gladius in the other hand, the big NCO scurried up the chasm. Behind him, Marcus landed a little better as only one of the staff officer's knees hit the rocks and dirt.

Near the top, the gully flattened and fanned out where it met level ground. Rising to his feet, the NCO rushed upward. His head came level with the land, and he caught a glimpse of two climbers collapsed and a third being forced back to the ravine. Bellowing his rage, the Legion NCO adjusted his angle, came fully out of the gulch, raced by the third climber, and smashed into the mercenaries.

With great slashes of his gladius and powerful swipes of his shield, Feri fought alone against twenty soldiers of the Empire. Then the third climber's shield snapped in next to the Sergeants. Another climber added his shield and when the fourth shield joined them, the mercenary's forward momentum stopped. For the moment, the mouth of the gully remained unguarded.

A voice, calling out a warning order, surprised the five-man Legion line. What were they expected to accomplish against four times their number?

"Stand by for advance, advance," Marcus Flamma notified them.

"Standing by Tribune," they shouted despite their reservations.

"Advance, Advance," Marcus instructed.

Feri and the four remaining climbers braced, hammered their shields forward, withdrew them, and stabbed. Five against twenty did not produce a lot of movement or injuries. The actions backed the soldiers up a half step but did no real damage.

Tribune Flamma had called for two advances. The NCO and the climbers expected the same results or to be enveloped by the enemy. Yet, following orders and accepting their fate, the five shields shot forward and met resistance. Then, the resistance vanished.

From either side of the thin shields wall, heavy infantrymen of the Legion plowed into the mercenary formation. At the stabbing phase of the advance, Feri and his climbers found flesh with their blades but no second line of soldiers. The next wave of Legionaries had arrived from the ravine.

"This is the Legion," Centurion Iacōbus shouted. "Finish killing the Qart Hadasht scum and get into formation."

Resembling ants, the heavy infantrymen emerged from the gully and spread out into an attack line. Feri fell back to find Marcus standing dangerously close to the ranks.

"Tribune," Feri greeted the staff officer.

"Optio," Marcus replied. "Nice work."

"Thank you, sir," Feri said to the calm staff officer.

"Centurion Iacōbus. I see slingers, bowmen, and spearmen on my cliff," Marcus observed in a loud voice.

"Yes, Tribune," Iacōbus responded. "Orders?"

"Non capimus!" Marcus replied.

At hearing the order for 'no prisoners', the Legionaries who had come up, responded, "Rah!"

"You heard Tribune Flamma," Iacōbus announced. "Forward."

***

Far upstream and down in the valley, Centurion Farciminis and what was left of the original Legion skirmishers fought against Empire heavy infantry. Out armored, the Velites battled under the overhang. Trapped between the infantry coming from the north and the Qart Hadasht forces swarming the First Maniple to the south, the skirmishers perished.

Around the bend, some of the First Maniple noticed the Irmimio River running red.

"It's the blood of our light infantrymen," an Optio remarked. "Poor souls. They didn't have a chance."

"As if we do," a young infantryman remarked.

"Let me assure you, Legionary," the NCO boasted. "As long as one infantryman has a gladius in his hand, we have a fighting chance."

"Optio. Does the river look clearer to you?" another Legionary asked.

Glancing at the flowing water, the NCO didn't see a change. But as he watched, the red indeed seemed to dissipate, if only a little.

A roar came from the squads at the end of his Century.

"What is it?" he asked while shoving his way towards the sound.

"Skirmishers are coming from around the bend," a Tesserarius reported.

"Theirs or ours?" the Sergeant demanded.

"They are Legion Velites, Optio," the Corporal responded. "Orders?"

"Tenth squad, advance and step forward nine paces," the NCO instructed. "Let's bring our light infantry home."

***

General Barca Hamilcar had planned the ambush down to which of his units would capture Consul Calatinus. The Iberian heavy infantrymen should have swept down the river, removed the Legion skirmishers, and continued around the next bend to destroy the Legionaries defending their General.

Instead of a swift assault, the Iberians were hampered by the narrowing of the river valley. And, they had gotten into a fight with light infantrymen who refused to give up. Rather than retreat, the accursed men of the Republic held their ground even as his infantry cut them to pieces.

In a way, General Hamilcar was now grateful for the stubbornness of the skirmishers. Somehow, the Legion had scaled the cliff and brought infantrymen to attack his archers and slingers.

"Pull the Iberians out of the valley," Hamilcar instructed one of his Captains. "Send them up to clear the Republic forces from the top of the cliff."

***

The mercenaries above the trapped Legion consisted of light infantry and specialists. On open ground, they had no chance against the heavy infantry of the Legion.

Wagons, filled with spears, sling rocks, and arrows were shoved in the way. To maintain the formation, Legionaries simply climbed up and over the obstacles. Dropping to the ground on the far side, they slew the Empire defenders before rushing to retake their place in the moving assault line. Even using those shortcuts, the rain of death on the Legion below the cliff continued.

"Not fast enough," Marcus advised the Centurion. "We need to clear the skies and let the Legion move."

"The only way to increase our pace is to break formation," Iacōbus told the staff officer.

"Send half of our detachment in a sweep around the wagons and have them come in from the far side," Marcus instructed. "We'll use a pincer movement and double our efficiency."

"I'll take the far side," Centurion Philetus offered.

Shortly after the staff meeting, one hundred and fifty Legionaries separated from the assault line. In a fast-moving file, they jogged away from the cliff's edge and took a parallel course to the opposite end of the geographical feature.

The Empire forces had attempted to run or so it seemed. But once they had gathered a force of two hundred and fifty and outnumbered the Legionaries, they counter attacked.

Their light infantry shouldn't have been effective. However, the skirmishers received help from arrows coming in on flat trajectories, rocks streaking over the top edge of the shields, and spears dropping from the sky. In the mismatch of close quarter's fighting, the Empire specialists aided in slowing the advance of Marcus and his element.

Optio Feri danced around Marcus Flamma using the shield to protect the Tribune.

"This isn't working," Marcus complained.

"Sir, you are whittling them down from two directions," Feri responded. "Beside a melee assault, there's not much you can do."

"Explain melee and why would that be preferable to a solid formation?" Marcus demanded.

"It is like-against-like, sir," the Optio said trying to sort his thoughts while leaping in front of the Tribune to block an arrow. "We present a formation, and they collect enough bodies to clog our route and slow us down."

Marcus squatted, grabbed Feri's armored skirt, and pulled the NCO down to his level. With both men stacked behind the infantry shield they were somewhat protected.

"Defend your reasoning," Marcus requested.

A horrified look appeared on Feri's face and under the helmet, the Optio's face blushed.

"Tribune. Sir, no offense was intended," Feri pleaded. "I would never question your thinking."

It took a heartbeat before the staff officer realized an NCO might not understand the language of a philosophic discussion. To the Sergeant, defending yourself, meant to voice a defense against an accusation.

"Tell me your reasons for suggesting a melee?" Marcus inquired slowly to take any edge off his voice.

"Well, sir, we are Legionaries and one on one, our guys can smash any three of theirs," Feri bragged. "Pair us up and we can run through them like merda through a sick goat."

"All of my training tells me to hold the formation," Marcus admitted. "But your experience has solid logic behind it."

"I don't know about logic, sir. But we train two-on-two drills several times a week," Feri told him.

"Two-on-two drills," Marcus repeated as he stood. "Tribune Sisera would appreciate that."

"It is one of Tribune Sisera's favorite exercises," the Optio informed Marcus.

"Really. Who does he team up with?" Marcus asked.

"No one, sir," Feri stated. "It's usually him against pairs of us."

"Centurion Iacōbus," Marcus shouted across the rear of the assault line. "We are employing a new tactic."

"Yes, sir," the combat officer responded. "I was about to suggest a change."

"Why is that, Centurion?" Marcus asked.

Iacōbus lifted his gladius and pointed at the distant Legion element. Where they had been facing Marcus and closing the distance, Centurion Philetus had halted his forward progress and circled his detachment.

On one side, Empire light infantry and archers assaulted the defensive circle and on the other, Iberian heavy infantry hammered at the Legion shields.

"Should we form a wedge, sir?" the Centurion inquired. By his tone, it was obvious the combat officer expected agreement from the staff officer. "We can easily fight our way over and rescue Philetus and his Legionaries."

Tribune Marcus Flamma doubled over so quickly Feri stepped in front of him. Covering them both with the shield, he searched the Tribune for an arrow shaft or a rock bruise.

But it wasn't exterior wounds hurting Marcus. The churning bile in his gut resulted from indecision. The Legion below needed him on the clifftop removing archers, spearmen, and slingers. Now, half his volunteers were falling to Qart Hadasht forces, and it was within his power to save them. At least temporarily, because the land at the top of the cliff for his Legionaries was a one-way gateway to Hades.

Marcus Flamma heaved before the content of his stomach, plus more fluid, gushed from his mouth. Spewing and splashing onto the ground went the bile and his doubt. Lifting his head, he stood erect.

"Centurion Iacōbus. Separate the men into pairs," Marcus got out before he had to spit another mouthful of puke onto the rocks and dirt. "We will clear the clifftop of threats before engaging the Iberians."

"As you wish, sir," Iacōbus said hiding his disappointment. "Squads, by twos, forward."

Without massed targets, the bowmen attempted to shoot pairs of infantrymen. But the big shields caught most and when the archers hesitated, they were trampled and stomped to death as roving pairs of Legionaries began clearing the clifftop.

In the distance, the fighting continued. Centurion Philetus' defensive circle contracted as Legionaries died and fell out of the formation. It would continue like that because reinforcements were not coming. The sacrifice of the few to save the many lay at the heart of the decision to abandoned them.

Although condemned, they were not forgotten. The death of each of the one hundred and fifty Legionaries weighed heavily on Marcus Flamma's heart. And the Tribune knew, shortly, he would meet them all on the Elysium Fields.

Chapter 8 - Violent Extraction

Alerio studied the rain of pain coming from the clifftop. At first nothing changed. Then an archer sailed over and splashed, still screaming, into the river. Following the dramatic announcement that Marcus Flamma had reached the top, the flights of arrows and rocks slowed and eventually stopped in the nearest sector.

"Good enough for me," Alerio announced. "Let's see about unplugging the cork and freeing the Legion."

Empire mercenaries were banging and stabbing along the shield wall of Second Maniple. While the soldiers attacked at will, the Legionaries, under orders to hold, remained stationary.

"Blatium, when we engage, feel free to advance on those fatherless urchins," Alerio advised the Maniple's senior combat officer.

"Tribune Sisera, I would like to protest the insult to the worlds urchins, but I won't," the Centurion replied. "And you can be sure, once you make contact, we will be there."

"I'm counting on it," Alerio told him.

Then Alerio fast walked along the eighty Legionaries of his attack Century. As he passed, each man received a punch on his shoulder armor from the Tribune. And Alerio received words of encouragement back.

"We are with you, sir."
"The same, Tribune."
"My blade is yours."

When Alerio reached the Centurion on the slope, his knuckles hurt. But there was no question, the infantrymen were alert and ready to go to work.

"Sixteenth Century, Second Maniple," Alerio called out. "You can stay here and suck on wineskins all afternoon. Or you can come with me to glory."

"With you Tribune," the men shouted back.

There was a vibration of anticipation coursing through the Century. Alerio waited for their nerves to stretch as tight as he dared.

"Follow me if you can," Alerio challenged, "you herd of one-legged donkeys."

The insult hung in the air as Alerio spun and raced up the hill. Seeing the Tribune out pacing them, the eighty men sprinted after him.

When given the command to 'go' in a footrace, some men got off rabbit quick. Others, at the start, needed to test their legs before reaching speed. With the insult on their minds and their Tribune racing away, there was no time to think. All eighty men started together and hit the top of the slope at full stride.

Alerio needed them sprinting in mass as they rounded the mound. On the far side they looked down on two distinct battles. Forming an 'L' shape, one clash pitted mercenaries against the end of the Legion line while the other conflict had Empire soldiers fighting along the Second Maniple's defensive wall. The plan required a rapid assault between the mercenary elements to begin extracting the Legion.

If Qart Hadasht commanders noticed Alerio's maneuver, they could counter it. Soldiers from both fights plus reserve Companies would be directed to intercept the sixteenth

Century. Being caught in a three-way confrontation was a sure way to get dead.

To prevent the interception, Alerio needed his people to arrive at the fight before the Empire officers realized they left the defensive line. And the only way to do that was speed.

At the bottom of the slope, the gap between fighting units was an empty field stretching to the river. Alerio paused for a couple of heartbeats to be sure his Legionaries had caught up. Then he sang as he dashed down the hill.

> *"Tullia Major, Tullia Major*
> *Leave the mug be*
> *Open your eyes and see*
> *The vino is tainted*
> *By jealousy."*

Legionaries preferred two things: good singing and controlled formations. The mercenaries were wrapped around the Legion like a dirty bandage on an injured hand. To peel back the layers and free the Legion, the sixteenth needed to conform to the enemy's shape. The grind of a straight-line attack would take too long. Thus, they charged as a mob.

The Tribune's raw voice cut through the sounds of men screaming and calling out for mercy or vengeance. In addition, the awful rendition motivated the Legionaries to end the fight quickly and thus stop the singing.

> *"Tullia Major, Tullia Major*
> *Beware your spouse*
> *He be an unfaithful louse*
> *Guard your position*

from abuse."

Alerio kicked a pair of legs out from under a soldier. The man fell away from the cluster at the Legion's end. With the soldier on the ground, the backs of the next two mercenaries were exposed. Alerio stabbed one, bashed the other with his shield, and parried the blade of the third.

On either side of Tribune Sisera, the sixteenth Century slammed into the knot of Qart Hadasht warriors. They began stabbing, hammering, and peeling the layers of mercenaries off the Legion.

"Tullia via your birth order
Your last sip brings death
Your last kiss becomes your last breath
All for naked ambition
All to drive your sister's ascension."

Alerio yanked a warrior back and found himself staring at a pair of Legion shields and the sharp ends of two gladii. Struck by the hollow and desperate look in the Legionaries' eyes, he forgot the man dangling at the end of his arm.

"Excuse me, sir," one of the Legionaries said as he reached out and stabbed the man in Alerio's hand.

From behind, Alerio heard a beautiful sound.

"Advance," Centurions ordered.

"Advance. Rah," Second Maniple replied.

Then again, but closer, the Maniple repeated the drill.

"Advance," Centurions ordered.

"Advance. Rah," Second Maniple replied.

Alerio and the sixteenth Century turned and folded into the Legion ranks. They fought until the end of the Maniple linked with the start of the Legion. Then as if a tube inserted into a pipe, a safe pathway opened. Legionaries began carrying wounded from the tunnel of shields, through the Second, and into the open field beyond.

"Tribune Flamma?" a voice asked. "Marcus, where are you?"

Senior Tribune Iterum and General Calatinus walked by Alerio. Iterum didn't ask for Tribune Sisera, so Alerio didn't volunteer himself.

Without the arrows and rocks from the cliff, the Legion shifted to a three-rank formation. And shortly after they began rotating fresh arms and legs into the front rank, the Qart Hadasht forces withdrew from the fight.

***

Gloom rolled over the battlefield and the Legion. Physically, it was the sunset. But mentally, the cause of the melancholy resulted from the loss of so many comrades.

In the twilight, Alerio and Centurion Blatium studied the top of the cliff. Their hearts sank when Iberian infantry appeared along the crest. As quickly as they appeared, the infantrymen marched out of view.

"That doesn't bode well for Tribune Flamma," the Centurion offered.

"Or our Legionaries," Alerio added. "We need to get up there and see what transpired."

"That could mean more dead Legionaries," Blatium cautioned, "if the Iberians are still up there."

Before they could say more, a Junior Tribune rode up behind them.

"Tribune Sisera, Colonel Digessi requests your presence at the General's tent," the young man informed him.

His armor was rinsed but still splattered with faded pink stains and his young face showed lines of worry. The gore would wash off, but the young nobleman would carry the memories of the battle with him for life.

"What do you think, Blatium," Alerio asked his senior combat officer, "am I presentable."

"No sir. You are a mess," the Centurion replied.

"Good," Alerio announced. "Set watches and get Second Maniple fed. I'll be back, I think, or…"

"Or what sir," Blatium questioned.

"Or you will be in charge until they send my replacement from the Capital," Alerio told him.

With those fateful words, Alerio jogged southward towards a cluster of distant campfires. The dots of light signified Centuries located outside the marching camp. Inside or out of the stockade didn't matter this night. No one would get much sleep as the Legion remained on alert. Because, if General Barca Hamilcar wanted to cross blades again, General Aulus Calatinus and his Legion would be ready.

***

All the officers in the command tent were dirty, exhausted, and on edge.

Colonel Digessi pulled his head out of a bucket of water. With one hand he wiped the water from his face and with the other he reached for a drying cloth.

"Marcus Flamma took three hundred of my infantrymen to the top of the cliff," the Battle Commander said clarifying the news. "And where were you, Tribune Sisera?"

Before Alerio could reply, a Tribune from Third Maniple stepped forward.

"Tribune Sisera was cutting a hole in the Qart Hadasht mercenaries," the staff officer declared. "His actions allowed us to join with the Second Maniple."

Because the Colonel sounded as if he was preparing to discipline Sisera, another Maniple staff officer stepped up to flank Alerio. Then struggling with injuries, two more Maniple Tribunes joined them.

"Is this a mutiny?" Digessi inquired.

The Senior Tribunes all raised arms as if to deliver lectures. But the Colonel waved them down. He ran his eyes over the staff officers as he finished drying his neck.

"I asked a question," Digessi reminded the Tribunes.

"No, sir, this is not a mutiny," the other Tribune from the veteran Third Maniple answered. "We fought together today. We stood with you then and we stand, united, with you now."

The use of the word united did not escape the Battle Commander's attention. After a near disaster, it would be easy to assign blame, point out failures, and find fault. But Digessi needed a functioning Legion not a divided one.

"As I was going to ask, do we know the fate of Tribune Flamma and his detachment?" Digessi questioned.

"No sir, I was ordered to organize the northern picket positions with the Second," Alerio told the Colonel. "With your permission, I'd like to go up to the cliff tonight."

"I can't justify sending Centuries off to search in the dark," Digessi admitted. "If the Iberians are there, it could cost me more Legionaries. We should wait for the morning and go up in force."

Three of the Tribunes nodded their agreement. Tribune Sisera did not.

"Sir. Let me go out tonight and perform reconnaissance," Alerio requested. "I think…"

Iterum, Second Maniple's commander, snapped out both arms and pointed them at Alerio.

"I believe you have done enough thinking for one day," the Senior Tribune scolded. "Because of you…"

"Iterum, that will be enough," a voice ordered from a side flap. Consul/General Calatinus strolled into the room and gazed around at his staff officers. "Gentlemen, today we were tested. Beat on and bruised by a foe superior in numbers only. However, we did not break. Tomorrow, I want recommendations for accommodations. Lots of accommodations. And not, I repeat, not one request for punishment. Now what were you saying Tribune Carvilius Sisera?"

Legion rank aside, social standing among staff officers, and a few Patricians who could only afford Centurion positions, carried weight. And General Calatinus had just reminded everyone in the tent that Alerio's adopted father was a powerful Senator.

"With your permission, General, I will sneak and peek around the heights," Alerio proposed," and investigate. If nothing else, we'll have intelligence for tomorrow's patrol."

"But General, I need Tribune Sisera in command of the Second Maniple," Iterum protested.

"Nonsense, Iterum," Calatinus insisted. "You can spend the night with your Maniple. It'll do the men good to see their Senior Tribune sleeping with them. Especially after they saved the Legion. I'll order vino sent up. You can share drinks and toast their bravery."

For Iterum, being a senior staff officer meant perks. And one of them provided him a bed in the command area. Banishment to the Centuries felt like unwarranted punishment. He started to protest when Digessi draped an arm over his shoulders.

"When the attack started, I assumed you were with your Maniple," the Colonel remarked. Dropping the thread of reminding the Senior Tribune that he was out of position, the Battle Commander continued. "Perhaps I will come by tonight and share a cup with you and your combat officers."

"That would be most pleasant, Colonel," Iterum acknowledged. "My Centurions will be honored."

***

Alerio grinned in the dark as he climbed. Despite his weariness, the miserable task ahead, and his need for sleep, the search of the wagons for the woolen pants and shirt brought a moment of levity to his mind. The teamsters were outraged that he tore apart an entire baggage transport while looking for this outfit. But the woolens had proved lucky in the past, and he felt he needed as much help from providence as he could muster.

Or maybe the smirk formed from the half-truth he told to General Calatinus.

While he certainly planned to look for Iberians and try to discern what transpired on the clifftop, his real thought was to bring Marcus Flamma home to the Legion. If Alerio could prevent it, Tribune Flamma's body would not rest as wolf bait for even one night.

Far below him, four squads of veterans held the approach. Located a mile south of the battlefield, the gully was wide enough for three columns of mercenaries to charge the Legion. In reality, they would rush headlong into the shields and gladii of men from the Third Maniple. As he reached the end of the ravine, Alerio was thankful that he hadn't met Empire soldiers coming from the other direction.

Once on level ground, he jogged northward. Stars twinkled overhead providing enough light to see bigger rocks and larger obstacles. The features didn't mean much until he reached an area almost parallel to where the Legion had been trapped. There he found the bodies of two Legionaries at a narrow gulch.

Several paces beyond the gully, Alerio squatted at the bodies of twenty soldiers of the Empire.

"Nice going, Tribune Flamma," he whispered as he moved by the bodies.

Farther along the clifftop, he found a pair of Legionaries and several Qart Hadasht light infantrymen. In his mind, he pieced together the circumstances as he identified the result of two-on-two drills against a dispersed enemy. Nodding his approval, the former Weapon's Instructor moved northward.

Wagons with bodies on one side showed him the route taken and disruption inflicted by Tribune Flamma's detachment. Then he began finding pairs of Legionaries.

At first three pairs, then four, with two more off to the side. Following the change in direction, he stumbled on five pairs of infantrymen. Almost fearing what he would find ahead, Alerio stopped to catch his breath. In the silence, he heard camp noises.

Rapping on armor, files gliding on blades, and indistinct voices drifted to him from the north. Several paces away, he rustled aside branches and peered through a bush. Two hundred feet from the hedgerow, fifty campfires blazed in the night. The Iberians had not retreated with the main body of the Empire's army. Perhaps they were rearguard or maybe an ambush for a small patrol from the Legion. In either case, he knew about them, and the Legion patrol would be a full Maniple. And they would not come slowly and timidly across the clifftop.

Returning to the trail of bodies, Alerio crept forward stepping over the Legionaries who almost carpeted the ground. Then the orientations of the bodies changed. They became as spokes on a wheel, radiating out from a hub. If Marcus had made it this far, Alerio was sure to find his corpse in the center of what had to be a terrifying battle.

Stacked and left as they had fallen, Alerio located the command staff. One Centurion, a big Optio, and a handful of Legionaries constituted the pile. But there was no sign of Tribune armor.

Alerio faced north and crouched. Having failed in his personal mission, he would have the satisfaction of finishing the official task and telling the Colonel how to bring pain down on the Iberians.

"Nenia Dea," Alerio whispered. "I pray that you took all of them into your arms quickly."

With reverence, he reached out and hovered his hand over the pile of dead. Seeking to give the Legionaries one final goodbye, he lowered the palm.

Under his touch, a warm hand jerked, and a groan escaped from a pair of very much alive lungs. Alerio was torn.

Whoever was alive in the pile couldn't have much life left. If he groaned loud enough, the Iberians would come to investigate. Alerio needed to be gone from here and on his way to warn Colonel Digessi.

But one of Marcus' men lived. And because Alerio respected the Tribune who loved King Leonidas, Alerio leaned over the stack and began untangling arms, legs, and torsos.

Another groan came from under the muscular Optio's body and Alerio almost stopped and fled.

"Be quiet you fool," he warned. "Do you…"

As the body of the big NCO rolled away, starlight reflected off Tribune armor.

Marcus Flamma groaned again. But Alerio didn't care. He pulled his fellow Tribune onto his shoulders and headed south as fast as he could travel.

Act 3

Chapter 9 – Heroes of the Legion

Alerio unstrapped Marcus' chest and shoulder armor and took his time easing the leather and iron around the twisted arm and the collection of bloody cloths. Then, he gently unstrapped the hobnailed boots and was extra cautious removing the footwear from the oddly bent leg. As he unbuckled the armored skirt, Alerio wondered how he could slip the gear from under Marcus without hurting his friend.

The tent flaps moved and rather than the servants with water, soap, vinegar, and clean bandages, a doctor breezed into the tent.

Physician Oisin, Consul/General Calatinus' personal doctor, crossed to the cot, stopped, and rubbed his chin as he studied Marcus Flamma.

"The Tribune needs to be clean for me to see his complexion," the Greek doctor announced. "And his issues collected so I can investigate his humors."

"What about the broken bones?" Alerio inquired. "And the sword wounds?"

"I treat ailments of the entire body," the physician explained. "You'll need a surgeon for the other maladies."

"Barley soup and vinegar drink," Alerio said in disgust.

"Excuse me?" Oisin demanded.

"At my father's farm, we treated our own wounds," Alerio informed the Greek. "My father calls over educated physicians barley soup and vinegar drink merchants."

"I don't have to stand here and be insulted," Oisin exclaimed.

"Just the fact that you are here makes that a lie," Alerio suggested. Three servants came in with the supplies. "You supervise getting him clean and the collection of his issues."

"Where are you going?" Oisin asked.

"To find a veteran infantryman and a sheep herder," Alerio replied. He addressed the half-conscious Marcus Flamma. "I apologize, Leonidas."

Lifting Marcus' lower back, Alerio slid the armored skirt free.

Marcus screamed.

"Can you treat his back?" Alerio asked the doctor.

Physician Oisin shrugged and said, "It could be internal bruising."

"Can you treat that?" Alerio questioned while standing.

"His humors will tell us more," the Greek assured him.

"Someday, every Legion will have doctors and surgeons assigned to them," Alerio complained as he headed for the exit. "Until then, we will depend on infantrymen and sheep herders."

***

Alerio returned to find a servant pushing and kneading Marcus' stomach. With his eyes squeezed tightly and face grimacing, Flamma endured the pain in silence.

"Is that a treatment?" Alerio inquired from the entrance.

"No. We are attempting to help Tribune Flamma void his bowels," Oisin replied.

"Stop. Just stop before I cut you, Doctor, and show you two of your humors," Alerio thundered.

"Two of my humors?" the physician gasped.

"The second is blood," Alerio described. "Because when I draw my blade, I bet you will deliver a healthy dose of merda. You can gaze upon them all you want but leave Marcus alone."

Alerio stepped clear of the entrance and two Legionaries followed him into the tent. One was older and the other barely out of his teens.

"As near as I can tell, Tribune Flamma has three deep gashes from the fighting," Alerio explained. "And a broken leg and a broken arm. Can you help?"

The older Legionary had battle scars covering his arms. Several were puckered and raised from old sutures showing the veteran had experience with blade cuts.

"I can sew him up better than most," the veteran infantryman declared. "Do we have vinegar?"

From a pouch, he pulled bronze needles and catgut thread made from twisted strands of sheep's intestine. He washed his hands and the needles in vinegar before lifting the bloody cloths. After examining the wounds, the veteran pressed the cloths back over two and located flaps of skin on the third.

"The Tribune is a fighter," the Legionary declared as he poked the needle through the skin at the end of the gash.

"How can you tell?" Alerio asked.

"A blade slashes front to back if you are advancing," the scarred veteran stated. "Or back to front of you are moving away. Based on these wounds, the Tribune was attacking into the swords when he won these cuts."

"You mean sword thrusts," Alerio corrected.

"No, sir. These three wounds were made by three different blades," the man described as he drew the needle and thread through Marcus' flesh. "He must have been fighting a running battle against multiple enemies."

"King Leonidas," Alerio commented subtly.

"Did you say something, Tribune?" the younger Legionary asked.

"Not important," Alerio admitted. "What about the breaks? Can you help?"

"While tending the herd in the mountains at home, we had to mend broken legs ourselves. I'll need two pairs of hands to help straighten the limbs," the shepherd Legionary described. "Give me them and enough wrapping to swaddle the limbs, and I'll have him trussed up like a prized ram before you know it. But first, I'll need to fashion slats to support the bones."

Alerio dispatched a servant to fetch pieces of wagon bed. Having been worn down by use, the boards would be flat and easily carved into slats.

"Where was the Tribune positioned during the action, sir?" the man pulling sutures asked. "It looks like he was mixing it up with the light infantry around the bend."

"Tribune Flamma was not with the Velites," Alerio told him. "Marcus took a detachment to the clifftop to stop the archers, slingers, and spearmen."

"My Third Maniple was under the cliffs catching those missiles," the veteran remarked while tying off a line of sutures. "It felt like we were down range of Queen Lampedo and her army of Amazon women archers. Then it all stopped, and we could concentrate on the mercenaries."

"You can thank Tribune Flamma for the reprieve," Alerio informed the Legionary.

The servant returned and handed flat planks to the other Legionary. Pulling his pugio, the former shepherd began whittling on one of the pieces of lumber.

"My Century was near the second bend in the river," he offered while shavings of wood fell around his feet. "We were in a narrow part of the valley. The archers were shooting almost directly down onto our shields. And the spears, the ones that didn't get through, nearly broke our arms when they hit. We were grateful when they stopped, and we could take revenge on the soldiers of the Empire."

"Again, that was due to Tribune Flamma and his detachment," Alerio explained. "They volunteered to clear the clifftop of mercenaries."

"Where are they being treated," the shepherd asked. "I'd like to thank them."

"Aye, as would I," the veteran said, seconding the thought.

"Tribune Marcus Flamma was the only man to make it off the clifftop," Alerio advised. "Iberian heavy infantry got the rest. But Marcus made it back to honor the fallen and to warn us that the Iberians are still up there."

In mid stitch, the veteran stopped sewing. And with a curl of wood dangling on the edge of a board, the shepherd stopped carving. They stared at Tribune Flamma with renewed curiosity.

"You saved First Maniple, sir," the younger Legionary exclaimed.

"You saved Third Maniple," the veteran barked. Then with a shake of his head, he looked at Alerio and rephrased the statement. "Not just Maniples. Tribune Flamma saved the entire Legion."

"Yes, the entire Legion," the young infantryman echoed.

***

Before the first rays of light graced the eastern sky, Third Maniple marched from the Legion camp. Two hundred paces from their bivouac, the eight hundred veterans split into two groups. One climbed a gully to the clifftop. The other half broke into a Legion jog and followed the river northward.

Out front of the fast-moving file of heavy infantrymen, Centurion Farciminis and three squads of light infantry acted as pathfinders in the dark. Their route took them along the river and around both bends. Where the eastern bank overhung and hundreds of Velites died, they waded across the Irmimio River.

The noise of over four hundred armed Legionaries splashing across might have reached the Iberians on the clifftop. No one cared if the Qart Hadasht force heard, anticipated, prepared, or tried to run. It was too late for them, too late for anything except to die.

Centurion Farciminis was the first up the winding trail. With his gladius in hand, he searched the clifftop praying for an Iberian sentry or one seeking to relieve himself in the early morning. Any of them would do to sate the officer's desire for revenge. Not finding any ready victims, Farciminis directed his skirmishers to form a line. Once the heavy infantry dispersed behind them, the Velites moved forward.

The Legionaries halted when the Iberian campfires came into view.

"Centurion Farciminis, you did a good job of getting us on location," Battle Commander Digessi complimented the light infantry officer. "Withdraw your squads. We will take it from here."

There was rustling of grasses and low voices requesting retribution as the skirmishers shuffled to the rear. They received promises of just that from the heavy infantrymen.

Once the maneuver was completed, near quiet settled on the early morning. It lasted for several moments.

Colonel Digessi's voice cut the silence, "Third Maniple, stand by."

"Standing by, Battle Commander," the four hundred Legionaries on either side of him responded.

Then, from the far side of the Iberian camp, an equal number of veteran Legionaries replied, "Standing by, Battle Commander."

Resembling a kicked hornet's nest, the Iberians rousted from their tents. But it was too late.

"Third Maniple, draw," Digessi ordered. "Forward."

"Forward. Rah!" the Legionaries responded.

"Forward. Rah!" echoed back from the other side of the enemy camp.

***

Consul/General Calatinus carried a chest to his camp desk. After resting it on the tabletop, he opened the lid and began sorting jewelry, coins, and bars of metal. In the lamplight, items of gold, silver, and copper reflected the flames in a variety of colors and shapes.

"General, the metalworkers you requested are here," his house manager announced.

"Bring them in," Aulus Calatinus instructed while making come-in-motions with one hand as his other selected less than desirable objects from the chest.

Two Legionnaires from the First Century entered and stepped to opposite corners of the General's tent. Following the bodyguards, five craftsmen, rubbing sleep from their eyes and yawning shuffled into the command area. Two more veterans from First Century entered on their heels.

"General, if this is about our grinding prices," one craftsman began. He looked at the armored Legionaries and shivered, "we can discuss lowering the price. There is plenty of work for all of us."

"I am sure First Centurion Sanctoris will be happy to hear that," Calatinus acknowledged. "But that is not the purpose of this visit. Are any of you proficient with sand casting?"

Three of the craftsmen raised their hands.

"Excellent. You three will pour and create the medals. The other two will clean and polish them," the General/Consul directed. "I am ordering a celebration and need awards for the heroes of the Legion."

"Sir, when do you need the medals?" a craftsman inquired.

"The day after tomorrow," Calatinus informed them.

"Sir, that's impossible," another metalworker offered. "We need weeks to create medals in quantity, and more days beyond to assure quality."

Calatinus' house manager carried a small set of scales to the desk.

"What's the name of this Legion?" Calatinus asked.

"Calatinus Legion South," a metalsmith responded.

"And my titles?" Calatinus questioned.

"Co-Consul of the Republic," two metalworkers conceded, "and General of the Legion."

"Exactly. Now step up and we will weigh out the metal for the castings," Calatinus offered. "And tradesman, I expect the finished awards to equal on the scale the amount you receive."

The five metalworkers crowded around the desk watching to be sure the scales were balanced. None of them wanted to be shorted and charged later for the lost gold, silver, or copper.

***

Two days later, the Centuries were lined up by Maniple. With the burials done and prayers uttered over graves, it was time for healing, a feast, and a celebration of the survivors. General Calatinus and Colonel Digessi stepped up on a platform to preside over the dawn sacrifices.

"Goddess Victoria, we thank you for delivering us from defeat," the General announced. "God Averruncus, we owe you for averting a calamity."

"Bellona, Goddess of War, we trust that you look down with pride on your fighting Legionaries and their officers," the Colonel continued intoning for the deities. "And as always, Goddess Algea, we strive to deliver your blessings to our foes."

Shouts of Euge! Euge! came from the ranks of Legionaries. Obviously, the bravos acknowledged the infantry's appreciation for the Goddess of Pain.

General Calatinus waited for the cheering to fade before adding other gods to the thanks.

"Jupiter, the Sky Father, we know you watch over us as any good shepherd guards his flock," Calatinus boomed. "And because we are the swords of Rome and the fighting men of the Republic, we give thanks to Mars, our God of War."

The Legionaries roared their approval and bonfires flared to life. In the backdrop of flames and crackling wood, priests ran to bulls, sheep, cows, goats, and chickens. And even through the screen of smoke, the Legionaries saw holy men cut the throats of the sacrificial beast.

When the drama drew to a close and the priests began towing the animals to the butchers, the General and Colonel raised their arms for attention.

"Together we experienced a narrow victory," Calatinus exclaimed. "But we fought our way free and with the heroism of a few, the Legion survived."

"As one, we will honor those who stepped forward in places and made a difference," Digessi inhaled deeply to gather breath for the rest of his pronouncements.

But, to everyone's surprise, Senior Centurion Sanctoris leaped to the platform.

"Pardon, General, Colonel. Before you continue," the Legion's senior combat officer declared. "The Centuries will have a voice."

"What say, the Legion?" General Calatinus inquired.

Sanctoris reached into a pouch and extracted a circular object. Lifting it overhead, he displayed a wreath of woven grass.

Cheering erupted in a volume that far exceeded any of the previous outbursts.

"The men have voted a unique award," the Senior Centurion exclaimed. "One not in the authority of a General or a Battle Commander to grant. Nor in the power of a Consul or the Senator or any High Priest even of the mightiest temple to confer. I hold before you the Grass Crown."

"The will of the Legion shall be done," Colonel Digessi promised. "But who deserves this great honor? And for what act of bravery?"

"Marcus Calpurnius Flamma, Tribune of Rome," Sanctoris bellowed the name in a voice that commanded thousands during a battle. It carried to the ranks and beyond. Then he called for the winner. "Rome's Tribune present yourself to the Legion."

Holding a pole upright, Alerio Sisera marched from the rear of the Centuries. At the top of the pole, Tribune armor, a staff officer's helmet, and a gladius hung from a cross piece. He stopped near the forward rank of the Legion and stood still for several moments.

Then six muscular Legionaries shouldering an open litter marched into view. Reclining on the litter, Marcus Flamma weakly raised his good arm and acknowledged the hailing.

The motion only served to increase the cheering and that motivated Marcus. As his porters reached the front rank and stopped beside Tribune Sisera, he added the splinted arm to his waving.

"Go easy there, King Leonidas," Alerio cautioned. "You are still recovering."

"Do you suppose this was what it was like?" Marcus inquired.

"What it was like?" Alerio questioned.

"When King Leonidas arrived at the Elysium Fields," Marcus told him.

"Tribune Flamma, you can ask him yourself someday," Alerio suggested. "Because you have earned your place in the fields for heroes."

"Forward, sirs?" an Optio of the porters asked.

"Forward," Marcus instructed.

Chapter 10 – Professional in All Things

A day after the celebration of heroes, a messenger arrived at Second Maniple.

"Tribune Sisera, you are wanted at the command tent," the Junior Tribune announced.

"Have someone take my gear," Alerio told Blatium. "I'll catch up with you on the route."

Around them, the Legionaries of the Maniple were packing and getting ready for the march.

"No, sir," the junior staff officer clarified. "You are to bring all of your belongings."

"They finally caught up with me, Centurion," Alerio offered. "Hopefully, my replacement, when he arrives from the Capital, will be a proper gentleman."

"You are a proper commander, Tribune Sisera," Blatium complimented him. Then the combat officer added. "You are a little rough around the edges for a staff officer. But sir, I'll fight besides you any day."

"That's all an officer can ask of this life," Alerio said before saluting the Centurion.

After picking up his gear and balancing it on his shoulder, Alerio marched to the command tent. The side tents for sleeping and storage were already packed in a wagon. He dropped his load outside the single big tent and marched through the entrance.

***

"Sirs. Tribune Sisera reporting," he announced himself.

It seemed the thing to do as the two commanders were the only ones in the tent. No Junior Tribunes or servants were around to do the formal announcement.

"Come over here, Alerio," General Calatinus invited him.

"You sent for me, sir?" Alerio said letting the General know, in case he forgot, that Alerio was answering a summons.

As soon as Alerio thought it, he checked his recent history. Had he done anything to warrant charges?

"Relax Sisera," Colonel Digessi offered as if he read Alerio's thoughts. "We have some questions for you."

"Yes, sir. I'll answer to the best of my ability," Alerio promised.

"Yesterday at the award ceremony," Calatinus inquired, "were you bothered or disgraced by the story of Marcus Flamma crawling back to warn the Legion about the Iberians?"

"No, sir," Alerio replied truthfully.

"Not troubled even a little by the acclaim showered on Flamma?" Digessi insisted. "Granted he took the three hundred to the cliff. But in reality, you brought him out. If it wasn't for you, he would have died up there. And that doesn't get under your skin, just a little?"

"No sir. To be honest, it was partially my fault the story spread like it did," Alerio informed them.

"Can you explain that?" Calatinus asked.

"Well General, I brought in a Legionary to stitch Tribune Flamma's wounds and another to set his broken bones," Alerio told him. "While they worked, I allowed them to think he made his way back alone to warn the Legion."

"I know your Father," Calatinus stated.

Alerio almost smiled. As a member of an opposing political faction, Aulus Calatinus sat across the Senate from Spurius Maximus. The phrase, 'I know your father', could be translated to 'I fear angering your adopted father'. That then gave reason for the questioning. They didn't want Alerio upset and running to his father with complaints.

"Yes, sir," Alerio acknowledged.

"He sent you a package," Digessi explained.

The Colonel picked up a bundle from behind his legs and handed it to Alerio.

"Somehow it got opened by a servant," Calatinus warned excusing the invasion when he noticed Alerio inspecting the ripped cloth. "But I can assure you, nothing is missing."

Resting the package on the ground, Alerio pulled his Legion dagger and sliced it open the rest of the way. He peeled the cloth back and his hand hovered over a gladius, a dagger, ten gold coins, and a letter.

Tribune Alerio Carvilius Sisera
Calatinus Legion South, Sicilia
Dear son,

I trust your health is good and your humors are in balance. Enclosed is a small token of my esteem and examples of the result from the northern expedition you suggested. We are getting close to where you must make a decision: Go into politics, or if you prefer, we can buy you an infantry Maniple. After the campaign season, we will talk more.

Your father, a citizen, and a Senator of the Republic
Spurius Carvilius Maximus

Alerio pulled his gladius and replaced it with the new sword. Then he gripped the dagger and tested the weight. Standing, he displayed the blade to Calatinus and Digessi.

"It's called Noric Steel," he described. "Harder and holds an edge without chipping. A fine gift, wouldn't you say."

"We have a dilemma," Digessi confessed after long moments of staring at the knife. "Tribune Flamma was supposed to go on a mission as a military attaché."

"But in his present condition," Calatinus exclaimed, "he is in no shape to represent the Legion of the Republic."

"I stand ready for whatever the Republic needs, sir," Alerio declared. "Why did you wait so long to ask me?"

"Because, you are not qualified for a diplomatic mission," the Colonel answered. "Not in education, breeding, or in temperament. We felt that you were more likely to start a war than to form an alliance."

"What changed?" Alerio inquired.

"While we are defeating the Empire forces on land, despite recent events," Calatinus stated referring to the ambush of the Legion. "Our fleet is still at a disadvantage and unable to cast a wide net of protection over our merchants. The Senate is desperate for treaties with countries that have fleets."

"Where am I going, sir?" Alerio asked.

"The Isle of Rhodes," Digessi told him. "You'll be heading east with Marcus Flamma and the other wounded. They will continue to Messina. But you will disembark at Syracuse. From there, you can catch a merchant vessel to Rhodes."

The Colonel handed Alerio a scroll with the written assignment. After reading it, Alerio squared his shoulders and looked Consul/General Calatinus in the eyes.

"Why are you really sending me to Rhodes, sir?" he demanded.

"The Rhodians are refined, organized, and professional in all things. You are arrogant, quick tempered, and hard to get along with," Calatinus confessed. "I am sending you because you will fail, tremendously. And when you fall on your face, your disgrace will reflect badly on your adopted father. And that, Tribune Sisera, is why I am sending you. Dismissed."

Alerio braced and saluted. Then he collected his package and marched out of the tent. As he repacked his gear, a thought occurred to Alerio. Although Calatinus' words seemed to be a blatant challenge, underneath the man's bravado, the Consul really did fear Senator Maximus.

Once packed, Alerio headed for the wagon park. While hiking through the vanishing structures of the marching camp, he mouthed these words over and over again, "I will not fail. I will not fail. I will not fail."

***

The warship shoved off the beach, the oarsmen took the quinquereme into deep water, and navigators turned the bow to an easterly heading.

"That is Sicilia for this year," Alerio remarked as the coastline glided by.

"More than this year," Marcus remarked.

"Whatever are you talking about?" Alerio inquired. Reaching down, he adjusted the blanket draped over Tribune Flamma's legs. "You will be healed before spring."

"I am retiring my position," Marcus confessed. He patted the broken leg and waved his broken arm in the air. "Thanks to you, I have earned all the glory I ever wanted. My family will be proud. And now, they will allow me to oversee my father's farms and continue my studies."

"They gave me your assignment to Rhodes," Alerio told him.

"You are a good choice," Marcus complimented his fellow Tribune. "I can't imagine a better representative from the Republic military."

"You and I aren't exactly harvested from the same field," Alerio observed. "You are a reader and a thinker. I am more brash and enjoy playing with blades. How can you say I am a good choice?"

"It goes to the approach," Marcus replied. "Should we present a deceitful face and attempt to falsely emulate the Rhodians? Or is it better to show them the strength of our planning, our will, and our discipline?"

"Me being successful as a diplomat is a sentiment not shared by Consul Calatinus or our esteemed Battle Commander," Alerio stated. "Based on their expectations, I worship at the feet of Coalemus and thrive off the God's blessings."

"You have nothing from the God of Stupid," Marcus assured Alerio. "Your common sense will carry you through the mission."

"What are the Rhodians like?" Alerio asked. "Colonel Digessi called them refined, organized, and professional in everything. In truth, I'm not sure what that means."

"I read a lot of travel journals and scrolls from the modern world," Marcus exclaimed. "How do I put this without frightening you? Rhodes is presented in all of the literature as a wealthy, educated paradise."

"It can't be that perfect," Alerio begged.

"Not to push the issue," Marcus cautioned. "But their main harbor is guarded by a one hundred and five-foot statue to their Sun God Helios. It is called the Colossus of Rhodes."

"Sounds impressive," Alerio granted. "But come on, Marcus, they are just people."

"The Rhodians have embraced the philosopher Aristotle's Golden Mean," Marcus explained. "They do all things in moderation as he proscribed."

"They sound like a fun group," Alerio commented.

"And the straight streets of their Capital are from a layout by Hippodamus, another philosopher," Marcus described. "Plus, although small, the Rhodians Navy is among the world's most feared. They fight piracy and enforce a set of maritime laws for their merchant ships."

"Marcus please stop before I break my own arm and leg to get out of this mission," Alerio complained. "How were you going to handle the assignment?"

"By keeping my gladius in its scabbard, my dagger in its sheath, and my mouth shut," Marcus listed. "My intake of vino to a minimum and my eyes and ears attuned for knowledge."

"Those Rhodians sound like Priests from a temple," Alerio noted. "Recently, I haven't had much luck with Priests."

"For this mission, you will have to be diplomatic," Marcus instructed. "The Republic's trade with Asia Minor depends on eventually reaching a mutual defense treaty with the Isle of Rhodes. You are the first step towards the agreement."

"Or the last pace before a political abyss," Alerio remarked.

He sat on the deck beside Marcus and, together, they watched the shoreline pass by.

***

Two days later, Marcus Flamma shifted onto the elbow of his good arm and watched Alerio march down the ramp to the dock. Then the navigators fluttered their rear oars and the warship nosed away from the pier. In moments, Marcus lost his view of the city as one hundred and eighty oars dug into the water. When the mouth of Syracuse Bay replaced his view of stone walls and buildings, the sails were raised. Smoothly, the ship tracked out of the sheltered waters and towards the mouth of the Messina Strait.

As the Republic warship left the bay, Alerio reached the end of the docks.

"Where is the Harbor Master's office," he asked a street urchin.

"I am not sure, Master," the boy exclaimed. Crossing his arms, he pointed to opposite sides of the busy harbor. "It might be to the east. Then again, it might be to the west."

After fishing a bronze coin from his money pouch, Alerio held it out.

"Does this help your recollection," he inquired. "Or should I ask someone with a better memory?"

"Four streets to your left," the boy explained as he snatched away the coin. "It's the big white building."

The urchin dashed off and Alerio looked around. Most of the buildings located at the harbor of Syracuse were painted white.

"Was the boy misleading for revenge or animosity towards a Latian?" Alerio mumbled. Then he addressed the absent boy. "Your problem little man is you went too far in the lie."

Legion NCOs learned quickly when an infantryman was dancing around the truth. The first hint of a lie always included too much detail. And the mention of a white building in a sea of white buildings qualified as an inessential fact.

He faced to his left instead of right, walked two blocks, and located the Harbor Master's office.

***

Alerio entered the building to find a gross waste of space. Small offices lined both sides of a large room. A well-attended feast would fit nicely in the area. But no multitude of diners or servers populated the expanse. Instead, a single man lounging on a couch, two armored guards, a slave, and a secretary occupied the space.

"I seek passage on a merchant ship," Alerio informed the man reclining on the sofa. The slave standing behind the Harbor Master fanned him with a linen cloth stretched over a framework of small rods. Curious about the framing material, he inquired. "Excuse me, but what wood is that?"

"The linen is held in place by Egyptian papyrus reeds," the Harbor Master reported. "Is Egypt your destination? If so, we have many merchants visiting from the river valley of the Nile. I can recommend several trustworthy Captains."

"No sir, my business is on the Isle of Rhodes," Alerio informed him. "And I think it would be best if I avoided Qart Hadasht ports."

"That is understandable considering the tensions between your two governments," the Harbor Master remarked. "Rhodes you say. The island is rumored to be populated by people who are professional in all things,"

"What does that mean?" Alerio asked.

Rather than an answer, a gesture from the Master brought the secretary and a logbook to the couch. They conferred in short, clipped phrases. No doubt the vernacular used to keep the uninitiated in the dark as to the flow of ships into and out of Syracuse harbor.

"Your best choice is to catch a ship to Peloponnese," the Harbor Master recommended. "From there you can make your way to the island."

"When does one leave?" Alerio asked.

"If Captain Tivadar follows his normal trading route, he should be here within the week," the Master replied. "His seventy-five-foot corbita is one of the few merchant vessels with the size to cross the sea."

"I could use a recommendation for a place to stay in the meanwhile," Alerio requested. While handing the Harbor Master several coins, he added. "Perhaps a room near Archimedes Phidias' College."

The Master laughed.

"Workshop is a better description," he corrected. "Archimedes is inventive, I'll give him that. But a philosopher with his own college. No, no."

"The recommendation?" Alerio reminded the Master.

"Yes, of course," the Harbor Master stated. "Try the Starfish Inn."

"Thank you," Alerio acknowledged before turning about and marching to the exit.

***

Across the city, three men entered the establishment next door to the Starfish Inn. Two were men-at-arms and the third a Judge for King Hiero the Second.

"Metalworker, Dryas Chrysós?" the Judge inquired.

"I am the metalsmith," Dryas replied.

"The King wishes a crown made for the Temple of Plutus," the Judge explained. He placed three wrapped bars of metal on the counter. "The King will honor the God of Abundance and Wealth in seven days. This offering and dedication will assure the continued success of our city."

"Without a doubt," Dryas agreed. Being a man of faith, he relished the opportunity to create a crown for a deity. Carefully, the metalsmith lifted the cloth and gazed at three bars of gold. Then with all his heart, he avowed. "The Crown of Plutus shall be the fairest coronet ever crafted by man."

"Well spoken, craftsman of Syracuse," the Judge declared before the men left the store.

In the doorway to the rear of the shop, but hidden behind a curtain, Febe Chrysós, wife to Dryas, eyed the gold with beady and greedy eyes.

Chapter 11 – Natural Defenses

Alerio looked out of the windows from the second-floor apartment. On one side of the flat, the Starfish Inn shared an alleyway with a metalsmith's shop. To the front, the suite overlooked a busy main street.

The abrupt change from sleeping in a tent or under the stars, but always close to the ground on a bedroll unnerved Alerio. For several months, he was surrounded by his men with little privacy. Now alone, he paced a room with a door, walls, and a ceiling. He missed the blue sky and the clouds overhead.

To see the sky, he bent, looked out of a window, and upwards. From the uncomfortable position required to see the heavens, Alerio lowered his head and peered down into the alleyway. A cat slinked along the far wall, being on guard as it roamed the city.

"I wonder if you would feel as trapped as me," he whispered to the feral cat, "if someone enclosed you in an apartment?"

He knew the uneasiness of adjusting to civilization would fade. But for now, he needed to get out of the room. Before he pulled back from the window, the cat's tail dropped, and the beast arched its back.

"Something frighten you?" Alerio questioned.

A door to the alleyway opened, and a slightly stooped woman came shuffling from the metalsmith's shop. Her posture matched the lines on a middle-aged face that once belonged to a very pretty girl. Also showing her age, her hips were wide. And as she ambled from the doorway, the movement of her legs under the dress material revealed thick thighs. Despite her matronly appearance, Alerio enjoyed his private observation of the woman.

"I really have been campaigning too long," he scolded himself.

111

The cat leaped in the opposite direction and sprinted from the alleyway.

"Good idea," Alerio stated, agreeing with the cat that it was time to go.

Then the stooped, plump woman transformed. Once the door closed, she threw her arms in the air and did a pirouette. Adding to the display of joy, she swung her hips suggestively, and pranced several paces along the alley before sashaying back to the doorway.

"Attitude is everything," Alerio offered to the room.

As he had witnessed hundreds of times, a Legionary's frame of mind reflected directly on his posture and performance. It seemed the woman was no different. Alone and unseen in the alley, she became vibrant and lively.

"Good for you, lady," Alerio complimented. "I'll leave you to your private moment."

Before he could pull back, her mouth opened as if to scream and her eyes opened wide. Fearing she was about to be assaulted, Alerio did a mental inventory of the weapons on his person. Only the Golden Valley dagger, and it would not be a good idea to publicly use the assassin weapon of the Sweet Fist. If he were going to dash downstairs and help the woman, he would…

She placed a fist at her lips and bit down on a knuckle to keep from shrieking with excitement. Her other arm extended and elevated, the hand cupped as if to caress a face.

"You don't seem to need rescuing," Alerio teased. He wanted to leave the room and get away from the private drama, but his curiosity held him rooted to the floor.

The delivery man was young. Tall and lean with broad shoulders, he walked to the woman and rested his cheek in her hand.

"A son perhaps," Alerio guessed. When the man stooped and delivered a passionate kiss on the woman's mouth, and a lusty embrace to her entire body, Alerio revised his thinking. "No, not a son. A secret lover. Well, Syracuse is Greek, and the people certainly enjoy their dramatic plays."

With the mystery of the woman in the alley solved, Alerio strapped on his Noric steel dagger and left the apartment. He needed a tall cup of vino and an invitation to dinner. The wine because he was thirsty. The invitation, however, depended on locating the residence of Gabriella DeMarco.

***

The two-story city home was taller than it was wide, and almost a city block long. An impressive residence in an upper-class neighborhood, it had taken a few questions and a good walk to locate it.

After rapping on the door, Alerio stood on the stoop scanning the fronts of nearby buildings. As he had noted on his last visit to Syracuse, the variety of building materials incorporated in all the structures made the street resemble a mural.

Brick, not as uniformed as bricks from the Republic, composed only a little of the construction. The rest consisted of painted mud and clay over wood, or granite, or lava stone, or stained wood. Mixed to form curious patterns on the facades, the materials made buildings in Syracuse works of art.

When a servant opened the door, he faced her.

113

"Master, can I help you?" the servant inquired.

"Alerio Carvilius Sisera to see Gabriella DeMarco," Alerio answered. His confidence came from having asked three different people for directions to the DeMarco residence. "Gabriella and I are old friends."

"Please wait there, sir," the servant requested as she shut the door.

The last time Alerio talked with her, Gabriella had denied any chance of a relationship. Her excuse being he was too committed to the Legion to be involved with her or any woman. And she didn't want to wait at home for a notification of his death or disfigurement. As a Tribune the chance of injury dropped considerably, but not the months of being away from home or the possibility of death in battle. He had just thought through the infallibility of her arguments when the door opened.

Alerio's breath caught in his throat. For a moment, he forgot her logic and his decorum. In the depth of his heart, he wanted to reach out and embrace her like the delivery guy who kissed the lady in the alleyway.

"Centurion Sisera, what a pleasant surprise," Gabriella greeted him with a smile. "Please come in."

The arch above her nose perfectly framed the brown of her eyes. Even in late afternoon, her eyes captured the sparkle of early morning light and the promise of a new day. She pivoted sideways to allow him to pass. In the graceful turn, her profile revealed the touch of Venus in her face.

"Tribune," Alerio stammered.

"Excuse me?" she asked.

"I am a Tribune, now," he said sounding like a raw recruit speaking to his training Optio. "I mean, I am a staff officer."

"Does that prevent you from coming inside?" she teased. "Is there a regulation against ceilings?"

"Well, no, I just," Alerio mumbled. Then he clamped his mouth shut, crossed the threshold, and moved deeper into the foyer.

"Congratulations on your promotion," she offered while closing the door.

"More than that, I was adopted by Senator Maximus," Alerio informed her. "You are looking at a lucky man who happens to be rich."

"How wealthy?" she inquired while putting her hands on her supple hips.

Sensing a challenge, Alerio paused before answering.

"I am a partner in a travertine quarry, and part of a trading agreement to bring iron ore to the Capital for blades," he listed. "Plus, the inheritor of the Senator's lands and property. Why do you ask?"

"Just checking to see if you are too important to ride on a wagon with me," Gabriella told him. "I suppose we could find you a horse so you can ride high and gaze down on the common folks."

"No, no," Alerio insisted. "I am, I am simply lucky. I certainly did not mean to use expressions that conveyed an admiration for the Goddess Petulantia. There was no intent of arrogance or bragging on my part."

"If you say so," Gabriella smirked. "I have to deliver the evening meal to Nicholas and Archimedes. Would you like to ride with me?"

"Yes, I would," Alerio responded.

"Come. You can help load the baskets," Gabriella proposed. She bumped his shoulder as she passed him and inquired. "That's not to lowly a task for a Legion staff officer, is it?"

Her touch weakened his knees and he stood immobilized for a moment. But she turned at the far end of the room and flashed a smile at him. The joyous expression freed his feet, and he crossed the room quickly. They exited a side door, crossed a courtyard, and entered the cook shed together.

***

The horse was spirited and stepped high and quickly. Too quickly for Alerio's taste. It wasn't that he disliked the beast. It was just a quick trip would separate his hip from Gabriella's when they reached their destination.

"The King asked Archimedes to refresh the defenses of Fort Euryalus," she explained as the wagon rolled northwest from the center of the city. "Nicholas and the inventor have been out there working for two weeks."

"I've seen the fortifications from outside the walls," Alerio told her. "They are tall, thick, and formidable. But I didn't notice a fort. Only a few buildings right behind the wall."

"Once Archimedes had the contract to improve the fort," she explained. "He and my brother sat up all night describing possibilities."

"I suppose you were there to capture their ideas on paper," Alerio joked.

He didn't for a moment expect that she stayed up all night drawing the inventor's thoughts on paper. She did that for her brother because most people could not follow Nicholas' thinking. But surely, the famous Archimedes would have assistants.

"I did," Gabriella admitted. "They used up my stock of paper, and it almost caused me to miss an appointment with a client."

"You have clients?" Alerio questioned. "Of course, you do, for your leather business."

"No Sisera. When my brother and I arrived in Syracuse, I discovered a need for an interpretive artist," she explained. When Alerio twisted up his face in confusion, Gabriella described an example. "Say a husband wants a jeweler to make a brooch for his wife. But his attempt to tell a metalsmith what he wants fails. The man refuses to pay for the brooch because it doesn't look like the one, he envisioned in his mind."

"You draw the idea on paper and the smith makes the brooch from the picture," Alerio summed up. "There is a metalsmith next door to the Starfish Inn."

"Master Craftsman Dryas Chrysós," Gabriella reported the name of the shop owner.

"Does he have a daughter or a sister?" Alerio asked remembering the lady in the alleyway.

"Dryas has a wife and no other family," Gabriella told him. "But Febe Chrysós is not anyone's prize."

"Ugly, is she?" Alerio questioned.

"No. Febe, for her age, is still attractive," Gabriella corrected. "She is just not a happy woman."

"I saw a plump lady meeting a deliveryman in the alley next to the Starfish Inn," Alerio told her. "They were closer than passing acquaintances. Like us."

Gabriella snapped the reigns and the horse started up the backside of a hills. At the top, Alerio saw a collection of buildings with low roofs.

"If that is Fort Euryalus," he remarked, "I don't see a lot of construction."

"And you won't," she told him. "Archimedes is focused on the defenses."

The wagon pulled up in front of one of the buildings and a servant began unloading the baskets of food.

"Come Sisera," Gabriella offered while climbing down from the wagon, "I'll introduce you to Archimedes Phidias."

***

From the top of the hill, Alerio could see the enormous walls of Syracuse stretching off into the distance to his right. To his left, the wall ran behind him heading for the swamp and eventually to the beach at Syracuse bay. But no wall filled the corner where the fort stood.

"You have opened the city to invasion," an older man in a military tunic complained. "We are doomed with this foolish plan."

He spoke to a slim man who appeared younger than thirty years old. Alerio couldn't tell how tall because the man stood in a wide trench below a short wall. Other trenches ran for a short way before zigzagging and converging with another ditch as equally twisted.

"General. If you have a plan please take it to the King," the man called from the bottom of the trench.

"The King only has eyes for your drawings," the General complained.

"Then leave me in peace and allow me to do the job I was hired to do," the man said as he began climbing a ladder.

"Archimedes, I have brought supper," Gabriella shouted to him. "Nicholas, food. The both of you, climb out of your digs. You need your strength."

A ladder materialized on the side of another ditch and Nicholas DeMarco's head appeared.

Upon seeing Alerio, Gabriella's brother cried out, "Centurion Alerio Sisera of the Republic's Legion, welcome. What do you think of our defenses?"

"Those will be almost impossible to decipher from below," Alerio informed him. "I would not attempt a breach at this location."

"What are you seeing that I am missing?" the General demanded. "I apologize. I am Pelle, General of the city's defenses. If you are a military man, please explain how you can call this bad excavation a fortification."

Archimedes and Nicholas met at a flat area above the trenches, turned their backs to the fort, and began pointing to other ditches.

"Archimedes and Nicholas, it is time to eat," Gabriella instructed. "You can work later, once your bellies are full."

The two men turned and Alerio noted the same vacant look in Archimedes' eyes that he had observed in Nicholas' eyes. The two men thought differently from the average man and saw possibilities where others saw mundane objects. When Gabriella said she was taking her brother to Syracuse to study with an inventor, Alerio didn't understand. Now he did.

"They dismantled our wall and replaced the high with the low," Pelle complained.

"The parabolas create a better defense," Archimedes stated as he walked by heading for a table being set with food.

119

"Intersecting triangles funnel the water to pools below the walls," Nicholas described while walking with the inventor. He jerked a thumb over his shoulder as if he had explained everything. "Sisera, dine with us."

"Lady DeMarco, can you help out an old campaigner," Pelle begged. "What are they talking about?"

"Tribune Sisera, you said you would not suggest a breach here," Gabriella solicited. "Tell General Peel why."

"An approaching enemy when confronted with your walls General, will focus on your gates," Alerio described. He neglected to inform Pelle that a few years before, he had stood at one of the gates with a Legion. If King Hiero hadn't negotiated, Alerio would have been part of the force attacking the walls.

"We have ballistae and onagers targeting the gates," Pele said defensively. "No one can take our walls."

"I could tell you three ways the Legion could defeat your barrier," Alerio assured him. "But if I saw the fort and no walls, I would attack at this location. At least I would have before I stood above the works."

"What are you seeing that I am not?" Pelle requested.

"A natural defense," Alerio replied. "From the fields down there, it seemed simple to line up and feed men into the trenches. But your artillery will hurt the reserves and force them back. In the meanwhile, what appears to be a simple line of ditches, will funnel my men into tight boxes where your archers and spearmen can butcher us. And for those who survive the missiles, you'll free water from reservoirs creating deep pools. I only realized that item from Nickolas' description."

Archimedes and Nicholas wandered over while nibbling on bread.

"Like spearing fish in a pond," Archimedes suggested.

"Unfortunately for an attacker who takes the easy route," Alerio admitted, "it is exactly like spear fishing. In those pools, men will die, being trapped by men coming in from behind. I hate to admit it, but your plan is ingenious."

Gabriella's face darkened and she walked away from the four men. Moments later, Alerio looked around but couldn't find her. After a quick search of the fort, he discovered her sitting quietly on the wagon.

"You should have told me," Alerio informed her. "I would have walked out with you."

"But I, Sisera, did not want to walk out with you," she replied.

"I don't understand," Alerio pleaded. "What did I do wrong?"

"Nothing that I didn't already know," she said with exhaustion in her voice. "You speak of being butchered so easily. Death and military maneuvers are in your heart. For a time on the ride over, I forgot what you are."

Alerio paused and thought. He had the question but resisted asking. Finally, his heart beating hard on his ribs forced him to voice it.

"And what am I?" Alerio asked.

"You, Alerio Sisera are a Tribune of the Legion," she complained.

Then Gabriella snapped the reins and the wagon rolled away leaving Alerio standing alone on the hilltop. With his mind numb from the confrontation, he remained in front of the fort until the sun set over the buildings. In full darkness, Alerio began the long walk back to the Starfish Inn.

Chapter 12 – Rejected and Unloved

The sunlight blanketed half the apartment. But to Alerio's sleep encrusted eyes, it lay backward. Morning sun should be along the west facing wall and floor. Only in the afternoon does it…

"I have slept the day away," Alerio grumbled as he rolled out of bed. In appreciation of the soft mattress, he offered. "Much better than sleeping on the ground."

After splashing water on his face, he strolled to the alley side window, bent, and looked at the sky.

"Does it mean anything, if it's a nice day?" he complained to the storm clouds overhead. "I've no where to be with nothing to command my attention."

Because he was bored, Alerio lowered his gaze. The door across the alleyway opened a crack and remained motionless for long moments. When it fully opened, the woman didn't shuffle from the doorway. She appeared hunched as she crept out of the metalsmith's shop. No prancing or bright eyes today, she remained near the door huddled next to the wall.

"Are you ill, Febe Chrysós?" Alerio whispered.

As if she sensed someone watching, Febe glanced over her shoulder at the other end of the alleyway. But she failed to look up and across the lane at Alerio's second floor window.

"I'll leave you to your business," Alerio mouthed in her direction.

One of Febe's arms jerked outward and she made hurry up motions towards the mouth of the alley. Caught up in another of the woman's miniplays, Alerio stayed to watch the act unfold.

The tall delivery man came into view. No cupped hand to stroke his face waited to greet him. Instead, she grabbed his shirt and pulled him in close to her.

Alerio expected a kiss and an embrace. Neither occurred. Rather in the narrow space between their bodies she displayed an object. The size of her palm, it was wrapped in a cloth and pushed into the young man's hands.

He took the item and lifted a corner of the cloth then quickly covered it. Only after the transfer did Febe hug the man's neck and draw him down to plant a kiss on his lips. They separated and the man jogged out of view. Febe on the other hand twirled and danced a few steps before opening the door and vanishing into the shop.

"A present for her young lover," Alerio laughed. "The young partner receives gifts, and the older half receives what? Love, companionship, or maybe simply a chance to recapture a more exciting time in her life?"

Alerio strapped on his dagger, straightened his tunic, and headed for the door. As he walked out of the apartment and took the stairs down, a thought occurred to him.

'Maybe I can find a rich older woman who I can meet in an alleyway,' he pondered. 'If not love, at least I'd have gifts.'

***

The rain fell in waves resembling sheets of sails blowing across the city. Unfortunately, the three-day weather delay left Tribune Sisera with nothing to do because no ships could row in or out during the storm. Rain and idle time guided Alerio to a pub and tavern games.

"It's all in the wrist and the balance of the blade," Alerio explained to the men lined up behind him. He took a long pull of Syracuse beer before offhandedly flipping the knife. It spun across the distance and landed point first in the center of the target. "Simple, see?"

To the groans of the crowd, he staggered to a table and collected his winnings. Someone handed him his knife and he fumbled and dropped it on the tabletop.

"For two days you have cleaned out coin pouches and defeated all comers," the gambler told him. "I am afraid Alerio, there are no more challengers for you."

"Then I shall attempt to drink this fine establishment dry," Alerio boasted as he slid the Noric blade into the sheath. He canted to one side before righting himself. "Indeed, I will give it a try."

At his table in the corner, Alerio watched a blurred image of a very young serving girl bring him another pitcher of beer.

"You are cute," she flirted. "I get off at sunset."

The words and meaning took a few heartbeats to pass through the alcohol barrier.

"Love, companionship, or a chance to be young again," he exclaimed. "Have you no wealthy older friends. No one to give you gifts?"

"I am not that kind of girl," she barked. "You are a pig. And not a gentleman and…"

Alerio raised his mug in salute as she stormed away. And like the ravings of the serving girl directed at Alerio, outside Tempestas, the Goddess of Storms, vented her rage on Syracuse.

When the front door of the tavern blew open, a woman in a hooded cape came in with the wind. A patron closed the door as the woman tossed back the cape. A pair of sparkling brown eyes scanned the room.

"This is the third tavern I have visited today. I am wet, tired, and angry," she shouted. "I am not thirsty, and I don't want to hear your life's story or entertain an offer of friendship. I am looking for Alerio Sisera. Is he here?"

Heads turned and peered at a table in the corner.

Oblivious to the woman's presence, Alerio attempted the difficult task of pouring beer from a pitcher into a mug. It wouldn't be hard if the mug and pitcher would remain stationary.

"You are drunk," a female voice accused.

"Not near enough," Alerio replied while trying to control the stream of beer flowing onto the tabletop. "But the owner assured me they have barrels of this stuff in the back."

"Tribune Sisera, I know you are disappointed in me," the woman told him.

"I'll have another pitcher and some beef, and bread," Alerio slurred. "Stew and bread, works as well."

"Sisera, I am talking to you," she said with aggravation. "Please understand."

The voice of a siren, her song as strong as one calling to a sailor awash in the sea, broke through the ocean of beer.

"Gabriella DeMarco, what are you doing here?" Alerio asked while attempting to stand. "Can I offer you a beer?"

"No Tribune, not a beer," she said while taking his arm and guiding him around the table. "But you can offer me your help."

"Help? I fear fair lady, I am in no shape to offer anything," Alerio said as he sagged against her shoulder.

"Come on, we are leaving," Gabriella instructed.

She pulled on his arm and the Tribune staggered in the general direction of the front door. Using his momentum and her control, they made it out of the tavern and into a carriage.

"To my residence, please," Gabriella instructed the driver.

"Is that who you were looking for in all those pubs?" the teamster offered. "A pretty woman like yourself, lady, can do better than a drunk."

"In this case," Gabriella replied, "I cannot do better, as you say. This drunk is precisely who I need."

***

Another platter of cold ham and carrots replaced the empty plate.

"Are you feeling better?" Gabriella asked. She added a smile of sympathy.

"How did you find me?" Alerio asked. Between bites of food, he drank water.

"First I went to the Starfish Inn," Gabriella replied. "When the proprietor told me, you hadn't been to your room in two days, I began a concentric search."

Alerio poured water on a cloth and placed it on the back of his neck.

"You began a what?" he inquired while squinting his eyes.

"I looked in all the neighboring taverns starting with the ones closest to the Starfish Inn," she informed him before lying. "You were in the seventh pub I checked."

She smiled a demure expression to hide the fact she had located him at the third pub. But she needed him to feel that she had worked hard to locate him.

"I apologize for putting you through the ordeal," Alerio acknowledged then stopped. "Hold on. Why am I apologizing to you? More importantly, why did you interrupt my drinking? Surely, it wasn't because you wanted my company."

"Sisera, my feelings for you are complicated. But we can discuss them later," Gabriella proposed. "Right now, I need your help."

"Who do you want killed?" he sneered while throwing the damp cloth down on the table. "Because, according to you, that is all I am good for."

"I told you it was complicated. But I can assure you, you mean more to me than a blade," she pushed back. Then softly, Gabriella mentioned. "Dryas Chrysós has been arrested. And you are the only one I know who can help him."

"Did he kill his cheating wife?" Alerio tossed out as a snide remark.

"That's what they are charging him with," Gabriella uttered. "How did you know?"

"Tell me what happened," Alerio urged.

Gabriella picked up a carrot and rapped it against the edge of the platter.

"It started with a golden crown," she related.

***

Dryas Chrysós carefully cut the Kings' gold bars into equal parts. Then he positioned the pieces on his work bench and prepared the small forge and the crucible. Usually, a single pot or two of molten gold provided enough metal for the construction of custom jewelry. But the crown for the Temple of Plutus required multiple castings.

"He brought me in to draw his vision of the crown," Gabriella reported. "We worked for half a day on the placement of the gold ropes, peaks, scrolls, and the band. It was magnificent."

After I left, Dryas sifted the molding sand in preparation for sculpting the shapes into forms. It took another day to get the separate molds completed. Then he poured in the molten gold. After allowing for a cooling period, he separated the molds. There were no gaps or bubbles from the pour, giving him perfect sections of the crown.

During the time he filed off excess gold, bent and twisted the ropes, carved the scrolls, and curled the band, Febe must have left the shop.

It wasn't until Dryas' stomach reminded him, he needed to eat, that he went upstairs. To his surprise, the living quarters were empty. Febe was nowhere to be found. After a snack, Dryas went to his shop, expecting his wife to return after a trip to the market.

"Men who craft with gold and silver are meticulous," Gabriella informed Alerio. "They have to be exact as the tiniest details of their work will be scrutinized by admirers. It is not unusual for those craftsmen to remain at their workbenches throughout the night to finish a commission."

The rain beating on the roof drowned out the banging on the door. Dryas set the pieces into a wooden frame. Then carefully, he dribbled molten gold into the seams. After piecing the segments together, he used a tool to smooth the still warm metal.

While buffing and polishing the surfaces of the crown, the front door crashed in, and city guardsmen invaded the workshop.

A dilemma presented itself when the guard Sergeant saw the golden crown. An officer was summoned and when he arrived, he sent for one of the King's Judges. Then, the guard took Dryas Chrysós to detention and the Judge carried the crown to the King.

"Word reached me and that's when I went looking for you," Gabriella concluded the narrative.

"What am I supposed to do?" Alerio asked. "Or rather, what do you expect of me?"

"I need you to prove Dryas Chrysós did not murder his wife," she replied.

Her face gazed at Alerio so open and trusting that he almost believed through strength of will, he could find a solution. But, in all honesty, he could not see a way to prove the innocence of the goldsmith.

"The trial is tomorrow," Alerio pointed out. "Even if I track down Febe's man friend, it'll be too late for Master Chrysós. He could be half dead on the nails before I bring back the man she possibly went to meet."

"I talked to Nicholas about that," Gabriella informed him. "He has a way to delay the process for at least a day."

Alerio stood, still a little unsteady on his feet.

"Where are you going?" Gabriella questioned.

"To start the investigation," Alerio replied. He grabbed the edge of the table to remain upright.

"Certainly not in the condition you are in," she observed.

"You may not like this, Gabriella" Alerio warned, "but I have fought in worse shape. Imbalance from drink or blood loss feels the same. Except rather than be in a hospital tent tomorrow, I'll be sober."

Alerio collected his red Legion cloak from the drying line and left the house. He was correct. Gabriella DeMarco did not like his remarks.

***

On the far side of the Temple district, Alerio located the gate and the gate post with the etching of a bee. After hammering on the wooden door, he contemplated leaving and getting a good night's sleep. Before he could act on the notion, the gate drew back, and darkness greeted him.

"I am a friend of the Golden Valley," he said to the opening.

"Enter friend," the manager invited. "Do you have something to show me?"

Alerio handed over the dagger identifying him as an ally of the valley.

"Please come into the office, Tribune Sisera," Milon, the manager of the trading house, greeted him.

"I trust you have been well?" Alerio inquired.

"The years, the goods, the apprentices come, and they go," the manager remarked. "We roll with the passage of time and hope to survive. And allies drop in for, what?"

They entered the building, trekked down a hallway, and turned into an office.

"A metalsmith has been arrested for murdering his wife," Alerio informed the house manager. "I know the wife

130

was having an affair with a tall, lean, but broad-shouldered delivery man. I need to find him."

"It is not often we receive such specific requests," Milton commented. "Is there a timeline?"

"Dryas Chrysós goes in front of a judge tomorrow," Alerio began then stopped. "You already know about the charges. Don't you?"

"Of the trial and charges, I have prior knowledge," Milton admitted. "But the wife having a lover is news to me. Can you give me something else to help identify the man?"

"I don't know much else," Alerio confessed. "He is young and Febe gave him a gift."

"Yes, the spring to winter paradox," Milton suggested.

"That is one way to put it," Alerio said as he accepted his dagger and sheathed it. "Thinking of the difference between lovers of different ages, the paradox is a fitting description."

"Dryas Chrysós is a good and honest man," Milton told Alerio. "I will have a messenger bring you any details we uncover."

"It's all I can ask," Alerio professed before backing out of the office.

It was never a good idea to turn your back on anyone in a Golden Valley trading house. Even one disguised as the friendly manager of a trading concern dealing in luxury merchandise. Because the other item for sale at the trading house was death by the skilled assassins of the Dulce Pugno.

Act 4

Chapter 13 – The Golden Crown

Alerio woke to a message placed under his door sometime during the night. It directed him to a hearing room at the King's Palace. When he arrived, Gabriella and Nicholas met him on the walkway.

"Have you found out anything?" Nicholas asked.

"Was it you who gave Gabriella the idea to contact me?" Alerio inquired, while ignoring the question.

Gabriella huffed, squared her shoulders, and fast walked ahead of the men.

"Oh no. It was the other way around," Nicholas assured him. "But once she told me, I pointed out that one night wasn't enough for you to find the real murderer."

"That's what I told her," Alerio stated. "There is not enough time for an investigation."

"There will be," Nicholas exclaimed. "I have…"

"Nicholas, Tribune Sisera, hold up," Archimedes called.

The tall, lean inventor jogged to them, took a place between the men, and draped his arms over their shoulders.

"I have just had the most amazing breakthrough," Archimedes explained. "I got into my bath this morning and Eureka."

"You got into a bath and discovered something?" Alerio teased. "Usually, I find out where my blisters and small cuts are located."

"My body displaced water," Archimedes declared.

Nicholas stopped and his mouth fell open. Alerio assumed Gabriella's brother was about to unload some good-hearted harassment on the inventor.

"Volume and density," Nicholas gushed. "That is so close to the formula you've been working on."

"There is still a missing element," Archimedes uttered. He shook his head slowly as if they were weighing the weight of the world.

"Can we get to the hearing?" Gabriella asked.

She had walked back to collect the men standing and blocking the walkway.

"Yes, of course," Alerio concurred.

He fell in beside her and the four entered a side door and found seats in the hearing room.

***

"Under authority of King Hiero the Second, the state of Syracuse brings charges against the metalsmith Dryas Chrysós," a Marshal announced. "His wife Febe Chrysós was found stabbed to death less than a block from their shop. Without an alibi, the guard officer in charge imagined the following scenario."

Alerio leaned over and whispered to Archimedes, "What is it with you Greeks? Does everything have to be a dramatic performance."

Gabriella tapped Alerio's shoulder, "Sisera, hush."

But to Alerio's delight, she laughed when she said it.

"This is the disclosure segment of the trial," the Judge announced. "I will not have interruptions from the choir during the presentation. Marshal."

Alerio smiled at the concept of the audience being called a choir. There was an older man standing to the side of the Judge. Alerio assumed it was Dryas Chrysós.

"In the scenario imagined by the evidence, the couple argued," the Marshal continued. "Febe fled into the rain. Dryas grabbed a knife and, in the downpour, chased his wife. Once he caught up with her, he stabbed her multiple times. Then leaving her dead in an alleyway, he coldly went back to his shop and continued working on the King's project."

To Alerio's surprise, Archimedes stood.

"What happened to the knife?" he asked.

Another person in the choir stood and questioned, "And why did she run into an alley, if she was attempting to escape?"

"Did you find damp clothing?" someone else inquired.

"We didn't find a knife at the scene," the Marshal stated. "We can only assume Dryas pulled his wife into the alleyway to avoid detection while he murdered her. And finally, we did not find wet clothing in the shop."

"I don't see any real defense," the Judge declared. "I submit to the choir…"

"Judge, if I might," Nicholas requested. The Judge nodded his approval. "Although Master Chrysós has a reputation as an honest craftsman, if he truly murdered his wife, how do we know the gold in the Crown of Plutus is pure?"

The room fell silent. The Judge and the Marshal exchanged serious looks.

"We do not know," the Judge admitted. "Justice for murder is a capital crime. However, a crime against the God of Abundance and Wealth has far reaching ramifications."

"To have an impure artifact residing in a Temple threatens the stability of Syracuse," the Marshal added. "We must discover if the God Plutus will be offended before we can reach a decision about the fate of Craftsman Chrysós."

From the choir a unified 'yes' echoed around the room.

"And there you have it," Nicholas boasted. "You now have time, Alerio, to investigate the murder."

Alerio had his eyes on Dryas Chrysós. At the postponement, he sagged against the Marshal. Most people watching would assume the collapse was a display of relief. But Weapons' Instructor Sisera knew toppling sideways was usually associated with fear. Without realizing it, the accused leaned away from the imagined punishment.

"Archimedes, you are called on to perform a civic duty," the Judge informed the inventor. "The Crown of Plutus will be delivered to your workshop. We expect a decision in two days. Is the crown pure gold?"

"It will be my pleasure," Archimedes confirmed.

"How can you tell the purity between a gold bar and a golden crown?" Gabriella asked the inventor. "Without destroying the artifact, I mean."

"It shouldn't matter because the craftsman is an honest man," Alerio suggested.

"No, no, Tribune Sisera," Archimedes declared. "I will solve this puzzle. I must."

He and Nicholas with their heads together rushed from the hearing room.

"Can I buy you breakfast?" Alerio asked Gabriella.

"That would be nice," she agreed.

Before they reached the door, a timid little girl stepped in front of Alerio. Her small arm reached up, and as she handed

135

him a piece of paper, he noticed callouses on the tiny assassin's fingers.

He opened the paper, glanced down at the writing, then upward searching for the child. She was gone and so were the moments for breakfast with Gabriella.

"I am sorry. I need to cancel our meal," Alerio apologized. "Something has come up."

"I understand," she replied. "Maybe we will breakfast together, another day."

Alerio bowed to her before running from the hearing room. After sprinting down the pathway, he raced off in the direction of the nearest stable.

***

The note from the girl informed Alerio of a tradesman matching the description of Febe's lover. Hyperion, the driver, had resigned from his job this very morning. After buying a horse and used tack, he left the city with a large bundle tied to the rear of the horse.

An 'informal group' at the Golden Valley trading house surmised that Hyperion planned on permanently moving away from Syracuse. Alerio smiled at Milton hiding his opinion behind a made-up collection of people. Misdirection, stealth, and camouflage were tools of the assassins and used to their advantage. It appeared the subterfuge of the Sweet Fists extended to the written word.

The intelligence seemed solid, and the actions of the tradesman fit a man fleeing his conscious and seeking a new life. Alerio continued running.

At the stable, he flipped more than enough coins to the owner for a saddle and the rental of a horse. Then he saddled the beast and rode north. According to the note, Hyperion left by the northwest gate but much earlier in the day. By the time Alerio reached the exit, the sun hung high above the horizon.

As an access point, the northwest gate created a small portal in the defensive wall. Being adjacent to the strong point of Fort Euryalus, the gate needed only to serve farmers bringing food to the market.

Kicking its flanks to encourage the mount, Alerio passed through the gate and drove the horse down the road. In long strides, it galloped from Syracuse chasing Febe's killer. At least that's what Alerio hoped.

***

Two of the King's men-at-arms arrived with a Judge holding a box. Nicholas DeMarco met them at the front door.

"Come in and watch your heads," he instructed while indicating the instruments hanging from the low ceiling. "We will place the crown on the far end of the workbench."

Nicholas guided them passed ceramic bowls of various sizes. They grew in volume from mugs easily held between the thumb and one finger to enormous clay fired tubs suitable for soaking an entire head.

Barrels of clean water spaced every few feet rested on the floor. A couple leaked creating wet pools. The crown's honor guard had to dodge around the containers and the damp spots to reach the end of the bench.

"This is it?" Archimedes declared when he rushed into the room.

Reaching into the package, he lifted out the golden crown.

"It certainly feels heavy enough to be gold," the inventor announced. "But opinion is not fact and untested theories make for bad judgements."

"How will you test the purity?" the King's Judge inquired.

"I propose to cut it into pieces," Archimedes told him. "Nicholas, I seem to have misplaced the saw. Please fetch my ax."

The Judge stepped forward while reaching with both hands.

"I cannot allow you to destroy the Crown of Plutus," he exclaimed.

Archimedes spun, moving the crown out of the man's reach, and began laughing.

"I have no intention of harming the coronet, Judge," the inventor assured him. "But I will need to experiment on it."

"Do you swear that no harm will come to the crown?" the Judge questioned.

"I am Archimedes, a great inventor and mathematician," he replied. "The task before me is daunting. But as always, I will rise to the challenge."

"You are Archimedes Phidias, a local of twenty-nine years," the Judge reminded him. "I remember you as a snot nosed boy. So, don't brag to me. Show me, King Hiero, the people of Syracuse, and the Priest of Plutus that the crown is made from pure gold."

"My humble beginnings offer no restraints to the level of success my genus will achieve," Archimedes professed.

"Your father is Phidias, a well-respected astronomer and navigator," the Judge corrected. "And you are a second cousin to King Hiero. Those are not humble beginnings. However, if you will stop promoting yourself and get to work, I will give you a round of applause."

With that the Judge clapped several times before walking to a chair in the corner. He planted himself there and glared across the workshop at Archimedes.

"Nicholas, fetch the lump of gold from my room," the inventor ordered. "We will start with untangling the volume of the objects."

***

Alerio urged the horse to the top of a hill. From the crest, he noted a tall, broad-shouldered man riding slowly in the distance. Even if he didn't recognize Hyperion, the huge bundle tied over the back of the horse identified him.

Nudging his horse forward, Alerio walked the mount down the slope. At the base he kicked the beast into a trot. Hyperion grew as the horse caught up with the unsuspecting tradesman.

"Don't run," Alerio warned.

Hyperion glanced to the rear to see a man holding a knife by the blade. Angled back as if in mid throw, the position told him he was targeted.

"Few men can stick a point at distance," Hyperion challenged. "Let alone do any real damage by throwing a knife."

The weapon flew from Alerio's hand. It blurred as it twirled before hitting and sinking up to the hilt in the bundle.

"I can," Alerio assured him as he pulled the Golden Valley dagger from the small of his back. "Get down. We need to talk."

Some tall men used their size to intimidate. With greater reach came the ability to hit an opponent while avoiding a counter punch. Others, when physically threatened, acted as if their height made them as frail as a young sapling. Alerio

139

realized which category Hyperion fell into when he dismounted.

"What do you want with me?" the tradesman demanded. With his head and shoulders visible over the horse's back, the tall man hid behind his horse. "I don't know you."

Alerio dropped off his mount, walked over, and retrieved his knife from the bundle.

"What happened to Febe?" Alerio inquired.

The tradesman shifted as if ducking a swing.

"I don't know anyone named Febe," he lied.

"Do you have a twin brother?" Alerio inquired.

"No, why?" Hyperion challenged.

"Because I saw you and Febe Chrysós in the alleyway swapping spit," Alerio told him. He flipped the knife and caught it at shoulder height as if preparing to throw it again.

"She was a friend," he rushed out the wording, then corrected himself. "I mean, she is a friend."

Alerio had learned from his experience in the Legion to observe as much as talk. Looking over the huge bundle, the older horse, and the used tack, he realized none were valuable. Yet, the young man had received one, if not more, gifts from the wife of a goldsmith.

"What did you do with it?" Alerio demanded.

Alerio had no answer for the test question and wasn't sure what to expect. When Hyperion looked down, Alerio prepared for an attack. But the tradesman stared so long, Alerio thought it might be remorse. But it was neither bracing for a fight or an act of repentance.

"It's right here," Hyperion admitted. He raised his hand and displayed a square piece of gold. "I couldn't sell it in Syracuse. When I get to Messina, we can split the coins."

"Why did you kill Febe?" Alerio asked.

"She wouldn't leave me alone," Hyperion said as tears welled up in his eyes. "I am young. She followed me, saying if I left, she would say I was a thief. Say I did horrible things to her. When she kept pulling my arm and screaming, I had to shut her up."

"So, you dragged her into the alleyway and stabbed her," Alerio offered, "ten times?"

"No, that is not correct," Hyperion stated. "She followed me into the alley."

Alerio sheathed his knife and rubbed his eyes. Last night's beer had worn off and he had a headache.

"Get on your horse," Alerio ordered. "We are going back to Syracuse."

***

Archimedes lowered the Crown of Plutus into a ceramic container of water.

"What's that," the Judge asked. "Are you washing it? Hoping to rinse away the gold?"

"We are ascertaining the volume of the crown," Nicholas told him.

Suspended by strings, the crown sank into the vessel and the water rose. Water displaced by the volume of the crown spilled out of the big container, rolled down a tube, and fell into a smaller bowl.

Nicholas replaced the bowl containing the measured amount of water with an empty bowl that matched the first. While he was refilling the larger container, Archimedes placed the crown on the benchtop and tied a string around a lump of gold.

"The crown is a lot bigger than that nugget," the Judge stated. "You cannot balance them on a scale."

"Very astute of you," Archimedes respond. "I can't balance uneven masses, but I can... Eureka."

"What did you see?" Nicholas asked. "You mentioned mass then went silent."

"Not mass, Master DeMarco," the inventor corrected. He ran to a desk in the workshop, opened a jar of ink, selected a pen, and began writing on the desktop. "I said, masses."

Nicholas leaned over and studied an equation scrawled on the desk.

"Density equals volume over mass," he read.

"What does that mean?" the Judge inquired.

"It means," Archimedes informed the Judge while puffing out his chest, "that by morning, Archimedes Phidias will have proof of the purity of the Crown of Plutus."

"From dipping it in water?" the King's man teased. "It sounds like alchemy to me."

"Sir, alchemy is the study of turning lead into gold," Nicholas described. "This formula will turn the weight of water into gold. Or reveal the crown as a mixture of gold and other metals."

Chapter 14 - And One Evil

No note was needed to remind him about the hearing. Having delivered Hyperion and his confession to the city guard yesterday evening, Alerio felt connected to the case. He wanted to see the final resolution. Plus, he felt good about completing a task important to Gabriella DeMarco.

"Maybe she will reward me," he whispered while stepping through the doorway.

"Who will do what?" Gabriella inquired.

Positioned just inside the hearing room, she obviously was waiting for her brother and possibly Alerio.

"Maybe Themis, the Goddess of Wisdom and Good Counsel will bless me. Because, yesterday, I captured Febe's murder," Alerio jabbered. "And delivered him to the authorities. I served justice. Maybe she will bless me was all I was saying."

Nicholas came through the door. His appearance saved Alerio from any more babbling.

"You found the murderer?" Gabriella cooed. "Sisera, that is wonderful."

She threw her arms around Alerio and crushed her body against his.

'Justice has its own rewards,' Alerio thought.

"Dryas didn't kill his wife?" Nicholas questioned.

After Gabriella freed him from her lusty embrace, Alerio responded.

"He did not," Alerio assured Nicholas. "It was a tradesman she loved who did not love her."

***

The Judge, Marshal, and Dryas Chrysós entered, and the attendees faced forward while moving to claim spots on the benches. Alerio guided the brother and sister to an empty section.

"Where is Archimedes?" Gabriella asked.

143

"We ran experiments and made notes until late in the night," Nicholas reported. Then he stared off into the distance before adding. "Archimedes is searching for time."

"What does that have to do with the hearing?" Alerio inquired.

"When I left him, the inventor had figures and symbols written on every flat surface," Nicholas described. "As Menander the dramatist said almost sixty years ago, time leads truth toward the light."

"The choir will settle," the Marshal announced. "Guards bring in the accused."

Murmurs and questions ran through the audience. 'Wasn't Dryas the accused?' 'Was there a second conspirator in the death of Febe?'

The idea of a love triangle or some other salacious activity drove the choir to loud talking and projecting. Then a guard escorted a tall and handsome young man into the hearing room. The attendees quieted.

"Hyperion the Tradesman, the Marshal and I," the Judge proclaimed, "have witnessed your confession to the murder of Febe Chrysós. Please enlighten us as to the motivation for committing this dreadful act."

"I admit, as a young man, I use my appearance to flirt with the wives of shop owners," Hyperion told the Judge and choir. "Mostly it's harmless. The women get the attention of an attractive and vibrant man when I make deliveries. And sometimes, I received gifts. No harm is done. In fact, I consider my flirtation acts of kindness to those poor, bored women."

An uncomfortable energy rolled over the choir. Some men wanted to rush home and shower love and attention on their wives. Others, the jealous types, thought of investigating their spouses' acquaintances and recent whereabouts.

"I ask for mercy because I never started any of the liaisons," Hyperion insisted. "It was always the women who made the first move."

"You are not accused of philandering," the Judge reminded him. "The charge is murder. If you will not discuss the crime, I will call for the voice of the choir."

The tradesman dropped his head as if it were too heavy to hold erect. Veins and tendons lining his long neck strained against his skin. And to accent his emotional state, his shoulder's shook as he cried.

"I liked Febe. She was entertaining, lively, and pretty for an older woman," Hyperion enlightened the attendees. In response to his compliments about another man's wife, eyes shifted to see Dryas' reaction. The metalsmith stood dry eyed and stiff. His hands clamped into fists and held rigid at his sides while the tradesman continued. "She started like the others. Light and loose just as I prefer. I make deliveries around the city and a scandal would hurt my business. But weeks after getting Febe's attention, she became bolder. Meeting me in the alleyway for a hug and a quick kiss. I was uncomfortable and told her so."

The crowd leaned forward so as not to miss any of his story. Not so much to evaluate Hyperion, they already knew he was guilty. What they wanted were titillating details to add when they recited the tale to their friends.

Alerio shifted uncomfortably. To the Tribune, none of this was an excuse or a reason to kill a woman and make a husband, a widower. Given a chance, Alerio would stab the tradesman in the heart and be done with the matter. To save him from this drawn-out trial, Alerio second guessed his decision to bring back the tradesman.

'Better I killed him on the trail,' Alerio thought, 'then sit through the drivel of a man with no honor.'

Unaware of the action, Alerio's hand moved to the hilt of his knife. A soft hand covered his preventing him from drawing the weapon. He had no intention of pulling the blade. But Gabriella's gentle touch felt wonderful. Alerio maintained a slight upward pressure as if her hand kept his in check. Assassins weren't the only ones who used subterfuge.

"In answer to my rejection of her affection," Hyperion resumed, "Febe began giving me gifts. It was precious stones a couple of times, slivers of silver at others. Then she began talking about leaving her husband and running away with me. I am a young man, why would I want an old woman for a mate? But I am also a tradesman and to reject her outright would cost me her husband's business."

'Not the heart,' Alerio reconsidered. 'Now I want to stab him in the eye.'

"To deflect her insistence on running away with me, I explained that I had no coins for such an adventure," Hyperion rationalized. "I went about my business, thinking I had calmed the frenzied female. However, on my next visit, she passed me a square of gold with instructions to meet her that night. You must understand, I didn't know what to do. I certainly did not want to take her away with me."

Alerio vibrated with pent up energy at the weak man's plea. Enough so that Gabriella removed her hand.

'Not the eye,' Alerio contemplated. 'I'll cut his throat and watch him choke on his own blood.'

Hyperion scanned the crowd looking for faces sympathetic to his dilemma.

"Please have mercy on me," he begged when no one seemed to side with him. "I did not ask her to steal the gold. Or to leap to conclusions. Or create a fantasy about me and her together. I tried to get away, yet she found me in the rain. We argued as I walked her back in the direction of the shop. Then she pulled a knife and forced me into an alley. She was going to cut me, then call the guard, and accuse me of lechery against her. We struggled, and somehow, I got the knife away from her."

The Marshal took a threatening step towards him but stopped.

"You stabbed Febe Chrysós ten times," the Judge commented. "That is not self-defense. I put it to the choir. Guilty or innocent?"

The voice of the choir was a unanimous, "Guilty."

"Hyperion the tradesman, you will be drowned in the sea," the Judge declared. "Or you may drink a mixture of hemlock. Decide now, the sentence is to be carried out immediately."

***

The tall tradesman's knees buckled, and he dropped downward before catching himself. From the change in posture, Alerio recognized the wabbly stance of a guilty man.

"I assume they will release Dryas Chrysós now," Alerio offered. "I was glad to help bring him justice."

"Unfortunately, Master Chrysós must await Archimedes' findings," Gabriella told him.

"But the goldsmith is an honest man," Nicholas protested. "Everyone says he is beyond reproach. His shop is

147

a favorite of the King. I only suggested deceit to stop the trial. And it did, didn't it?"

Alerio recalled Dryas' leaning when the purity issue was introduced.

"Nicholas. Did you question Dryas before challenging the purity of the crown?" Alerio asked.

"No. He is a well-respected..." Nicholas stopped when Archimedes appeared.

It wasn't the presence of the inventor or his sudden entrance. What stopped Nicholas DeMarco were the hat and robes of a scholar. With the robe streaming behind him, Archimedes marched to the front of the room.

"I have findings to present," the inventor declared.

"Please, by all means Master Phidias, present your conclusions," the Judge invited.

"After extensive study and experimentation," Archimedes announced. "I find the Crown of Plutus light in gold. It is my learned opinion that the coronet is far from being pure gold."

"Dryas Chrysós, you stand accused of crimes against the people of Syracuse, an attempted conspiracy to defraud your King," the Judge listed, "and most grievous of all, instituting a scheme to insult and disgrace the God Plutus, his Temple, and his followers."

Jeers rose from the attendees. The Marshal allowed for a short display before he signaled for them to settle.

"What do you have to say for yourself, Master Chrysós?" the Judge inquired.

"Febe was younger than me, but I loved her with all of my soul," Dryas admitted. "When the gold went missing, I knew Febe took the piece. I knew but could do nothing about the theft. Nothing my heart would allow. So, to keep her secret, I added silver to the molten gold and made up the difference. Before I could speak to Febe, the guards broke in and informed me of her death."

Dryas folded his arms in front of his chest, closed his eyes, and stood as if waiting for the roof to fall on him. Then, it did.

"For your horrendous crimes against humanity and the Gods," the Judge decreed, "you will be strapped to a plank by iron about the neck, wrists, and ankles. Raised to the sky, you will bake and plead with the Sun God Helios for relief. If exposure does not end your life, eventually the crows feasting on your flesh will deliver justice. As it is ordered, let it be, take the condemned away."

Alerio's mouth dropped open and he shook his head to clear his thoughts. He had used his contacts and brought back the killer only to have the goldsmith receive a punishment harsher than the tradesman.

While Alerio contemplated Dryas' sacrifice for love and Alerio's part in the man's awful punishment, Archimedes rushed to Nicholas. The men hugged in celebration. Gabriella smiled and gazed upon her brother and the inventor with delight.

"We did it," Archimedes shouted. "The calculations need better measurements, but the formula works."

With their arms linked, Nicholas and Archimedes hopped and danced around.

"Your calculations just sent a good man to a gruesome death," Alerio pointed out. "Doesn't that bother you?"

"As the Philosopher Socrates stated," Nicholas lectured Alerio. "There is only one good, knowledge. And one evil, ignorance."

Alerio glared at Gabriella and before thinking, he exploded.

"You accuse me of being a blood thirsty warrior. And that's not good enough for you," Alerio lambasted her. "Yet you stand by smiling while academics use science to build inhumane traps and send a sweet, lovestruck man to suffer under the beaks of crows. And for that you smile."

Alerio stomped to the doorway shoving his way through the crowd. Once out of the hearing room, he jogged back to the inn to burn off his anger.

***

In the morning, a messenger arrived at the Starfish inn.

"I have a message for Alerio Sisera," he informed the proprietor.

"Sisera checked out last night," the inn keeper replied. "His passage to the Isle of Rhodes came into port."

"When does it row out?" the courier asked.

"This morning, if I remember Sisera's comment about, not soon enough," the inn keeper related. "I'm afraid it's too late to get a message to him. Who is it from?"

"It can't be that important," the messenger described. "It's an invitation to breakfast from Lady Gabriella DeMarco."

Chapter 15 – Wind Dancer

The sun climbed high but had yet to reach the summit of the sky. Below the orange ball, the water of Syracuse Bay was glazed over in the calm of late morning. Until the mouth of the harbor, the bay rested as flat as a wheat field, except for the wake behind a single transport.

"Stroke, stroke," Captain Tivadar called from the rear oar. Six oarsmen went through the repetitions of rowing a merchant ship as he steered. "Walk it together. Stroke, stroke."

From the protected harbor, the ship rowed into the Ionian Sea and rolled gently in the rougher waters.

"Not to worry," Tivadar guaranteed the crew when a high wave rocked the deck. "The Aura is a wind dancer."

Alerio glanced fore and aft and stepped while pulling and pushing his oar.

"Not to be rude," Alerio remarked, "but this is a floating bowl. I can't imagine naming this boat after a nymph of the breeze."

"She is seventy-five feet long, eighteen feet across at the beam," the Captain described. "But the key to her dancing and sea worthiness are the twelve feet of draft. Her big belly keeps the Aura flowing with the wind and as stable as a Spartan shield wall."

From the Captain's choice of words, Alerio knew he was Peloponnesian and a fan of Sparta. A wind whipped across the deck blowing from the Southeast. Another caught the side boards and the deck tilted.

"Unroll the sails. Let's give her some air," Tivadar instructed. "Now Sisera, you'll see her dance."

The two sails dropped and filled with wind. As the Captain promised, the big merchant ship steadied and began smoothly rocking up and down while cutting through the waves. Although slow, the rhythmic movement could be called a dance.

"What do you think, now?" Tivadar inquired.

"It…"

"She, Sisera. Do not insult the Aura," the Captain warned. "It will be two days before we see land again. And the only solid surface for miles upon miles is the deck of my girl."

"She dances well," Alerio complimented as he shoved his oar under the steering platform. "The sun is off my right shoulder. If we are sailing east, shouldn't it be in my eyes?"

"You must have an understanding of navigation because you are correct," Tivadar submitted. "Our track to the northeast is to offset the sea current coming from the north. Closer to Peloponnese, the current will come from the south."

"What happens in the center?" Alerio questioned.

"We become a hole in the water for a black night, a day, and another black night," Tivadar answered. "But not to worry, the Aura will see us through."

Offered the rear oar, Alerio stepped up on the platform. With the handle under his right arm, he kept the sun on his right shoulder. To his surprise, the ship did not track to the northeast in the direction he steered. But due to the force of the current, the Aura ran almost directly eastward.

***

Syracuse had faded below the horizon long before the sun dipped below the same empty skyline. Almost as if a beneficial tradeoff for an ocean-going vessel, the view of the deck and the rolling waves gave way to a sky filled with stars.

"I have traveled on the sea overnight," Alerio told the crew. "And I've seen the night sky from valleys and mountain tops. But nothing compares to this overhead dome."

"We are traveling via the circle of the bears," Tivadar announced from the steering platform. The Captain held a wedge-shaped structure against the sky and directed the sailor on the rear oar. "Bring us to port. A little more. Good, hold that track."

"Circle of the bears?" Alerio asked.

"There are two spots of light in the northern sky that never move," Tivadar described. "The Egyptians call them the Indestructibles. From sunset to dawn, and some claim during the day, the heavenly bodies of Kochab and Mizar remain stationary in the sky. The Little Bear cluster revolves around Kochab. And Mizar anchors the center of Big Bear. When I line up this triangle with the Indestructibles, we are traveling in the circle of the bears."

Throughout the night, crew members took turns on the rear oar. Standing with him, another sailor held the triangle up to the sky to keep the Aura in the circle of the bears and heading east.

***

At the start of the second day, Tivadar stowed his triangle sticks and used his hand.

"Starboard," he directed the oarsman. With his hand held up to the side of the rising sun, the Captain judged their direction eastward. His experience dictated how many fingers off the blazing orb were required to stay on course. "A little more starboard. Good."

The sailor on the rear oar swung the handle. In jerking movements, the bow of the Aura shifted further to the right.

As Tivadar used the sun to reset the heading, three sailors pulled out fishing lines. Another seaman unpacked what appeared to be a bronze shield.

"Is there a threat?" Alerio asked. He stood and drew his gladius. "I don't see an enemy."

"Oh, it'll heat up soon enough," the sailor advised as he placed the shield face down on a circle of bricks. "Once we have fish to put in the fire."

From bundles, the sailor pulled branches and chunks of charcoal. While the fishermen began landing and cleaning fish, flint struck iron and the wood flared to life. Alerio put away the gladius, drew his knife, and helped clean fish.

The only fluid being spilled would be fish blood and the only slashes required were to remove scales. Baked fish, bread, and watered wine help the crew pass the day.

Just before sunset, Tivadar did a hand check of their position. After adjusting the Aura, he pulled the triangle and waited for the Indestructibles to become visible in the evening sky.

***

The steady whoosh of water passing along the hull seemed to grow louder with the setting of the sun. Part of it might be the lack of birds squawking. But sailors speaking in hushed tones was another reason. The lowered voices were a natural reflex handed down from ancestors attempting to hide from night predators and raiders.

"Sisera. Do you know the story of how the Ionian Sea received its name?" Tivadar asked. His low-pitched voice was perfect for telling tales around a campfire.

"I do not, Captain," Alerio replied.

"Then allow me to enlighten you. There once was a city on the edge of an unnamed sea," Tivadar related. He sat on the steering platform and dangled his legs over the deck. "Today the land is part of Illyria. But at the time of this tale, King Epidamnus ruled a small kingdom by the sea. A stingy and mean man, King Epidamnus guarded his power carefully. One way was to forbid tradesmen and craftsmen from holding public office or serving as community leaders. His tightly controlled oligarchy consisted of his three sons and himself."

Tivadar reached for a wineskin. During the pause, the four off duty sailors moved closer to their Captain and Alerio so they could hear.

"Dyrrhachus, the King's eldest son married and had a son," Tivadar continued. "Because he produced the only heir, Dyrrhachus became the country's Magistrate. With nothing to occupy their time, the other two brothers grew lazy, caustic in their language, and bold with their criticisms. Noticing the shameful behavior, King Epidamnus banished them from the palace."

The Captain shifted, reached for a piece of fish and bread, put them in his mouth, and chewed for a few moments. When done, he rinsed down the food before returning to the story.

"Dyrrhachus the Magistrate took pity on his brothers. He gave them gold to start businesses," Tivadar described. "They prospered and became rich men. However, because of the King's law neither could hold public office or have a say in the rules that regulated their businesses. These captains of commerce grew irate and jealous at the lack of control. Forgetting their time in the palace, or maybe remembering it

155

too fondly, they bridled at the sight of Dyrrhachus' son and heir to the throne living the life of a nobleman. Together, the two brothers plotted an overthrow of their sibling and their father."

The Captain stood and crossed the steering platform. After checking their course against the circle of the bears, he returned to the edge of the deck.

"Where was I? Ah, with their wealth, the tradesmen brothers raised an army and marched towards the capital city of Durrës," Tivadar told Alerio and the sailors. "By coincidence, the hero Heracles arrived for a visit with King Epidamnus. Despite the looming threat, a midday feast was organized for the demigod. Dyrrhachus' son became enamored with Heracles and choose to sit beside the hero. While they dined, the army of mercenaries arrived, and the brothers called challenges to Dyrrhachus and the King. Hearing his host insulted, Heracles donned his armor and went to face the brothers. Seeing an advantage with the demigod on his side, Dyrrhachus called out his army and marched them from the palace. Unknown to Dyrrhachus, his son Ionius put on his grandfather's old armor and marched out with the Durrës army."

The Captain took a sip of wine and glanced up at the stars. Figuring the Aura was on course, he continued.

"On one side, Magistrate Dyrrhachus commanded the King's army," Tivadar explained, "facing him were the usurpers. When the brothers saw Heracles, they trembled. But having invested so much gold in the venture, they concentrated their forces and sent wave upon wave of soldiers against the hero. Time and time again, Heracles was surrounded. And after each skirmish, the hero remained among the living while the mercenaries died. Rather than attack the distracted enemy, Dyrrhachus and his army idled in their formations, watching the hero fight their battle. But war takes a toll, and even heroes get tired. When Heracles staggered from blood loss, only one warrior from Durrës raced to the hero's side. The fighting was furious with blades cutting armor and slicing flesh. After the frenzy ended, only Heracles lived. At his feet lay a body dressed in Durrës armor. The bronze was shredded by slashes only a demigod could have delivered."

Tivadar yawned and stretched as if exhaustion would end the tale.

"No, finish the story," the sailors protested.

"If I must," Tivadar said giving in to them. He smiled in the dark and continued. "Seeing the serrated armor, Dyrrhachus finally sent his army against his brothers while he rode to the body. Turning the warrior over, the Magistrate gazed at the face of his son, Ionius. Heracles bent and lifted the boy to his chest. Then with the grieving father in tow, the demigod walked from the battlefield to the edge of the unnamed waters. There Heracles declared, I anoint these waters with the body of this hero. Then he tossed Ionius into the sea. And that is how this body of water came to be called the Ionian Sea."

"Is that true?" Alerio asked.

"Who knows," Tivadar admitted. "It's one of many legends about the Ionian. But Aristotle used the story to demonstrate one of his ideas."

"Which one?" Alerio questioned.

"The philosopher proposed that the most perfect political community is one in which the middle class is in control, and outnumbers both of the other classes," Tivadar quoted.

"Myth, legend, or an example for a dissertation," Alerio remarked, "none of that matters. What happened was a failure of command."

"How so?" the Captain asked.

"First, King Epidamnus needed to leave his palace and make an appearance on the battlefield. The absence of their General hurt the morale of his army. Had they been motivated, the soldiers would not have stood by while others fought for them," Alerio explained. "And Dyrrhachus missed an opportunity. Any quality Battle Commander would have taken advantage of an enemy combat line that collapsed to focus on one unit. In this case Heracles."

"That's a very practical take on the story," Tivadar pointed out. "What are you, a Hoplite?"

"No, sir," Alerio replied. "I am a Tribune in the Legion of the Republic."

***

Dawn found the deck of the Aura wind swept and enclosed in torrents of rain.

"Stroke, stroke, walk them together," Tivadar shouted.

Most of his words were brushed away by the storm. But the sailors and Alerio got the idea. And although they couldn't see across the deck to their counterparts, the three on either side managed to coordinate the dips and lifts of their oars.

With no sun or stars to guide the ship, Alerio hoped Captain Tivadar's experience would hold the transport to the proper heading. And while the question of direction without navigation caused a concern, the Aura moved stately through the rolling swells. She might have been a sow compared to a sleek warship, but her size kept the top boards above the water line.

"This is not good," Tivadar bellowed the warning.

"Is there a problem?" Alerio called to the Captain.

"We are half a day's journey from the Peloponnesian coast," Tivadar called back.

As he walked the oar, Alerio worried about being lost a sea.

"How long can we last?" Alerio screamed into the wind.

"The ship?" Tivadar questioned. "She'll float for months. I was complaining that we might miss Vromoneri when we reach land."

"Captain, please, not that," the rower behind Alerio whined.

During a raging storm far from the coast and blind to navigational aids, the crew and the Captain were not panicked. They took the weather in stride. Except for the possibility of making landfall somewhere other than a place named Vromoneri.

"What is Vromoneri?" Alerio asked.

"A sheltered harbor with deep water," Tivadar replied. "Merchants from up and down the coast land there. It makes for a good trading market."

"And there's a gentlemen's club," the front rower exclaimed. "with the most dramatic women in the world. You will love them."

Alerio did not respond. But his mind offered an unspoken thought, 'I left enough drama in Syracuse to last me for the year. At this point in my life, I don't need any more.'

Chapter 15 – Drama and Thieves

The sheets of rain parted and after a few last drops on the deck, the vista over the fore deck cleared. A distant mound of land appeared off the right side of the bow.

"Raise the sails," Tivadar ordered, "but keep your oars."

"Is that Vromoneri?" Alerio questioned.

"That, Sisera, is the coastal island of Porti," the Captain whined. "It breaks the surface five miles north of Vromoneri.

"Sir, you navigated to within five miles of our destination across open water," Alerio complimented. "Surely you have a gift from Hermes."

"The God of Travel and Trade does deserve a sacrifice," Tivadar acknowledged. "But I was aiming for Methoni, twenty-two miles south of here. It was the crewmen who wanted Vromoneri."

"And we'll make a sacrifice to Hedone for the landing," a crew member shouted.

"You'll be thanking the Goddess of Pleasure when you are hungover, holding a belly full of sour wine, and rowing against the current," Tivadar offered. Then he explained to Alerio. "Methoni is farther south. From there, I planned to move up the coast to the Gulf of Corinth. But now, we will stop at Vromoneri first."

"Can we stop again on the way back?" another sailor asked.

"No, we'll sail right passed it," the Captain scolded. "I pay you to move cargo. Not to waste my time while you nurse a wine head."

"If it is a struggle to fight the current southward, why not skip Methoni and head north from Vromoneri?" Alerio asked.

"During the Trojan War, King Agamemnon took Achilles prize for the sacking of the fortress at Lyrnessus," Tivadar told him. "Deeply offended, Achilles not only refused to fight, but he prayed for defeat to punish the King."

"I can see the issue," Alerio agreed. "But to pray for defeat over a little wealth sounds disrespectful to me."

"The prize for capturing the fortress, Sisera, was the stunning Briseis," Tivadar pointed out. "And Achilles was infatuated with her."

"It wasn't gold or silver causing dissension in the command structure," Alerio considered. "The division came from a dispute over a woman."

"You say that like you have experience with women and drama," Tivadar proposed.

"Just one woman but lots of drama," Alerio replied. "Please continue."

"King Agamemnon begged his hero to engage in the fighting. Achilles refused and withheld his men from the battle for Troy," the Captain related. "During the pleading, Agamemnon offered populated cities as numerous as leaves on a vine. There were seven and the last city offered to Achilles was Methoni."

"You make it a port-of-call for historical reasons?" Alerio questioned.

"No, Sisera, for sentimental reasons," Tivadar replied. "Methoni is the place of my birth and where my wife and children live. But first we suffer Vromoneri. Stroke, stroke, stroke."

161

***

The Aura rolled out of the current and into the protective arms of the cove. On shore, campfires sent smoke into the air. High up, it drifted away on the breeze. But at ground level, the smog hugged the earth. Through the gray fog, Alerio could see buildings. One appeared to be a roof supported by columns over a raised floor.

"That is the Melodrámatos Club," Tivadar pointed out. "Drama girls dance there day and night. As long as there are men with coins, they put on shows. Later, if you want, a girl will invite you to her quarters in the small buildings. You can see them arranged around the backside of the club."

"No thanks," Alerio stated. "I understand war and training men. Recently, I have discovered my inability to understand women."

"An ago old problem for men, Sisera, I can assure you," Tivadar told him. "The wine and beer are usually good and there are other games."

"How long will we be here?" Alerio asked.

"No longer than two days. One for my crew to indulge themselves," Tivadar reported. "And another for them to sleep it off."

"That's very kind of you," Alerio observed.

"Not as much as you might think," Tivadar informed him. He indicated two of the five ships in the cove. "Unlike a coastal trader, the Aura only serves deep harbors. Deep harbors attract all kind of vessels. And a wide variety of mariners and thieves. Two of those ships belong to Illyrian pirates. Usually, I would sail up the coast in a convoy. Or keep the crew on board to guard the ship."

162

"But here, you'll allow them to go ashore," Alerio guessed. "And you'll do what? Stand guard by yourself."

"I don't expect trouble," Tivadar replied. "But just in case Phthonos whispers into the ears of a drunken Illyrian crew, I will remain on my ship."

Alerio glanced at the other vessels in the cove. The smallest transport, barely larger than a river craft, had little value while the two coastal traders contained cargo but lacked value as captured ships. Tivadar's transport however, bobbed seductively in the swells, making her a tempting prize for the two Illyrian biremes.

"No offense, but what will you do if the God of Envy does sends one hundred and twenty pirates to take your transport?" Alerio asked. "Die?"

"Possibly," Tivadar admitted. "But my crew deserves a little fun."

"Let me propose something to you," Alerio offered. "Bring me a shield, food and drink, and I will stay and protect the Aura."

"I will personally deliver a feast and the shield," Tivadar promised. Then to the crew he shouted. "Hold water. Prepare to drop anchor."

The big transport drifted to a stop as the idled oars resisted the forward momentum. Shortly after, two splashes, one fore and the other aft, announced the release of the anchors. With the transport stationary, the sailors dipped pails, pulled up buckets of water, and bathed.

"You are going to miss the fun," one sailor advised Alerio.

"Then you have twice as much fun," Alerio responded. "Once for you and another for me."

163

"Twice as much fun," the five crewmen shouted as they shoved a ramp from the deck to a large rock jutting from the water. After walking the ramp, they leaped into the water on the other side. "Twice as much fun."

Splashing to shore, they continued the chant while weaving through the campfires on the beach.

"I'll be back with your food," Tivadar told Alerio.

No one on the beach paid attention to the Aura. At least they didn't appear to be interested. But Alerio caught more than one Illyrian making side-eyes in the direction of the fat merchant vessel.

"Don't forget the shield," Alerio reminded the Captain.

Tivadar strolled down the ramp and splashed ashore. When he left, Alerio pulled out the bundle with his armor, helmet, red cape, and grooming kit.

Before dark, he planned on putting on a show for the pirates. A cautionary tale that would hopefully dissuade them from trying to seize the Aura.

***

From the beach of Vromoneri, a pair of eyes scanned the Aura.

"Murat. I may leave that transport to you in my will," an Illyrian offered.

Murat looked across the campfire at his Captain before gazing at the cove.

"I was unaware you owned that ship," Murat remarked.

"I don't as yet," Bujar told his Lieutenant. "But I will, by dawn."

"In that case Captain, what can I do to enhance my inheritance?" Murat asked.

He shifted around the fire until he sat next to Bujar. The Illyrians leaned inward and conversed in whispers.

***

As good as his word, Tivadar returned with a shield laying across his arms. A two-fisted hunk of roasted beef, a loaf of bread, and a wineskin were heaped on the Hoplite shield.

"I hope this is satisfactory," he said while placing the load on the steering platform.

Alerio unstacked the food and drink and strapped the shields to his forearm. Snapping his arm outward, the Legion Weapons' Instructor shoved the shield forward before bringing it back in front of him. Constructed of stiff leather with a bronze face, the shield was old and dented, but also well-oiled and polished.

The heavy and stout mankiller pleased Alerio.

"Excellent shield," he announced.

"I was talking about the quantity of beef and bread," Tivadar pointed out.

"The food looks fine. But it is not a feast suitable for a last supper," Alerio replied. "With this shield, it needn't be."

The Captain departed, Alerio ate, and the sun moved steadily for its meeting with the sea. In the late afternoon, sounds of drums, pipes, and men laughing and cheering carried from the Melodrámatos Club.

Before dark, Alerio stripped off his workman's woolen shirt and pants. He picked up the bucket and prepared to put on a show of his own.

***

In the back of the crowd at the Melodrámatos Club, two men watched as a girl twirled, dipped, and pranced.

"Is their anybody on the transport?" Bujar asked.

Murat walked away from the club, located a point of land where he could see the merchant ship, and peered at the Aura. After a long look, he went back inside.

"One crewman is still onboard. I thought he was stripping for a swim," Murat told his Captain. "But he didn't. He is washing from a bucket."

"If he follows the normal practice," Bujar proposed, "he'll be heading for the club once he has bathed. I've paid the girls to occupy the crew and their Captain for a long time. Select a salvage crew and have them ready to take the ship after dark. Go watch our straggler and keep me informed."

The Illyrian Lieutenant moved back outside. After speaking to a few of his crew, Murat went to his vantage point. Expecting to see the sailor dressing, he was puzzled as the man poured olive oil into his hands. Then he began to rub the oil into his naked flesh. After coating his body with oil, the crewman began rubbing it off with a metal scraper.

"Not the actions of a sailor," Murat said with a shiver. "Rather than preparing for a night of drunken debauchery, he is performing a ritual."

When the man pulled on a short sleeved red tunic and picked up a set of chest armor, the Lieutenant understood. He raced back inside.

"He is not a sailor," Murat warned his Captain. "The straggler is a Legionary. And he has washed, oiled, and is dressing for battle."

"One man will not stand between me and that trophy," Bujar declared. "Pick your salvage team from our best fighters. And to be sure no one interferes, send another seven to the beach."

"We'll have your prize out of the cove and gone before the crew knows their ship is missing," Murat vowed.

"My ship," Bujar said.

"What was that, Captain?" Murat inquired.

"Before they know 'my' ship is missing," Bujar replied. He turned to watch the dancing girl but added. "And kill that Legionary."

***

Lounging in a Roman bath allowed for an obligatory soak. The opposite held for field washing. A quick cleaning, get dressed, and get back to business was the norm. Leisurely washing, oiling, and scraping as Alerio had done wasted moments of one's life. But he had to be sure the Illyrians saw him preparing for battle. Hopefully, seeing a Legionary would cause them to back away from attacking the Aura.

Before sunset, Alerio pulled on his armor, locked the armored skirt around his waist, draped the red cape over his shoulders, and slipped on his Tribune's helmet. Once dressed, the fully armored Legion officer began patrolling the deck.

The sun wasn't completely set when the first pair of pirates came for the Aura. Taking advantage of the sun's rays streaming into the Legionary's eyes, they swam to the seaward side and climbed the aft section.

Alerio had demonstrated his readiness to fight with the display of armor, helmet, and gladius. And although he had put himself on view, he went with the doctrine of not showing an enemy all his gear.

The first two pirates crept up the back of the merchant ship. Climbing with confidence that the sun would blind the man guarding the vessel, they expected to make the steering deck before being discovered. They were wrong. The Hoplite

167

shield arched down from the platform. It cracked the first one in the head and launched him back into the water. Then, the big, bronze oval rocked back and scraped the second Illyrian off the side boards. He splashed down and came up sputtering and bleeding.

"Watch out for sharks," Alerio warned while pulling back from where he leaned over the railing.

A sneak attack served one of two purposes. Either it preceded an attack from that direction, or it acted as a diversion to draw guards out of position.

Alerio could see the water behind the transport. There were no other swimmers or small boats. After delivering the warning about swimming with predators, he straightened from the rail and sprinted towards the fore deck to face the main attack.

***

The aft assault had attempted to use the sun in Alerio's eyes as cover. At the bow, the fading rays of the sun outlined the Legion officer and put the pirates in deep shadows.

Two Illyrians had scrambled onto the fore deck and crouched for a moment. They might have been looking for the Legionary or waiting for help. The hands and heads of two more were just coming into view from over the side.

Seventy-five feet of deck required twenty-two strides to cross. When Alerio reached his twentieth pace, he pushed off with his front leg. Holding his arms folded into his chest, he flew the last six feet, and touched down between the pirates on the fore deck.

The Legion officer bent his knees to absorb the shock. Rocking his hips forward to torque his arms and back, he paused for a breath and held his arms together.

A Hoplite's shield measured two and a half feet across its face and could launch an unprepared man back and onto his butt. Or locking with neighboring shields, it could smash into an enemy's shield wall while protecting the Hoplite.

Alerio uncoiled to the left and swung with the edge of the shield. Rather than hammering the pirate, he caught the man with the rim. Three feet of curved, narrow bronze shattered the man's bones, cut flesh, but did not launch the pirate. The Illyrian dropped to the deck when Alerio retracted the shield.

Taking a wide step to his right, Alerio stabbed with his gladius. The pirate on that side anticipated a slash. He raised his sica to parry. But the gladius snaked under the man's arm. The blade shattered ribs as it pierced the pirate's lungs.

With the deck cleared of active foes, Alerio turned his attention to the two emerging from over the side. One ate a mouthful of bronze and the other swallowed a length of sharp Noric steel. One screamed as he fell. The other tumbled silently, unable to voice any sound. Both splashed into the cove with no chance of survival.

Alerio patrolled around the deck of the Aura while monitoring the ramp. It was the next likely approach. He maintained a vigil between glances over the side, searching for more swimmers.

Finally satisfied the waters were calm and empty of combatants, Tribune Sisera faced the ramp, braced behind the shield, and waited for the next wave of attackers. The pirates never came. But that did not mean Captain Bujar had given up on capturing the prize transport.

Act 5

Chapter 16 – Fingertips to a Mile

A loud splash alerted Alerio to the assault. But the sloshing around in the shallow water confused him. What enemy force announced their presence by stomping around before attacking?

When the first man reached the top of the ramp he paused, which saved his life. Not the stopping, Alerio could have easily stabbed the dark shape. It was the puking over the side of the ramp that saved the mariner's life.

"Sisera?" the second crewman on the ramp whispered. "The Illyrians have taken Captain Tivadar."

"Hold right there," Alerio ordered. Many a fort had fallen when the gates were opened for citizens only to allow attackers to follow them inside. Holding a shield at the top of a ramp entailed the same caution. "How many are you?"

"Just us, the five crewmen," another replied.

"Come aboard slowly so I can identify you," Alerio instructed.

One got under the sick man's arm and together they stepped onto the deck.

"Put him on the steering platform and out of my way," Alerio directed. When the other three staggered off the ramp, Alerio herded them to the side with the shield and warned. "Step away from me."

"What's wrong?" one demanded.

"I don't want a traitor's blade in my back," he told the sailor.

"That won't happen, Sisera," a crewman assured him. "By birth or marriage, we are all related to Tivadar. And we know once the Illyrians take a fancy to a vessel, the crew becomes dead or slaves."

"What do we do?" another begged.

"Tell me what happened?" Alerio questioned. Confident that none of the crew represented a threat, he handed the shield to one of the crewmen. Then Alerio drew his gladius and passed it to another sailor before unfastening his armored skirt.

"We were drinking and talking with the drama girls," the shield bearer related. The other crew members laughed and encouraged him. "They seemed really interested in spending time with us. When Captain Tivadar joined us, we all toasted our crossing of the sea. Then a girl suggested that I..."

"But you five are here," Alerio pointed out, "and your Captain is not."

Other than bragging about physical deeds, young men enjoyed expounding on how and why women were attracted to them. Given a chance, even in the middle of a crisis, the shield bearer would explain the woman's reaction to his irresistible charm. Alerio needed a description of the layout of the Melodrámatos Club grounds and where the Captain was being held. He did not require boasting about dancing with a drama girl.

"Where is Tivadar?" Alerio demanded.

"The party was getting fun until it got dark," the bearer answered. "Suddenly, armed Illyrians surrounded our table.

They pulled Tivadar out of a chair and forced him at knife point to a building near the back of the Melodrámatos compound. And they sent us here with a warning and a promise."

"What's the promise?" Alerio asked.

"They promised that we could go free," the bearer told him. "All they want is our ship. Don't you want to know the warning?"

"No need," Alerio responded as he slipped the chest armor off and placed it on the steering platform. "I have killed six of them. It's too late to heed their warning. Now, tell me about the compound."

***

All Legionaries could swim. In training they took swimmers and made them better while non-swimmers were brought up to Legion standards. Crossing rivers, ponds, or even coves while lightly armed gave the army of the Republic an advantage.

Alerio reached the far end of the beach but remained in the water. After crawling to the shallows, he lay partially submerged. Unnoticed, he studied men standing guard on the beach while others slept. All of them were Illyrian. The crews from the trading ships were sleeping on their vessels.

The rocky shoreline of the cove's southern arm offered no flat or comfortable areas for sleeping. It was camp far inland or on their boats for anyone wanting to avoid Illyrians.

Music from pipes and drums drifted to him from the club. As Tivadar had described, as long as there were men with coins, the drama girls would perform. While Alerio recalled the conversation, the lure of the entertainment proved too much for two of the guards. They began walking off the beach in the direction of the Melodrámatos Club. As they reached solid ground, a big man ran to them. Between episodes of verbal chastising, he pushed and slapped the fugitives back to the beach.

Using the disturbance as cover, Alerio rushed from the water and made it unseen to the corner of a building.

"Obviously, an Illyrian officer,' he thought.

Then while moving behind the building, he deliberated going to the officer and explaining the danger of distracting the other guards by disciplining one or two in the middle of the night. The idea made him chuckle because there was no way he would help his enemy.

Slipping from building to building, he avoided contact with anyone who might call out a warning. It proved both easier and harder than he imagined. Easier than he assumed because the buildings were erected in a semicircle around the club. Due to the curved layout, the corners of the roofs were only five feet apart. He moved out of sight from customers, club guards, and drama girls cruising in the center of the compound. However, for Alerio to move undetected behind the buildings required him to hide from servants washing clothes and tending garments drying on clotheslines.

Near the back of the compound, he tucked his shoulder against a building and snuck forward. Settling behind a bush and under a window, he peered between the walls and studied the neighboring building.

***

Even without directions from the crew of the Aura, Alerio knew he had located the building where Tivadar was being held. Three guards lounged at the front door. Confirming the guards were not from the club, a drama girl with a friend walked a wide path around the Illyrian sentries. Having found Tivadar still left Alerio with the problem of getting by the trio and freeing the Captain.

'At least Tivadar's cell is nice,' Alerio considered.

He had seen jails and prison houses made from everything from wooden beams, to dirt, rocks, and bricks. Some ancient and others newly constructed, but none as far as he could remember smelled good. Based on the aroma of the perfume wafting from the window above him, he wondered if Captain Tivadar's prison smelled as enticing.

An idea of how to get passed the guards came to Alerio. He raised up and peered through the window. The room was dark and empty. Drawing his knife, the Legion officer began prying the bars out of the wooden frame.

***

The cloud of perfume extended to the three Illyrian sentries before the drama girl reached the entrance. She was heavy but so were a lot of the drama girls. It didn't matter that her features were hidden under a silk veil and flowing scarfs. Their eyes were drawn to the swaying of her hips.

"I'm for Tivadar," she spoke in a voice that was too husky.

Two of the Illyrians pulled back when they realized she was a boy. But one leaned in close.

"What say later," he suggested, "you and I have a drink together?"

A calloused hand reached from under the flowing cloth and briefly caressed the man's cheek. Then the drama worker was passed the guards and inside the building.

"I don't need company," Tivadar spit out.

His tone reflected the bruising on his face and his attitude.

"That's good Captain, because I am not here to hold hands and listen to your life's story," Alerio informed him while tossing off the drama girl garments.

"Sisera?" Tivadar questioned. "How? Why?"

"I needed the coins," he teased while going to the window. "Watch the door while I remove a few bars."

"What good will that do?" Tivadar complained. "The Illyrians have two boat crews between here and my transport."

"Minus six pirates," Alerio told him as he pulled the Noric steel knife from its sheath. "Let me worry about the Illyrians. You watch the door."

***

The last bar was removed and Tivadar and Alerio slid through the window. Tivadar tumbled out and landed on the grass. Alerio's loin cloth caught, and for a moment he hung on the sill, before falling to the ground.

"Now what?" the Captain demanded as he squatted beside Alerio. "We are out. But we have nowhere to go."

"You have a direction," Alerio told him. "Climb on my shoulders and onto the roof."

"What about you?" Tivadar asked as he lifted his foot.

"I have to let the guards know you escaped," Alerio informed him.

Before he could question the Legion officer's sanity, Alerio cupped the foot and hoisted the Captain to his shoulders. From there, Tivadar hung by his fingertips before scrambling onto the tiles of the roof.

Below him, Alerio jogged away.

Traveling along the buildings on the opposite side of the complex from where he first came in, Alerio was less worried about being seen. An almost naked man running around the Melodrámatos compound might be a novelty, but it wouldn't draw undue attention. At the last building, he paused and studied the beach.

While the sleeping pirates snored, the ones on guard duty nodded from boredom. They as well wouldn't care about a near naked man approaching from the direction of the club. Walking slowly, Alerio reached a campsite on the beach. He picked the location because smoldering branches extended from the embers.

He sat on the sand, extended his hands to the warmth of the campfire, and gazed at the cove. Out on the water, stars in the distant sky back lit the shape of the transport. Although not completely invisible in the night, the Aura blended with the dark water beyond the cove. Trusting fate and his plan, Alerio wrapped his fingers around a branch and pulled it from the fire.

"What?" he shouted. Jumping to his feet and spinning around to face the compound, Alerio waved the glowing brand above his head. Then, bellowing so every Illyrian on the beach could hear, he announced. "The merchant Captain has escaped. Everyone, get up, get up. Search the compound. Our Captain wants him found."

As he waved the burning branch, the end glowed and left traces of light above Alerio's head. Around him, the call for a search was picked up and repeated.

'Even if the crewmen on the Aura missed the fire in the air,' Alerio thought, 'the riot on the beach should signal them."

Those awake were the first to run for the compound. A break formed between the runners and the ones just getting up. Alerio sprinted off the beach behind the first group.

***

One pirate, having been forced to remain on guard duty all evening, burned with anger. All he wanted was a drink and the company of a drama girl for a short while. But Lieutenant Murat had struck him, threatened him in front of his friends, and forced him back to the beach. Of course, he would join his crew mates in the search. But he would take his own sweet time about it.

The impact of a shoulder in the small of his back plowed him into and through a row of bushes. He began to struggle with his attacker when…

Moments later, Alerio stepped through the hedgerow dressed in the man's clothing.

"This area is clear," he told the stragglers. "Try the other side of the compound."

They ran onward and Alerio jogged behind them. With two hundred oarsmen from the two Illyrian ships awake and prowling the compound, the drama girls came out to investigate.

Soon clusters of pirates gathered around the girls as if they were islands in the ocean. Seeing the commotion in the courtyard, the musicians moved outside and began playing. Not to be denied, the bartenders rolled out kegs and wine barrels and serving girls began rushing around selling drinks.

Alerio had planned to use the confusion of a mass hunt for him and Tivadar to slip away. Around the back of the buildings, he saw no search parties of pirates and heard no signs of a search. What he did hear were cheers and calls of delight at the development of the massive, middle of the night party.

After calling Tivadar down from the roof, they clasped arms in relief. Then the two fast walked from the compound and took a trail heading south. Meanwhile at the front of the compound, three people experienced different emotions.

Captain Bujar roared his anger at Tivadar's escape while demanding that someone return to the beach and keep an eye on the merchant transport. The target of his rage, Lieutenant Murat, waited for an opening in the barrage of insults to make an escape of his own. And from the bushes near the front, a pirate crawled out of the shrubs, glanced around, and climbed to his feet.

"Finally, I can have a drink," he said while strolling to a group from his crew.

"Hey, you are naked," a shipmate pointed out.

He looked down, rubbed the knot on his head, and asked, "Are we drinking or comparing fashion notes?"

"Drinking," the group shouted.

The noises faded as Alerio and Tivadar moved quickly along the trail.

"Sisera, I appreciate you getting me out of there," Tivadar stated. He stopped and turned around. "But my ship and crew are back in the cove. I should be with them."

"I agree. You should be with your ship," Alerio comforted him. "And we would return to the cove, if your transport was there."

178

"If not in the cove," Tivadar asked. "Where is my Aura?"

Chapter 17 – Satire, Mockery, Poetry

Two thousand six hundred paces from the compound, Alerio took Tivadar by the elbow and guided him off the path. They walked carefully over rocks until the ground smoothed.

"This is the beach south of Vromoneri," the Captain announced.

"A mile and a half south according to your crew," Alerio confirmed.

"How did you know where the beach started?" Tivadar inquired. "If we had left the trail earlier, we would be walking the top of a cliff."

"I counted steps," Alerio informed him. "Now, less talking, more walking and looking."

The black waters of the Ionian Sea extended out to where it met the dome of stars on the horizon. But no transport appeared in the transition between the sky and the water.

"I told them to pull the anchors but wait for my signal before pushing off the rocks," Alerio advised while the two walked along the water's edge. "The signal was clear. But I didn't have an opportunity to stick around and see if they rowed out."

"They are good boys," Tivadar offered. "If they could get the Aura out of the cove, they did. If not…"

"If not, we have a sixteen-mile hike ahead of us," Alerio said steering the conversation away from the morbid reality.

They strolled along in silence with their eyes scanning the black water. Then oar splashed, a curse followed by bickering, and finally, the sound of a keel grinding on sand came to them.

"Captain, your ship has arrived," Alerio announced.

"If the crew hasn't put a hole in her hull," Tivadar complained.

But his tone was light, and the two men picked up their feet and jogged forward to where a great black shape rested in the shallow water.

"The Aura needs twelve feet to rest comfortably," Tivadar shouted up to the deck. "Twelve. More than two of me tall. Drop the ramp."

"Tivadar. We couldn't see the shoreline," a crewman protested. "We brought her in too fast."

"Are we stuck?" Alerio asked as he followed the Captain up the ramp.

"I can feel the aft end floating," Tivadar explained. "But it'll take all six of you to refloat her. Are you up for getting wet after the night you've had?"

"Between pushing a hull and fighting pirates, I'll take relaunching the Aura," Alerio assured him. "Besides, these leather trousers and this linen shirt need washing."

"Everyone over the side," Tivadar instructed. He stepped on the fore deck and waited. When Alerio and the five crewmen called out their readiness, the Captain shouted. "Push. Push."

The Aura held for a moment, then the big belly slid free, and the crew scrambled up the sides.

"What about the Illyrians?" Alerio asked as he took an oar.

"If they dare row into Methoni's harbor, they will not receive a cordial greeting," Tivadar promised him. Then with joy in his voice at being back in control of his ship, he called out. "Starboard side, stroke, stroke. Port side, ship oars."

The transport rotated until the bow pointed south.

"All together stroke, walk it together, stroke," Tivadar ordered.

***

The sun popped into the sky over the mountains to the west. Shortly after Sol Indiges, the Sun God, returned light to the earth, Tivadar turned the Aura. They rounded a point of land, and a large city came into view.

"My home," Tivadar declared. "Methoni, one of the prize leaves on the vine."

"It's bigger than I imagined," Alerio remarked. "Too bad I don't have time for exploring. But duty requires me to push on for the Isle of Rhodes."

"Then it's good that you have time to dine with my family," Tivadar exclaimed, "while I find you a ship for the next leg of your journey."

"I hate to impose," Alerio commented.

"Nonsense," Tivadar declared. "My wife will want to know who to blame."

"Blamed for what?" a shocked Alerio inquired.

"For her not being rid of me so she can marry a young and handsome man," Tivadar announced. "But let me warn you. She may poison us both for your transgressions."

***

Home port or not, the Aura did business when she docked. Cargo came out of the hold, coins were exchanged, and new merchandise went onto the ship. At midday, a guard arrived. As soon as he was installed on the deck, the crew dispersed down different streets of the city.

"Come Sisera, time to meet your fate," Tivadar invited.

They caught a carriage and a mile north of the bay, they arrived at a large farm. A plump woman marched out of the house trailed by five children. She stomped up to Tivadar and glared at him.

"Husband, you returned safe from the sea," she remarked.

"I have, wife," the Captain replied.

"I suppose you are hungry," she stated. Then with a curious look at Alerio, she added. "Brought another mouth to feed?"

"I have," Tivadar answered.

"Fine, one more can't hurt," she declared before throwing her arms around the Captain's neck. "The children have missed you. And, so have I."

Tivadar lifted her off the ground and returned the hug. Alerio's fear of being poisoned faded as the children crowded around him. They asked questions while escorting him to the house.

***

Over a table piled high with food, the Captain explained about his capture and Alerio's rescue. Then Tivadar announced.

"Tribune Sisera is traveling to Rhodes," he described. "I need to find him suitable transportation for the next leg of his journey."

"Rehor," his wife offered.

"No," Tivadar responded quickly, "no."

182

"But, Tivadar, he is the best coastal trader around," she insisted. "You've said as much yourself."

"Your brother is a good trader," Tivadar acknowledged. "But his crew are almost pirates. Plus, they are young and have no respect for authority. Or any manners."

"You aren't afraid of rude people, are you Tribune Sisera?" she asked.

"No ma'am," Alerio assured her. "I am mostly around infantrymen, and they aren't the gentlest of creatures."

"There, Tivadar," she told her husband, "that settles it. Now you two take your wine to the patio while I see to the cleanup."

Alerio and the Captain moved from the dining room to a stone outdoor seating area. The five children moved with them as tightly packed as a Century formation on field maneuvers. Tivadar ruffled hair and patted shoulders as the group moved, while Alerio worried about stepping on little bare feet.

"Do you like being married?" Alerio asked once he was settled in a wicker chair.

"When you marry, Sisera," Tivadar replied, "the center of your world shifts from your forehead. You no longer think only of yourself and your own needs."

"Where does it shift to?" Alerio questioned.

"Away," the Captain informed him. He took a sip and smiled. "As far away as your wife is from you. Even across the sea, your thoughts are with her."

"And her thoughts are with you," Tivadar's wife chimed in. "I came out to defend Rehor if my husband thinks to argue against my brother."

"Wife, the subject has not come up," Tivadar scolded.

"Then finish your drink and come inside," she instructed. "You've been gone far too long."

"If you'll excuse me," Tivadar stated. Then before going to the house, he bent down and whispered. "Be glad she didn't poison us."

"I don't think there's much chance of that," Alerio whispered back. "She seems to have you where she wants you."

"It appears she does," the Captain laughed. "Children entertain Tribune Sisera. And warn him about Uncle Lex."

"He pilots the Momus with ingenuity, sails the seas heroically, on a boat named for the God of Satire, Mockery, and Poetry," they cried. "We love Uncle Lex."

"I cannot get my own way in my own house," Tivadar protested. "Maybe I should poison myself."

"Us too," the children shouted.

Alerio watched the transport Captain strut to the house. While the Legion officer was distracted, a little girl crawled into his lap.

"Are you a Hoplite?" she inquired. "Like the ones at Ther, Ther, Ther…"

"Thermopylae," Alerio suggested.

"Yes, there," she gushed. "Are you?"

"In a way," he replied. "I am heavy infantry but not a Hoplite. I'm a Legionary."

Alerio spent the rest of the day teaching the children about the Legion and the Republic's heavy infantry. To his surprise, they listened to his every word and never once seemed bored. Then, the little girl rested her head on Alerio's chest.

"Do you have any children?" she questioned with a sleepy yawn.

"No, I am not married," Alerio told her.

"That is a shame," she said sounding like a little old lady. "Someday, you must marry and have children. You will be a great father."

She snuggled into his chest and, as her breathing shallowed, a strange feeling engulfed Alerio. Suddenly, he felt an urge to protect the innocent child and make the world a better place for her.

The feeling faded when Tivadar's wife lifted the child from his arms.

"Are you married, Sisera?" she inquired.

"No, ma'am," Alerio replied. "Why do you ask?"

"You are very good with children," she complimented before carrying the sleeping child to the house.

Looking up at the darkening sky, Alerio inhaled and relaxed. Then an image of Gabriella DeMarco crossed his mind. He attempted to hold the image. But as quickly as it arrived, the vision vanished, leaving Alerio feeling lonely.

***

The coastal trader Momus boasted a length of thirty-five feet, nine across its beam, and had a meager draft of just 5 feet. There were few harbors, coves, or intercoastal settlements the boat couldn't service.

"You will need to cut down on your stops," Tivadar instructed a young man who vaguely resembled the Captain's wife. "Sisera is traveling to the Isle of Rhodes. And I owe him."

"I can get him to the Island of Kithira," the man offered. "He'll easily get a sea snail trader from there."

"That works. Just be sure you take care of him and treat him with respect," Tivadar ordered before turning to Alerio. "Sisera, this is Rehor Lex, skipper of the trader Momus."

"Captain, it's good to meet you," Alerio stated.

The crewmen on the Momus, all younger than their youthful skipper, burst out laughing. Overcome with the humor, all three fell off the bundles stacked on the deck.

"Call me Rehor, or Lex, but Captain is a bit much for a trader of this size," Rehor Lex proclaimed.

"As you wish Rehor," Alerio started again. "I am Alerio Sisera. Call me anything you want, just not late for supper."

A new round of laughter burst from the deck.

"It wasn't that funny," Alerio told the three.

"Or that clever," one reflected.

"Or that original," another observed.

"You are correct, it wasn't that funny," the third man offered.

Alerio studied the three. One lacked the mass to be a threat in a fight. The second carried lean muscle and the third was doughy soft. None appeared to be a fighter although with their attitudes and absence of discipline, they would need some martial skills. At least enough to defend themselves against offended drunks.

"No thanks, I'm not drunk enough," Alerio commented.

"No thanks to what?" one inquired.

The second questioned, "Drunk enough for what?"

"For me to take offense and drown you like rats," Alerio replied pleasantly with a smile on his face. "But with enough wine, I could be convinced."

"Who are you?" Rehor asked. "Better yet, what are you?"

"I am a Tribune in the Legion of the Republic," Alerio replied. "And I don't take umbrage easily."

"Filib is my first oar," Rehor introduced the man with the lean muscle mass. "The fat youth with the blond hair is Isyllus."

"I take offense at that," Isyllus protested.

"The fat or the blond part?" the third crewman inquired.

"And the mouth is Olek," Rehor said while pointing out a lean darkhaired youth. "He is the one most likely to get us run out of a village."

"Chased by a jilted husband or an angry father," Isyllus offered. "and sometimes by brothers."

"He likes the ladies?" Alerio guessed.

"Worse than that," Filib remarked. "The ladies can't resist Olek's charms."

Alerio studied the first oar and revised his initial impression. Lean yes, but the man carried a curved sica with a black oyster shell hilt. Not a cheap weapon or one likely carried by an unskilled swordsman.

Just as Legionaries in a squad filled roles to fit in, the crew of the Momus assumed identities. Rehor no doubt was the leader, Isyllus the clown, Olek the lover, leaving Filib to fill the position of enforcer. If the parts fit together well, the crew would be tightly bonded and dependable. If not, they would lose unit integrity in a crisis.

"We have clear skies, smooth water," Rehor declared, "and a fair morning to make Foinikounta."

Isyllus and Olek moaned.

"What?" Filib challenged. "You don't like snails?"

"They smell," Isyllus protested.

"Sisera, toss your gear onboard," Rehor directed. "Filib, get us off this beach."

As the crew pushed the Momus into the bay, Rehor Lex spilled helpings of wine and olive oil over the side.

"Poseidon, God of the Sea. We beseech you for mercy during our travels over your domain," Rehor prayed as he poured. "Keep the seas calm, the monsters in their depths, and the birds flying along our route. For a safe voyage from sheltered harbor to sheltered harbor, we give you thanks with these humble offerings."

Alerio took an oar and with four rowers dipping, the trader Momus glided quickly from the bay.

Chapter 18 – Indigo Snails

At first, the coastline had beaches suitable for landing with access to green grass and trees above a gentle slope. Then slowly, the expanse of beach shrank to a ribbon of sand at the base of uneven rock cliffs.

At midmorning, Rehor Lex steered the Momus eastward and the shoreline rose twenty-five feet from the sea. It seemed as if a giant had broken off a section of land like a man would rip off the end of a loaf of bread.

"It looks desolate," Olek suggested to Alerio, "but watch ahead."

Eventually, the high cliffs flowed into rolling hills. And where rocks had risen above the sea, the forest and farmland spread to the edge of the water.

"There's nothing like traveling by boat," Filib told him. "Your view changes with the wind."

"Enjoy the fresh air," Isyllus warned Alerio. "For, I swear, by mid-day the stink of snail will assail every breath you inhale."

"So, the Momus is a snail trader?" Alerio asked. He heard Rehor use the phrase and thought it fit the discussion.

"No," Filib came back. "We are a coastal trader. We only haul snails when we need extra coins."

"Or when we have to travel fast and skip ports-of-call," Rehor added. "The snails pay a premium. But the cost is cleaning the smell from the boat and your senses afterward."

By midday, a village with a fleet of small boats came into view.

"Welcome to Foinikounta," Olek stated. "The sea snails grow in abundance in the shallow waters of the cove. And the fleet of boats are used to harvest them."

"The snails grow, are plucked from the cove," Isyllus chanted, "end parts ground to overflow, to make cloth that glows in indigo. And into a cook pots the other end goes."

"It needs work," Rehor offered. "Roll the sail and dip the oars."

Rehor angled the Momus towards the beach but steered away from one area. A field of light brown with spits of blue covered a portion of the sand. Behind the defined area, men sat at stones cutting and separating objects. After dividing the parts, one segment went into a pot suspended over a fire, the split shell got tossed to the light brown area, while the other object was dropped into a clay bowl.

As the boat drew closer to shore, Alerio could see that thousands of crushed shells created the brown field.

"Broken snails' shells," Olek mentioned. "From a distance the golden brown is pretty."

Then the wind shifted, and a rank aroma drifted over the boat.

"Aha, do you know what that smell is?" Filib asked.

"Rotting snails in the sun," Alerio offered.

"No Sisera, that is the smell of ready coins," Rehor corrected. Then he commanded. "Ship oars. Get us up on the beach."

Alerio and the three crewmen jumped into the surf and shoved the Momus onto the sand. Men with blue stains on their hands walked over to begin the trading session.

***

When Rehor mentioned sea snail traders, Alerio assumed he referred to transporting snail shells. Unfortunately, while the hard shells could be rinsed of rotting aroma, the valuable parts of the snails could not be washed. And they stunk.

"The harvesters want to know if we are staying for lunch," Olek mentioned to Alerio. "After cutting out the gut that makes the dye, they boil the snail bodies in those pots with garlic."

The two stood beside the Momus holding cloth covered bowls that easily fit in their cupped hands. The stench from the bowls also saturated the beach. Just the idea of eating brought bile into Alerio's throat. It left a nasty taste in his mouth. Between the horrid smell and the vile taste, he was close to throwing up the content of his stomach.

"I am not hungry," Alerio assured Olek. Then he wondered. "If they are cooking the snail bodies, what do we have in these bowls?"

"Snail excretion and guts," the crewman announced. "You are holding snail merda and snail cūlī."

"That is disgusting," Alerio pointed out.

Filib's face appeared over the rail of the boat.

"Not disgusting, valuable," he corrected. "Each bowl is worth a stack of silver. Now, hand me the bowl and be careful not to drop it."

He reached down and Olek offered up his bowl as if it was a sacrifice. Filib took the container and vanished. He would stow it with others in a cocoon of cloth to protect the clay bowls and the valuable indigo snail parts.

Still holding his bowl, Alerio asked, "Are you going to eat?"

"Gods no," Olek spit as he answered. "Who could even consider it with this smell?"

***

As soon as Rehor Lex finished the exchange, they pushed the boat into the surf and rowed away. Yet, even as they put distance between themselves and the beach with crushed shells, a reminder of the aroma wafted from under the forward boards.

Alerio wrinkled his nose at the smell when a breeze sent a whiff of snail in his direction.

"It smells like coins," Filib reminded Alerio before he could complain.

By mid-afternoon, the Momus turned off the southern heading onto an eastern track. Changing course removed wind from the sail and the crewmen resorted to oars. After rowing between two points of land, Rehor angled the trader northward and wind filled the sail.

"If the wind keeps steady, the crossing will be an easy sail," Olek commented.

"What crossing?" Alerio asked.

"We'll spend the night at Koroni point," Filib replied. "In the morning, we'll set out across the water to Stoupa on the other coast."

"How many days to cross?" Alerio inquired.

His thinking was based on the journey between Syracuse and Vromoneri.

"Take a look around you, Sisera," Isyllus offered, "the boat is narrow, from aft to forward, it is scarcely a meander. Our belly is a limited shallow hold with no depth for control. To sea we are not fit to go, the shoreline is our home."

"You are saying," Alerio summarized, "the Momus is too small for sea voyages."

"A little better, Isyllus," Filib critiqued. "Maybe less rhyme and more lyric verse."

"Everyone is a critic," Isyllus grumbled. But then he said. "I will reflect on your suggestion."

"What am I missing?" Alerio asked.

"Isyllus went to a play in Athens last year," Rehor told him. "After leaving the theater, he asked a beggar…"

"He was a stoic philosopher," Isyllus protested.

"Fine. Isyllus asked a stoic philosopher how he could become a dramatist and a poet," Rehor described. "The old fake told our young friend, that any fish in the sky could write, if they practiced flying and rhyming to the same degree."

"That is…," Alerio began to point out the absurdity.

"Save your breath," Olek advised. "We've been over the explanation way too often."

"And so, our young dramatist works on his craft," Rehor stated. "And we help him by being his audience."

"We are still waiting for him to fly," Filib added.

By late in the afternoon, they rolled the sail and rowed around a hook of land. At the back of a large harbor, Koroni filled the landscape. Obviously, an affluent town as demonstrated by the temples Alerio could see from the boat.

"In the center of Koroni is a copper statue of Zeus," Olek informed Alerio.

"I'd like to see that statue," Alerio responded.

"Take Olek and your blade with you," Rehor advised. "Koroni is a launch and landing harbor for towns on the other side of the water. And like any beach, it collects driftwood and wreckage. Some of the wreckage in Koroni is dangerous."

"But there are women," Olek cooed.

"I just want to see the statue of Zeus," Alerio informed him. "I'm not interested in romance."

"Neither am I," Olek agreed. "But I do like to eat. And women look at my sad eyes, my flat stomach, and conclude that I need to be fed."

"If it's food," Alerio exclaimed. "I am interested in meeting your woman."

"Not woman, Sisera," Olek corrected. "Women, and meals."

"Olek is our scavenger," Isyllus informed Alerio. "And he is very good at the task."

"I take it, I am part of a scheme to feed the crew?" Alerio inquired.

"You are the one who wants to see Zeus," Filib pointed out.

The Momus glided to the shoreline and the crew splashed into the water. Once the boat was high on the sand, Alerio followed Olek into town.

***

Late in the afternoon, some of the booths and stalls of Koroni's agorá sat empty. With so many closed, the remaining vendors had customers due to the reduced competition.

"The market is closing for the day," Alerio pointed to the small groups of women and men moving from stall to stall.

"It's a perfect part of the day for what I do," Olek assured him. "You stay here and admire the God of Sky and Thunder. While you are visiting, pray for fair weather for our crossing."

The green-blue streaks of patina gave Zeus the appearance of standing in an out worldly deluge. Fierce and strong, the copper statue of the god stood at a street leading to several temples. His presence challenged any nonbelievers or barbarians to tread carefully or else, face Zeus' fury.

But staring at a statue, no matter how mighty, became boring. Knowing that Olek didn't want any company, Alerio walked to the backside of Zeus and peered around the marble base.

The crewman browsed and chatted with people as he strolled from booth to booth. A pattern emerged when he moved to a third booth. Three women who didn't talk or associate with one another, engaged with Olek. One would hold an item and solicit his opinion. Another handed him produce and waited for his pronouncement of its weight or quality. Alerio could not decipher which. And the third woman hovered beside Olek as if he were in danger from the other two.

After touring all the open booths, Olek and one of the women stepped away from the other women. As the pair walked from the market, Olek put a hand behind his back and signaled for Alerio to follow.

Four blocks from the market, they came up behind a row of residential houses. Before the couple went into the building, Olek put a hand behind his back and pointed to an alley beside the home. Following directions, Alerio strolled into the lane and stopped.

"Pssst," Olek whispered from a window. "Take this."

A big clay pot appeared on the sill. When Alerio touched it, the covered bowl felt hot. But under the influence of the spicy aroma, he ignored the heat and snatched the bowl from the window.

"Take it to the boat," Olek instructed.

Before Alerio could question the theft, the crewman vanished into the house. Alerio stood confused for a moment before heading to the beach and the Momus.

***

"What have you brought us?" Rehor asked.

The skipper and the other two members of his crew crowded around Alerio.

"It's beef stew. Thankfully, we have bread for the gravy," Olek called as he came from town. He raised a sack in the air, shook it, and added. "I hate to eat and run, but I have another appointment."

The five men sat around the pot dipping bread and munching on chunks of meat and vegetables. Before the others finished, Olek jumped up and walked away.

"Is he always like that?" Alerio asked.

"Not always," Filib replied. "Sometimes he comes back early and there is no problem. At other times, he is like a feral cat."

"And that's a problem?" Alerio questioned.

"We'll know that when he gets back," Isyllus proclaimed. "Early to sleep, early to rise, launch the boat, before someone dies."

"Needs work," Rehor offered.

"Everyone is a critic," Isyllus muttered before shoving more stew into his mouth.

***

The moon rested low in the sky, but no hint of the coming sunrise touched the horizon. While the rest of the world slept, Rehor walked to each of his crewmembers.

"Get up, stretch, and get ready," he said to each of them.

"Why so early?" Alerio inquired.

"There is a storm coming," Rehor described. Although just a black shape moving in the dark night, Alerio saw an arm lift to the sky. "The wind is blowing westward, and it is increasing in velocity."

"You must have a sense for these things," Alerio suggested. "Being a seaman and all."

"Don't let Rehor fool you," Filib growled. "Olek did not come back last night. And that usually foretells a need for a quick departure."

"Plus, there is a storm coming," Rehor said in his own defense. "Stow your gear and launch the Momus. But keep it near the shoreline."

Once the bow of the coastal trader bobbed in the surf, and the aft rested on the beach, the crew sat on the deck boards.

"How long will we be at sea?" Alerio inquired.

"Most of the morning provided the wind holds steady," Filib told him. "And the water stays calm.

***

A faint cry came from the streets above the beach. In response, the skipper instructed. "Everyone, get your feet wet and grab a section of side boards."

The next shout came clearer. Not enough to make out the words. But enough to warn the crew of approaching trouble.

Olek traveled fast through the streets of Koroni, and his next shout reached the beach clearly.

"Launch the boat," he screamed as he ran through the last blocks of the town. "Launch the boat."

"Push," Rehor ordered. "Push. He can swim out to meet us."

Chapter 19 – Baskets of Heat

The Momus slid free of the beach and Alerio and the two crewmen scampered onboard. With oars dipping, they rowed the trading vessel away from the shoreline.

Dark shapes flickered through the black morning. Briefly one shape was silhouetted at the top of the beach then closely following, three more profiles popped into view before blending into the background of the black morning.

"Catch," Olek bellowed to the men on the boat.

Something landed on the deck then the voices of three men cursing and threatening covered the sounds of legs splashing through the surf.

"Reel him in," Rehor instructed while swinging the rear oar back and forth. Under his manipulations, the Momus turned parallel to the beach.

Filib left the rowing to Isyllus and Alerio and snatched up a rope. Listening to the splashes of a man swimming, he judged the distance and direction then tossed the rope at the sounds.

"Got him," the lead oar announced when there was a tug from the end of the line.

As the boat pivoted and nosed away from shore, Olek walked his hands along the rope. At the boat, Filib reached down and hoisted him onto the deck boards. From the beach, a trio of men shouted insults and threats.

"The bag has pears and quinces," Olek informed the crew, referring to the item that hit the deck earlier. Then he added. "Sorry about the hasty departure."

Alerio expected a scolding from Rehor or possibly a threat to abandon the troublesome crewman at the next port-of-call. The trader did neither. Instead of demanding discipline, Rehor Lex laughed. And not simply a chuckle. The expression of joy came from deep in his gut. Filib, Isyllus, and Olek joined in the merriment.

"They are so young," Alerio mused.

The boat wallowed when the four crewmen dropped to their knees trying to catch their breath and regain their composure. And just when they started to calm down, one would burst out in giggles and set the crew off into another round of howling.

Alerio took the rear oar from Rehor when the vessel began to drift towards shore. Rocking the oar from side to side, he got the Momus headed westward, away from Koroni and the angry men on the beach.

***

The sun rose, the sail dropped and filled with wind, and Olek passed out pears and quinces from the sack he threw onto the boat.

"What's this?" Alerio asked. Using one hand, he took the piece of yellow fruit. The other hand he kept on the rear oar. "I'm not keen on quinces. I find the raw fruit too tart."

"But you have been at sea for several days," Rehor described. "The salt in the sea suppresses the bitterness. Even if you can't appreciate the fruit now, by the time you reach the Isle of Rhodes, you will."

Cooked with dribbles of honey, the quince fruit provided a soft and delicious side dish. But raw, the pulp was woody, oddly spongy, and so tart to be almost inedible. Alerio dug his teeth into the quince and gnawed for a moment before freeing a little piece.

"It's bitter," Alerio complained while squinting his eyes in reaction to the tartness.

The crew of the Momus fell to the deck as peels of laughter racked their throats and the exertion caused pains in their sides.

"Of course, it is," Filib agreed, "because it is a quince."

Alerio wanted to be mad and strike out. Then he recalled his temper as a younger man and the cruel jokes and situations he thought were funny.

"But you were right," Alerio lied. "It must be the sea salt air, or could it be this one is ripened to perfection. It's delicious once you get by the initial taste."

He bit off another piece, smiled, and chewed while gazing at the sky. In response to the subject of their prank enjoying the fruit, the three men each took a quince. They worked off pieces and munched on the pulp. Their noses wrinkled and their eyes watered at the acidity.

"Keep eating. The next bite will bring out the sweetness," Alerio encouraged as he appeared to take another morsel. "Yummy, aren't they."

Rehor, Filib, Isyllus, and Olek took up the challenge, as young men do, and proceeded to eat the fruit. What they failed to notice was the piece of quince in Alerio's hand, and the fact that his piece of fruit did not get smaller as he faked eating it.

"Keep chewing," Alerio cheered them on. "Any moment now, you'll figure out the secret of the quince."

***

The wind increased keeping the sail taut. Shortly after losing sight of the land around Koroni, the western shore rose above the horizon.

"See there Sisera, we are not truly at sea," Rehor pointed out before throwing the quince into the ocean. He licked his lips and moved his tongue around the inside of his mouth trying to clear away the bitterness. "How can you eat that?"

"I am older, and my taste is more refined," Alerio told him. Keeping his hand behind his back, Alerio tossed the uneaten fruit into the water.

"You aren't much older than us," Filib observed.

"True. But I have been in the Legion a long time," Alerio responded. He pointed at his leather sandals. "In war you eat whatever you can. One time, we ran out of food rations."

"What did you do?" Olek asked. "Go hunting?"

"When you are surrounded by Qart Hadasht mercenaries the only thing you hunt are soldiers. But human flesh tastes bad," Alerio said embellishing the tale. "So, we boiled our sandals, dribbled some bear fat on them, and ate our footwear."

"What did it taste like?" Olek questioned.

Alerio couldn't tell. Was the scrunched-up expression on the chubby man's face a result of the quince, or a reaction to eating sandal leather?

"The crewing was tough and the flavor bad," Alerio described. "But we grew to enjoy them after a few days. We even gave the dish a name."

"What did you call it?" Olek asked. He studied his own sandals and turned his foot to examine every section of the leatherwork.

"Barefoot stew," Alerio replied. "Others called it, bear-foot stew."

***

Once the boat drew close enough for Rehor to make out details on shore, he took control of the rear oar. Overhead, dark clouds closed off the morning sky. Wind gusted and whipped across the water rocking the boat.

"Roll the sail and man your oars," he ordered.

From loose and lounging young men, the crew jumped to their tasks. One pushed the material and dumped the air from the sail. The two others rolled and tied the fabric. Then the three secured their oars and joined Alerio at their rowing positions.

The Legion officer was impressed by the quick response to Rehor's instructions.

"We are north of Stoupa," Filib pointed out, "and coming in with a storm. Do you know what that means?"

Assuming the question was aimed at him, Alerio answered, "No. What does that mean?"

Isyllus and Olek hooted as they performed the next stroke.

"The storm renders us invisible," Rehor proclaimed, letting Alerio know Filib's question was rhetorical. "Stroke, stroke. Walk it together, we have work to do. Stroke, stroke."

Alerio walked and rowed, oblivious to what the head rower and the skipper meant by going to work after coming in with the storm. Rowing in rough water should be considered work, but according to Filib and Rehor getting to shore wasn't the real job.

The boat rocked and Alerio had to take a cross step to keep his balance. Thinking he was alone in getting caught off guard, he looked around. The other three oarsmen had also danced extra steps to stay upright and off the tilted deck. It made the Legionary feel better knowing experienced sailors also faltered.

"Are we heading for the beach?" Alerio shouted over the rising wind.

Off the starboard side, white sand met white caps offering an escape from the storm. But the Momus maintained a course cruising along the coastline.

"No," Rehor answered. "It's not far to Stoupa."

"Or the bottom of the sea," Alerio ventured.

"Relax Sisera," Filip instructed. "We do this regularly."

"Do what?" Alerio asked. "Challenge Tempestas."

"Who?" Filip inquired.

"The Goddess of Storms," Alerio responded.

"You mean the God Zeus," Filip corrected him. "He provided the storm. It would be ungracious of us to ignore the gift and the opportunity."

"What opportunity?" Alerio questioned.

The coastal trader cut a righthanded slice in the water. Running with the wind, the Momus entered a cove and raced towards the beach. Just before reaching the sand, rain fell in sheets and visibility dropped to several feet.

"Great navigation," Alerio called to Rehor.

"And with the rain just now, lucky," the skipper responded. Then he shouted out commands. "Backstroke, backstroke. Hold water, let it drift."

From charging at the shoreline, the vessel almost paused in the surf before bottoming out on the sand. Making it to shore just before the rain started was an impressive feat. Alerio expected the crew to pull out waterproof wraps and hunker down on the deck.

"Sisera, stay here and guard the boat," Rehor directed. "Filib, spin us."

The skipper, the head oarsmen, Isyllus, and Olek splashed into the water. They turned the boat until the bow faced the mouth of the cove. On a big wave, they shoved the Momus up onto the sand.

"Don't let it drift away," Rehor called to Alerio.

He and the three crewmen splashed onto the beach and jogged away.

"Sure, I'll watch your boat," Alerio mocked. "It's not that I'm going anywhere. Or even know my location."

After unpacking an oiled skin, he located some dried beef strips, and carried the snacks to the rear of the boat. There he sat dangling his legs over the side, ate the beef, and waited.

***

The storm intensified and the limited visibility closed in around Alerio. Looking back, he could only see half the deck of the boat and very little of the beach around it. For that reason, the cart's arrival startled him.

"Get down here," Rehor called as he pushed, and Olek pulled a two wheeled wagon from the curtain of rain.

"What are you hauling?" Alerio questioned.

He jumped from the deck, landed, and walked a few steps to the cart.

"Baskets of heat," Rehor instructed. "We'll stow them when we are away."

"Away from where?" Alerio asked.

A basket with low sides and a sagging middle landed in Alerio's arms. Chunks of coal filled the container. At the side of the boat, he handed the basket up to Rehor.

"Where are the others?" Alerio questioned.

"They should be here," Olek complained. He jerked a basket from the cart and stated. "I thought Filib and Isyllus were behind us. But I lost them in the rain."

Alerio lifted another basket of coal from the cart and carried it to the boat.

"I'm surprised any merchants were open in this weather," he offered along with the coal.

"Who said they were open?" Rehor commented as he took the basket from Alerio.

"Stoupa has the biggest coal mine in the area," Olek told Alerio as he nudged in next to the Legion officer with another basket. "And the biggest stockpile of unguarded coal."

"We learned a few trips back the guards don't like to walk the backside of the pile in the rain," Rehor added. "If we get rain, we hit the pile, and take a load of coal."

"But that's theft," Alerio remarked.

"No, no Sisera," Olek commented defending the action. "You see, the coal is there for anyone to dig out of the ground. We are simply skipping a step."

"I don't think that's how commerce works," Alerio protested.

From the curtain of rain, voices called out in angry tones.

"That's Isyllus," Olek announced.

He drew a knife and managed a step towards the commotion. Alerio's hand stopped him in midstride.

"Rehor. My gladius is under my pack," he called to the deck. "Hand it to me. Olek, you get ready to push us off the beach."

"What are you doing, Sisera?" Rehor questioned as he handed the sword down to Alerio.

"You read the coastlines, Olek breaks hearts, Isyllus rhymes, and Filib steals," Alerio replied. He gripped the sheath with one hand and the hilt with the other. Then he drew the Noric blade and informed the skipper. "This is what I do."

Rehor ducked under the leather sheath when it flew up to the deck. Even bent at the waist, he managed to see Alerio Sisera dash into the rain with the sword in one hand and a knife in the other.

***

Heavy rain did five things well. It soaked the ground, filled rain barrels, contorted sounds, and hid objects behind its silvery shroud. Backtracking Rehor and Olek's path gave Alerio a relative direction but no target.

Some commanders used tact and caution when approaching an opposing force. Their Legionaries stepped forward carefully, held formation, and met the enemy almost hesitatingly.

Tribune Sisera believed in a different philosophy. He liked to arrive first, fast, and ready to attack. Thus, he quick stepped through the rain with his gladius extended and the knife held high to fend off an assault from the side.

"Get off me," Isyllus' voice stood out from the pounding rain. Maybe due to it being shriller or because he yelled the words, the voice carried. Alerio focused on the chubby young man. Also aiding the Legion officer to find him, the poet repeated his complaint. "Get off me."

The second objection allowed Alerio to adjust his course and increase his pace. That's when the fifth effect of heavy rain came into play.

Fat drops of water hit and splashed off everything. And a man moving through the deluge deflected drops by the thousands creating an aura of liquid beads.

Shimmering in the torrent of falling and rebounding pearls of water, Alerio Sisera came to a second cart and four uniformed guardsmen. One held the tip of his sword against the underside of Isyllus' throat. A second guardsman, no doubt the person receiving the poet's wrath, had him bent back over the cart. And a third stood watching a swordfight.

Filib's short sword faced off with the fourth guardsman's blade. They appeared to be frozen in their stances. But that was an optical illusion created by the limited visibility and the fact Alerio had no knowledge of what transpired before his arrival.

Using the blurring effect, Alerio slammed his elbow into the guardsman's ribs, ducked by Filib, and moved to the one with his sword under Isyllus' jaw.

When his opponent flinched and crunched to the side, Filib stepped forward and ran the tip of his short sword through the guardsman's side. As he withdrew the blade, the lead oarsmen stepped again but this time he drove his knee into the injured man's face. His foe spun away and fell to the ground.

Filib searched in the rain for Isyllus. But his support was unnecessary. As if a spirit from Hades, a specter moved in a squall of splashing and flying water, and a gale of striking legs and blades.

Sisera hooked an elbow around the next guardsman. With the arm bone on the man's back, the Legion officer shoved the man out of the way. Then Sisera raised his leg and dropped his heel on the shoulder of the next guardsman. The blade under Isyllus' throat fell away with the wielder.

Alerio's leg followed the guard to the ground and stomped the man's chest before disengaging. The precaution was prudent as the man held a naked blade in his hand. If he didn't go down hard, he might pop back up. A great exhaustion of air announced the guard was out of the fight.

Alerio turned his attention to the guardsman pinning the poet against the cart. From his squatting position, Alerio powered forward and upward. Springing as if a feline, the Legion officer went from hovering over the downed guard to driving the hilt of his sword into the man's forehead. In every instance, steel beats flesh. The guardsman fell, freeing Isyllus.

The final guard stumbled forward a few steps from the blow to his back. Once recovered, he drew his sword, and spun to face the…

"I have not killed anyone yet," Alerio advised the man. With his sword extended at arm's length, he held the tip of his blade against the guardsman's nose.

The top of a nose has many nerve endings, but that was not the deciding factor. Having a sharp point suspended between his eyes and a width of steel threatening to blind him was the deciding factor.

Isyllus came abreast of Alerio's shoulder and pointed a finger at the guardsman.

"Flee, flea, before you anger me," the poet ordered. "Take flight, before I take slight, and my friend's sword takes a bite. Afore you are undone, know that I have won, and you, flea, should run. Run!"

The guard dropped his sword and raced away into the sheets of rain.

"What are you doing?" Alerio demanded.

Filib had stepped between the shafts and lifted the front of the cart.

"I almost died for this load of coal," he declared. "I will not leave without it."

Isyllus hurried to the rear of the small wagon and pushed. Resigning himself to the theft, Alerio turned about and walked backwards, keeping his eyes open for more guards from the mine. But they reached the Momus without further mishaps.

Once the coal baskets were loaded, the crew pushed the boat off the shore and rowed into the storm.

Act 6

Chapter 20 – Tyrian Purple

The coastal trader rolled and one of the baskets fell off a pile and slid towards the edge of the deck. Filib turned from his oar station as if to save the basket.

"Let it go," Rehor shouted to him. "If it falls overboard, it'll be a nice offering for Poseidon. Maybe he will ignore us while he plays with the coal."

"What does the God of the Sea need with coal?" Olek called out. Although the rain let up a little, water dripped from the crewman's head and spewed on his breath with each word. "He can't make fire."

"Stroke, stroke," Rehor ordered. "We are three miles from the nearest beach. Stroke, stroke. If we can distract the God until we reach the sand, it'll be worth the loss."

Isyllus stepped away from his oar position, hooked a foot under the basket, and flipped it over. Chunks of coal rolled across the deck and several large pieces fell overboard.

"That should reach Poseidon," the poet exclaimed. "Let him who commands the sea, allow us the nearest beach, to escape the storm by a wide degree."

"Well said," Rehor stated. "Stroke, stroke."

Lurching and tossing in the rough water, the Momus fought the crewmen as hard as it fought the sea. Although the sea kept the swells and white caps, the sky allowed the rain to fade to a drizzle. Three miles south of Stoupa, the exhausted crew rowed to an expanse of white sand.

"Filib, get us high, and get us dry," Rehor instructed between deep breaths.

The young skipper collapsed from manning the rear oar during a storm. And although they were tired, the four rowers jumped into the surf and shoved the boat onto the beach. Then, they sank to the sand to catch their breath.

***

The fire crackled and the crew sat waiting for the water to boil, the grain to cook, and the vegetables to soften.

"When I found you, you had one of the mine guards isolated," Alerio mentioned to Filib. "How did you convince him to fight you in single combat?"

"The guardsman is the local swordfight champion. He needed to practice cutting someone up and I was handy," Filib answered. "He ordered the other guards to back off. They went after Isyllus. I wanted to help the poet, but I got busy."

"I understand your issue," Alerio informed him. "Dueling with swordfighters is tricky work. I've faced a few in my life."

The head oarsman stared at Alerio with hard eyes.

"Is something wrong?" Alerio asked.

"Drunk or not, you really could drown us. I mean all of us," Filib responded. "Or kill us if you desired."

"I have the training and the skills, so yes," Alerio assured him. "However, I won't. I just want to get to the Isle of Rhodes with the least amount of trouble. But you and the crew are making it harder and harder not to consider murder."

"We have always danced around morality," Filib admitted. "It helps break the boredom of coastal trading. But we might have gone a little too far on this trip."

"I don't care about your youthful indiscretions," Alerio remarked. "Unless it gets in the way of my journey. And having two of the crew killed on a beach over a few lumps of coal qualifies as a hinderance. Maybe when we reach the next town, I should find another transport."

"Tivadar will kill me if I fail you," Rehor declared. He dipped his head, then glanced up. "If we promise to stick to honest trading, will you stay with us?"

Alerio hesitated while thinking about the possibility of remaining on the Momus.

"I owe you, Sisera," Isyllus told him. His hand touched the soft skin under his jaw. "Hades was just beyond the veil of rain. And a short, sword stroke away. Then, like an epic hero from mythology, you removed the steel from my throat. Sisera, you have my pledge to complete this trip with no further trouble."

Olek stirred the content of the pot and looked into Alerio's eyes.

"And my pledge as well," he added.

"If I stay, I'll need an itinerary," Alerio insisted. "And no more theft."

"We are thirty miles from Gerolimenas," Rehor listed. "Kokkinogeia is twelve miles beyond there. Then we have twenty miles to the island of Kithira. And that is as far as we go."

"Why stop at Kithira?" Alerio inquired.

"We don't have the crew to fend off Cilicians or the knowledge of which coves are good for hiding from the pirates," Filib stated. "The only reason we'll go to the island is to get a better rate for the coal and the indigo snails."

"And to put me on a snail trader?" Alerio ventured.

"It is your best choice," Rehor assured Alerio, "and the safest."

***

Three nights and four days later, a rocky island grew out of the water. Greenery consisted of stubby trees and bushes. Everything else was rock and sand.

"The island of Kithira," Rehor exclaimed while pointing at the land mass.

"It doesn't look like much," Alerio observed. "Who would live on a rock in the middle of the water?"

"The center of the island rises fifteen hundred feet above sea level," Rehor described. "That feature catches rainwater which feeds two rivers. So, while there is little farming, there is fresh water, fish, and sea snails."

The trading vessel Momus angled to port, straighten its track, and sailed along the coast of the island. For most of the way, shallow water with a rocky bottom prevented landing on the shore. When the submerged danger gave way to a sandy shoreline, Rehor swung the boat towards the beach.

Alerio rowed at the port side position. With the sea to one side and a limited view of the land across the boat, he didn't pay attention until the vessel turned.

"I recognize the small fishing boats. Those are for snail hunting," he declared. "But I don't see many broken shells."

"Here, they harvest the snails' excretion differently," Filib offered. "On Kithira, they massage the snails to collect the merda."

"But I see some crushed snail shells on the beach," Alerio noted.

"Those are the wrong type of snails," Olek told him.

"What's wrong with them?" Alerio inquired.

Men strolled to the beach and waved greetings at the coastal trader. Their hands were stained a vibrant purple.

"The dead sails don't produce the right color dye," Rehor responded. "Hold water. Backstroke."

The vessel bumped gently into the sand and the crew leaped into the water to manhandle the boat up and onto the beach. The men who harvested royal purple snails waited to begin trading.

***

Lacking hardwood for cookfires, the residents of the island traded valuable merchandise for the coal. When the Momus made its way back along the coast, Rehor would trade up and turn a healthy profit from the theft.

On the other hand, the pots of indigo snails required no trading. They were sold, as Filib described it, for stacks of silver.

After the trades, the crew stowed the goods, set up tents, and sat in a circle drinking wine and talking.

"We are staying until you catch another transport," Rehor told Alerio.

"How long will that take?" Alerio questioned.

Rehor peered at a residential hut where over a hundred pots of snail dye rested in the afternoon sun.

"I'd say two days at the most," he guessed. "The collection of pots tells me they haven't had a trader through here in a while."

"The pots are just sitting there," Filib noted, "unguarded."

"Don't we have an agreement?" Alerio asked.

"He's just teasing you, Sisera," Isyllus remarked. "But if we were going to take a few pots, it would be just before we rowed out."

Seeing Alerio bristle at the idea of another theft, Olek cleared his throat to get everyone's attention.

"Did you know Heracles walked this very beach?" he described. Observing the attention his question generated, Olek continued. "In his efforts to court the nymph Tyrus, Heracles persuaded her to stroll with him along the beach. Obviously, the Hero did not possess my charms or wiles with the ladies."

"Save your conceit for the merchants' daughters," Filib scolded. "Get on with the tale."

"Certainly. I was simply pointing out the truth about the shortcomings of heroes," Olek boasted. All the crewmen glared at him until he shrugged and got back to the story. "Heracles, I imagine, flexed his big muscles. and talked of his prowess in battles. Or he crowed about his twelve labors and the deeds he accomplished. All while trying to endear himself to the nymph with hero talk. I can tell you that approach does not work."

"Is your approach boring women until they fall asleep?" Rehor accused. "And then robbing them? If so, we can all see how you do it."

"I was only trying to tell you why he wasn't getting anywhere with the seduction," Olek protested. "One thing he did right, Heracles brought his dog. Women love dogs. I guess they were walking along the beach and Heracles put his

214

arm around Tyrus figuring to pull her in close. Well, it failed, and they got into an argument. What do you want? Heracles asked. Nothing you can provide, the nymph countered."

"It sounds as if you've had experience with that argument," Filib suggested.

"Me, oh no, never," Olek assured him. But he went back to the tale before anyone else could offer an opinion. "While Tyrus and Heracles exchanged words, the hero's dog found a sea snail on the beach and began chewing on the shelled creature. Heracles being a demigod, challenged her. What do you want? I am from Olympus, and I do hero stuff. She was not impressed but then the nymph looked at the dog. The dog's muzzle was bright purple and Tyrus became spellbound. Heracles, if you want to be my lover, the nymph declared, bring me a dress of that color purple."

"Wait. The snail color is called Tyrian purple?" Alerio asked. "Because Heracles gave the nymph Tyrus a purple dress?"

"Right here on this very beach," Olek swore. "Or possibly the beach on the other side of the island. Or one at Crete, or…"

The wineskin flew across the circle and smacked him in the face.

"It is called Tyrian purple," Olek insisted.

He took a stream of wine and smiled.

"Maybe I should have a purple dress made," Isyllus reflected. "As gifts, you understand, for the ladies."

"Even that wouldn't help your love life, poet," Rehor scoffed.

Olek chuckled. Filib added his expression of humor. Soon the entire crew was laughing. Alerio sat back and watch

215

them be young men full of life. They would learn soon enough the world was harsh. Then the infectious humor of stupid laughing caught up with Alerio and he joined in their mirth.

***

The profile of the snail trader resembled a bow floating on its handle with the ends curved towards the sky.

"Two days, just like I predicted," Rehor pointed out. "An Egyptian ship with a Greek crew. You'll be as safe as if you were a baby in your mother's arms with that one."

"And young seer," Alerio teased, "you can gather all that from a single glance?"

At first sighting, the Egyptian ship sailed far offshore. It was how they saw the shape from the beach. Although Rehor seemed to know about the vessel, Alerio remained clueless. Even when the ship turned bow onto the island the Legion officer remained in the dark about the ship. The crew furled a fore sail and a huge midship sail as the vessel headed to the beach.

"There are Hoplite shields along the ship's rails," Rehor told Alerio. "I counted four shields and sighted eight oars."

"Not enough to be a ship of war," Alerio reflected. "But sixteen oars are too many to be a merchant vessel."

"She is not a wallowing transport tub," Rehor explained. "That's a snail trader with an oversized sail to catch more wind. A keel turned up fore and aft to cut the water like a blade. And a squad of eight Hoplite rowers for protection."

"All that for dyes made from snails?" Alerio questioned.

"Egypt is known for linen and silk production. The dyes, especially indigo and purple from snails, increases the value of the cloth tremendously," Rehor informed him. "Plus,

216

depending on her ports-of-call, the ship will take on loads of cedar wood, incense, myrrh, and aromatic oils. Or bars of gold, copper, and iron."

"All high value cargos," Filib mentioned as he emerged from a tent. "They can afford the best."

"If the merchant ship travels so far," Alerio inquired, "how do I know it is heading in the direction of Rhodes?"

"Kithira is as far west as they travel," Rehor informed him. "From here they will head to Asia Minor or home to Alexandria. In both cases, it is the right direction for you."

The elegant Egyptian ship approached the shoreline. Then in a flurry of oars counter rowing on either side of the vessel, she spun, and backed her curved aft to the beach.

"The Egyptian might be able to transit longer distances. Go about with armed guards. And boast sixteen oars. But she can't avoid everything a coastal trader does," Olek commented when crewmen leaped into the water. "They still have to beach their ship."

***

More impressive on land than at sea, the Egyptian's curled tail and tall bow beam extending over the fore deck added to her graceful lines. Although only half the ninety-foot hull rested on the shoreline, enough was in view to dwarf the coastal trader.

A ramp slid from the deck and dropped to the sand. Alerio recognized the first man off. Not the individual, but his weapons, measured pace, and the carriage of his shoulders identified him as a Hoplite. From one heavy infantryman to another, Alerio gave him a nod. Although the Greek Hoplite did not respond to the greeting, he did scrutinize the crew of the Momus.

Following the guard, a man in an expensive robe strolled to the sand and crossed the beach to the hut and the field of snail pots.

"We will let the Captain finish his business before we approach him about you," Rehor suggested.

"Busy day at the beach," Isyllus remarked.

"How so?" Filib inquired.

Two ships appeared from the south. They came in fast, not bothering to backstroke before their keels ran up onto the beach.

"Ah Hades!" Rehor swore. He stepped back and ordered. "Defend the Momus."

Then he spun and the four crewmen ran to their vessel. Olek and Isyllus climbed onto the ship while Rehor and Filib waited in front of the coastal trader and watched.

"Who are they?" Alerio asked.

"Cilician pirates," Rehor uttered. "They must have been watching for the Egyptian."

From the deck of the Momus, Isyllus called down to Alerio.

"Sisera. Do you want this?" he inquired.

In the chubby poet's arms was the Hoplite shield from Vromoneri. He and Olek had stacked oars, knives, and anything they could use to defend the ship on the deck.

"Yes, please," Alerio said. After taking the shield, he requested. "Now if you would be so kind as to go to my bundle and get my gladius."

Chapter 21 – Milk for Blood

218

"How many do you figure?" Alerio inquired.

"Forty fighters from each Cilician vessel," Rehor answered. "Enough to capture the Egyptian and take my ship."

"What about the sea snail dye?" Alerio asked. "Isn't that the real prize?"

"If they can take the snails, yes," Rehor informed him. "But if the Hoplites make it too costly, the Cilicians will settle for the vessels."

Heavy infantrymen, identified by their big shields, jogged down the ramp. On the sand, the eight Hoplites set a curved barrier between the pirates and the rear of the Egyptian ship.

A handful of pirates, noting an easier target, headed for the Momus.

"Rehor, Filib, Isyllus, Olek," Alerio announced. "It has been interesting traveling with you."

"Are you going somewhere, Sisera?" Isyllus inquired.

"No. But you are," Alerio responded.

The two fastest pirates reached Alerio and the line of crewmen. Their mistake was shuffling their feet to slowdown. Had they run around the Legion officer they would have broken the crewmen's line. By hesitating and waiting for help, the pair gave Alerio a heartbeat.

In that brief period, Alerio crossed his legs at the ankles then stepped to his left. Extending his leg, he stepped out wide, and bent his knees. From the low position he shot upward, his left arm powering the shield up and into the pirate on that side. The Cilician stumbled from the impact and Filib stabbed him.

The shield did not remain stationary. Resembling a full moon racing across the sky, the big shield arched overhead as Alerio shuffled to the right.

The second quick Cilician noticed the shield moving away from him. Feeling safe from the round mass, he started to attack. Just before reaching Rehor and Olek, a shadow passed over him. Before his mind could register the shade, the bronze shield hammered him to the ground.

"Where are we going?" Olek asked.

"You are getting the Momus off this beach," Alerio instructed. "Away from the pirates and back to the coast."

"What about you?" Filib asked.

"Throw down my bundles on your way out," Alerio instructed. Then he added a blessing from a Latian Goddess. "Now launch and go. And may the Goddess Fortuna go with you."

"Who?" Isyllus inquired.

"He means the Goddess Tyche," Olek corrected him by using the Greek Goddess.

"We will take luck from either Goddess," Rehor bellowed. "Launch us."

A moment later, the crewmen plowed into the aft section of the coastal trader. Driving with their legs, they shoved the Momus off the beach and scrambled aboard when it floated free.

"Oars," Rehor ordered. "Stroke, stroke."

As his vessel moved away from the beach, the young skipper glanced back. Alerio Sisera was backing up the beach. Arranged in a semi-circle to his front, pirates pressed forward. In response, the Tribune swung the bronze oval from side to side to keep the pirates from getting around the shield.

Although there were opportunities, Sisera did not stab or slash with his gladius. Rather, he held the blade upright behind the top of the shield, almost like a priest displaying a ceremonial knife before starting a sacrifice.

***

In a Legion Century struggling with a breakdown of their combat line, Alerio's maneuver would receive Euges and other cheers. But isolated on the beach and being an unknown entity, his drawing pirates away from the battle at the Egyptian ship and the fighting by the Captain and his security officer had no effect. None of the combatants acknowledged his efforts.

"It was worth a try," Alerio submitted. Then he prayed. "Goddess Nenia, memento mori I sing. Remembering, we all will die. I ask only that you take me fast if I fall."

An icy breeze swept the beach and the hairs on the back of his neck bristled. The gladius of its own accord rotated downward to rest against the side of the bronze oval. And, as if someone looked over his shoulder, he felt pressure against his right shoulder blade.

"To you, Nenia Dea," Alerio submitted, "I commend these souls."

The retreating stopped. Alerio Carvilius Sisera paused for a heartbeat. Then he and his personal deity stepped forward and waded into the crowd of pirates.

***

The shield powered out and around to the left. With it went half the front rank of pirates. Those behind, making noise but not fighting, were unprepared when the Legion blade sliced to the right. Between Alerio's two weapons, a hole developed in the crowd of Cilicians.

221

The Tribune strolled through the gap, rotated, and attacked from a new direction. With both his left and right arm at high guard, Alerio crushed two pirates with the bronze oval while chopping down two more with the gladius.

***

Bleeding bodies on the ground made movement hazardous and uncomfortable for the attackers. Judging the locations of their comrades' limbs, three pirates struggled to reach the man with the Hoplite shield. In their attempt to avoid stepping on the dead and the injured, they divided their focus. It left them unready when the infantryman came from the sky.

Alerio stepped around two stacked bodies. Having fallen together, the pirates provided a grizzly barrier. When three moved to attack him but approached gingerly, Alerio bent and tensed his legs.

The eyes of a swordfighter communicated movement and the sword's direction of travel. Conversely, the opposing eyes watched for clues. And the clues from the three attackers were unorganized and tentative.

Using the bodies as a step, Alerio pushed off and vaulted into the air.

The three attackers glanced ahead at the Hoplite shield. Then, they looked down to avoid stepping on the arms of friends. Then, ahead again. But the shield and the infantryman had vanished. A rustle overhead drew…

Alerio landed on one, driving him into the sand with his feet. Another caught the end of the shield with his elbow. The bones shattered and he fell to the ground gripping his arm. A stomp took the fight out of the first and Alerio searched for the third pirate.

As if a scarecrow hanging limp in a grain field, the pirate dangled in the midair. Around the Cilician's body, Alerio saw the security man from the Egyptian trader. This time it was the Greek nodding his acknowledgement at Alerio.

"You took down nine of them," the man stated while shaking the dead pirate from his blade. "The Captain suggested we join forces."

Alerio peered beyond the Greek. Bodies littered the ground at the hut where the pots of snail dye were staged.

"You did a lot of damage yourself," Alerio complimented him.

"So far Cilician command hasn't noticed us," the Greek pointed out. "What is your decision?"

"I need passage to Rhodes," Alerio mentioned.

"Then it's milk for blood," the Greek declared. "Let's finish this."

***

The Egyptian Captain, although he gripped a bloody knife, hung back. He understood military men. And when his Sergeant of Hoplites locked shoulders with the Latian, he knew they understood each other.

At the Egyptian ship, the eight infantrymen had held positions. Three were wounded, but their shields and pride kept them in the fight. And as happens with all infantrymen when ordered to remain in place they were teeth grinding mad.

But their adherence to orders had prevented the pirates from reaching the aft boards and launching the vessel. Now, the infantrymen looked over the heads of screaming pirates to see their Sergeant locked in with another Hoplite. Where he came from, they didn't care. What they cared about was one side of the ship had double protection. And that meant an end to the passive defense.

"Give me three butchers," a section leader shouted.

Three of the healthy Hoplites replied, "Take my blade, its thirsty."

"On me," the leader ordered. When the four oval shields snapped together, he shouted. "Forward."

In a static battle, things slowed down. In fact, when not in direct contact with the enemy, the second and third rows behind the attack line became lethargic. Laughing, joking, planning for…

The big oval shields that had been stationary surged forward. With each pitch, the four Hoplites tore into the lightly armored pirates. Screams replaced war cries. Then, from the Cilician's rear, more shrieks of anguish carried to the front. Both were drowned out by horns sounding the recall.

Cilician command had finally realized they had been fighting on three fronts. With the consolidation of the Egyptian ship's defenders, the leadership decided it was time to go.

"Orders, Sergeant Abrax?" the section leader asked when the four Hoplites joined with their Sergeant and the stranger. "We'd like more of the cultural exchange."

"Let them go," Abrax explained. "I want us loaded and off this beach before they bring back friends. Oh, and I don't want us to leave any living pirates on this beach."

"You heard the Sergeant," the section leader instructed. "Clean up the beach and load the sea snails."

While oarsmen and sailors rushed down the ramp heading for the snail pots, the Hoplites walked to each wounded pirate. Mostly their blades were driven through throats. The chest and ribs making a heart stab difficult with the broad bladed swords.

"Do you have a problem with killing wounded?" Abrax asked.

"I am a Tribune in the Legion of the Republic," Alerio replied. "We are far from reinforcements and outnumbered. I'd say it was a sound tactic."

"Tribune. That's an officer, right?" Abrax remarked. He thought for a moment before asking. "What is your name, sir?"

"Alerio Sisera. But I'm not sure the sir is necessary," Alerio suggested.

"The way you fight is not from studying dusty scrolls about ancient battles," Abrax commented. "Your style shows me you came up from the infantry. So, you see, Tribune, you rate the sir. Come, let me introduce you to Captain Khnurn."

As they walked to where Khnurn supervised the loading of the pots, Alerio asked, "What did you mean about milk for blood?"

"Our ship is the Gála apó Hathor," Abrax replied, "in honor of Hathor, the Goddess of Motherhood and Fertility. And because the ship feeds us, the name means Milk of Hathor."

"Milk for blood was your way of granting me passage?" Alerio inquired.

"Not my right to grant anything," Abrax warned. "But seeing as you defended the ship, I can't see how the Captain can turn you down."

"Plus, you could use an extra oarsman," Alerio advised while pointing to the wounded Hoplites.

"Now there is something I do have control over," Abrax boomed. "Welcome aboard, Tribune Sisera. This is going to be fun."

"How so?" Alerio inquired.

"It's not often, I get the chance to boss around an officer," Abrax stated. "But as I tell all my infantrymen, you follow my orders, and we will get along just fine."

"Spoken like a true Sergeant," Alerio acknowledged.

Chapter 22 – Seaworthy Ship

The Gála apó Hathor caught the wind with her two sails. After traveling on the coastal boat, Alerio appreciated the speed as the sleek ship cut through the water.

"The land off our starboard side is the island of Antikythera," Khnurn instructed. He pointed at a big rock with a few spots of green. "As we pass Xiropotamos Beach, you'll notice buildings on the hillside."

Tiered streets rose from behind a defensive wall to just short of the top of the island. Well defined buildings bordered the levels of streets. Oddly, while the stone buildings were sturdy, the roofs were constructed of cloth or reeds or remained gaps facing the sky.

"What town is that?" Alerio asked the Captain.

"It's not a permanent settlement," Khnurn replied. "The Cilicians built the defensive walls and the homes from the island's natural stone. But they never imported other building materials."

"If those are pirates," Alerio questioned, "shouldn't we be sailing away from the island?"

"They don't have anything that can catch the Gála," Khnurn boasted.

Alerio studied the streets and the walls that divided the town into blocks. The Cilicians knew what they were building. While women, children, and families might be in residence, it wasn't a permanent settlement. The town was a fortress. Then the island fell behind and Alerio lost sight of Xiropotamos Beach and, shortly after, the island itself.

***

The sun had yet to touch the horizon when the Captain ordered the sails struck and the rowers to dip their oars. It seemed a strange order. They were surrounded by water and Alerio wondered at the call to row so far from a suitable beach. But Khnurn's experience proved correct when a rocky coast emerged in the distance. Closer to land, they rowed around a point and the navigator guided the ship into a narrow cove.

"Menies Beach," the Hoplite behind Alerio told him. "Welcome to the island of Crete."

"There is nothing here," Alerio reported. "No village or market. No fresh water, not even a tree. Why stop here?"

"For those reasons," the Hoplite informed him. "There are no other ships here. The beach is small so we're not likely to get visitors. And the location is easily defended."

Alerio noted the high rock and dirt walls and the narrow beach tucked into a corner of the cove. Hidden from the view of passing ships and boats, the snail trader landed for the night on the isolated beach at Menies.

While the ship's crew prepared for the evening, Alerio walked aft to speak with the ship's navigator.

"I can't tell exactly. Did we go beyond the range of a coastal trader today?" Alerio mentioned while scrambling up the steps to the steering platform.

"If you are referring to the island-hopping barge you came off of," the man suggested, "then yes. A coastal trader would take over half a day to cover the distance from the island of Antikythera to Menies. The Gála, a seaworthy ship, did Kithira to Menies in the same period."

"At that speed, how long until we reach the Isle of Rhodes?" Alerio inquired.

"It'll take us two days to traverse Crete," the navigator described. "Then another day of sailing to reach the island of Kasos. And that is as far as we will take you."

"Because Rhodes is off your route?" Alerio guessed.

"Not at all. The logical track to Rhodes from Crete is Kasos to the island of Karpathos and then to the Isle of Rhodes," the navigator described. "Two and a half days sailing. However, we won't be taking that tract."

"Are you unwelcomed in Rhodian ports?" Alerio asked. "I mean, is there bad blood between Egypt and Rhodes?"

"As far as I know, not right now. But that can change with the weather," the navigator submitted. "We'll avoid Karpathos and Rhodes to save from paying docking fees."

"The protection of the Rhodian Navy is expensive," Abrax announced as he climbed to the steering platform. "It's cheaper to sail overnight to Kas on the coast of Asia Minor."

"There are regular patrols to Kasos," the navigator assured Alerio. "You can get transportation to Rhodes on a trihemiolia."

"A trihemiolia?" Alerio questioned.

"Athens once used triremes with one hundred and seventy oarsmen," Abrax reported. "They have since advanced from the 'threes' to quinqueremes, which are better battle platforms. But the Rhodians don't care about archers, boarding parties, or bolt throwers on their decks. They added twenty-six more rowers, widened the center of the standard trireme to allow for double oarsmen, and created the trihemiolia, a 'three-and-a-half'."

"The Rhodians don't negotiate at sea, or board and ask questions," the navigator said with a shudder. "With one hundred and ninety-six oarsmen, the trihemiolia has one purpose. And that is to sink any ship that offends them."

"Now that you've had a history lesson, Tribune," Abrax stated. "My infantrymen are going to run two on two drills. Would you like to watch?"

"I'll do more than watch," Alerio told him.

"You are an unusual Legion officer," Abrax offered.

"How many have you met?" Alerio asked.

"Enough to know most staff officers from your Republic are more diplomat than warrior," the Sergeant replied.

"Let me get my shield and gladius," Alerio suggested. "Then we'll see if I can change your mind."

***

Three days later, the Gála apó Hathor rowed across a deep bay to Helatros Beach on the island of Kasos. For the first time since Alerio boarded the ship, the crew and Hoplites move slower and without purpose. Even Khnurn and Abrax relaxed their discipline. To reflect the attitude, almost everyone left the ship and began drinking wine while setting up campsites.

229

"Abrax. At every stop, you've had infantrymen in armor guarding the beach," Alerio observed. "Yet here, you have two sailors patrolling the deck. Everyone else is on the beach and on holiday."

"Kasos is under the protection of the Rhodian Navy, sir," the Sergeant responded. He rotated his sore right shoulder to loosen the bruised muscles. "No pirate will come closer than Crete to an area controlled by the Isle of Rhodes. At least none who want to stay on the surface of the water."

When Tribune Sisera joined in the sword and shield drills, the NCO did as well. His view of Republic officers had undergone a drastic revision thanks to Alerio's demonstration of Legion shield work.

"How is the shoulder?" Alerio asked.

"It's not the pain, Tribune," Abrax responded. "It's the bruising to my pride that hurts."

From the mouth of the bay, a warship turned head on to the beach. For a moment, Alerio thought it was a trireme. But as the ship drew closer, he noted the stretched center section. The trihemiolia came on fast, then in a show of seamanship, all one hundred and seventy oars backstroked. And it stopped dead in the water.

Alerio had taught Legion rowing and appreciated the training that went into the coordinated backstroke. But the cessation of motion, as if the warship hit a submerged rock, went beyond a unified stroke. To change from full strokes to a sudden halt required power. Then as if to confirm his thoughts, the warship spun a half turn and rowed aft end to the beach.

"The Rhodian Navy has arrived," Abrax announced. "If you'll excuse me, I need to speak with Captain Khnurn."

"Is there going to be trouble?" Alerio asked as the two men strolled to where Captain Khnurn watched the maneuvers of the warship.

"They have one hundred and ninety-six Rhodian citizen rowers, plus infantrymen. I have eight Hoplites and eight oarsmen," Abrax told him. "What do you think?"

***

The naval officer swaggered down the ramp, reached the beach, and marched directly to Captain Khnurn.

"What is the purpose of your visit to Kasos?" he demanded.

From beside Khnurn, Alerio studied the ship's officer. He carried his shoulders stiff and rigid with one hand on the hilt of his sword and the other in the small of his back. Haughtiness rolled off him like sweat from a farmworker on a hot day.

"I am the Master of the Gála apó Hathor," Khnurn replied. "We are a snail trader heading home to Alexandria."

The naval officer nodded once, about faced, and started to walk away.

"Plus, one more thing," Khnurn advised.

As if the Captain's words were a prelude to a duel, the Rhodian officer spun around.

"And that is?" he asked.

"I have a diplomatic passenger for you," Khnurn replied. He lifted an arm and indicated Alerio. "May I introduce Tribune Alerio Carvilius Sisera of the Roman Republic."

"Another politician from across the Ionian Sea?" the officer stated without introducing himself. "Collect your things and get on board. Somehow, we'll get you to Rhodes."

"I don't think so," Alerio responded.

231

"You are on a mission to kiss Rhodian cōleī," the officer submitted. "Get on board and let's get you puckering."

Alerio did not respond physically to the insult. But he did inquire, "Do you really want to do this?"

"Do what?" the naval officer challenged.

"Bleed out on the sand," Alerio responded. "Be aware, I can gut you before any of your pretty sailors can come to your aid."

The Rhodian officer drew his sword, stepped out with a leg, and lunged. Alerio's palm smacked the side of the blade driving it off to the side. He pivoted his hip, jumped inside the naval officer's guard, and chopped the wrist on the hand holding the weapon. The sword tumbled to the ground.

Alerio slugged the officer in the jaw and caught the Rhodian before he fell to the ground. None of the moves went unnoticed.

Shouts from the Rhodian warship preceded the squad of infantrymen. Dressed in armor with mid-sized shields, the ten scurried down the ramp and crossed the beach. They moved quickly, until stopping two body lengths from their officer. The reason for their hesitation, a knife blade hovered at his throat.

"I have a dilemma," Alerio exclaimed. When the naval officer did not reply, Alerio drove a knee into the back of the Rhodian's thigh. "I am speaking to you."

"You are a dead man," the naval officer snarled.

"No, I am Tribune Alerio Sisera," Alerio corrected him. "And I am here as a military attaché."

"Kill him," the naval officer ordered his men.

"Hold," Alerio instructed. "Someone please, tell me this idiot's name. And the name of his father."

232

When none of the infantrymen replied, Alerio violently jerked the naval officer from side to side. Despite his efforts to prevent it, the officer's head flopped in rhythm with the abuse.

"Let me guess," Alerio offered. "His father is an important man and bought his sad excuse for a progeny a commission in the Rhodian Navy."

None of the infantrymen spoke but neither did they attack. They acted as if they were waiting for something. One glanced back, not at their warship but at the mouth of the inlet.

Two more trihemiolia warships power stroked into the bay. More impressive than the backstroke stop, before turning towards each other, the pair split apart. Just missing a ram-on-ram collision, they curved in half circles. Both ships, then backstroked for the beach.

***

He came off the warship with an air of authority and two bodyguards. Unlike the first officer, who believed his status granted him influence, this naval officer had muscle and steel to enforce his will.

"Lieutenant Niels. Are you still investigating the Egyptian ship on the beach?" the senior Rhodian officer inquired.

"This savage laid hands on me, Commander," Niels complained. "I demand satisfaction."

"You there, holding the pretty blade against my Lieutenant's neck," the Commander asked, "can I get your name?"

The knee snapped up and drove into Niels' leg. With pressure from Alerio's forearm, the Lieutenant sank to the

233

beach. Even as his leg buckled, his hand snaked out for the sword. But Alerio noticed the reach and planted a foot on the blade. Niels' ended up on his hands and knees, the fingers of one hand trapped under the steel of his sword.

"I am Alerio Carvilius Sisera," Alerio declared, "Tribune of the Republic's Legion. I travel to the Isle of Rhodes as a military attaché."

"Is that supposed to mean something to me?" the senior Naval officer questioned.

With the tips of his fingers, Alerio rotated the knife and without looking, slid the blade into its sheath.

"How about, I didn't slit the throat of your silly little brat?" Alerio ventured.

"There is some value to that," the Commander acknowledged.

Alerio noted that the Commander did not mention releasing Niels.

"Your name, sir?" Alerio requested.

"I am Izador, of the Rhodian Navy and Commander of Three Warships," the officer answered.

"Allow me to make an observation," Alerio offered without waiting for permission. "You are a more than competent commander. With a reputation for excellence, loyalty, and precision."

"I like to think all Rhodian Captains fit that description," Izador boasted.

"But not all Commanders of three are asked to babysit an important man's son," Alerio commented. "Who is Niels' father? And is Daddy proud of him?"

"Very astute of you, Tribune Sisera," Izador praised Alerio. "Lieutenant Evzen Niels is the eldest son of Chief Magistrate Kolya Niels."

"By Chief Magistrate you mean for a township, a city, or a region?" Alerio inquired.

"Oh no, Tribune Sisera. Kolya Niels is Chief Magistrate for the Democracy of Rhodes and all our territories," Izador inform him. "And you are under arrest. Please release my Lieutenant."

Izador's two bodyguards were faster than one would expect from big men. Each locked onto one of Alerio's arms. Picking him up, they carried the Tribune for a body's length.

Alerio fully expected to be slammed to the ground as punishment.

"Lieutenant Niels, one more step, and I will send you home," Izador threatened, "bound in rope, alongside the Legion officer."

"But Commander, he assaulted me," Evzen Niels whined. "I demand the opportunity to fight him."

"Tribune Sisera. What would happen if you fought my Lieutenant?" Izador inquired.

The bodyguards turned Alerio and switched sides. Once the three faced the Commander, Alerio looked at Abrax.

"Sergeant, because I am humble," Alerio mused, "please explained to the Commander the result of a fight between me and Lieutenant Niels."

The testimony of an authority figure would be more convincing than a brag from Alerio. Even if they didn't know Abrax, the Commander had to recognize the words of a Hoplite NCO.

"I would never assume to judge an officer's skill level. But, sir, I have been training Hoplites and serving in phalanx formations for sixteen years," Abrax attested. He reached to his right shoulder and removed the clasp. When the tunic material fell away, an injury to his right shoulder became obvious. The entire deltoid muscle was coated in black and purple bruises. "Tribune Sisera did this to me while he fended off an attack from another infantryman. It's not my place to tell you what to do, sir. But I would not allow any of my men to fight the Tribune."

"The words of an experienced NCO are good enough for me," Izador declared. "Permission denied. Lieutenant Niels put your blade away and resume command of your ship."

For several heartbeats, the Naval Commander and Alerio waited to see what the Lieutenant decided. Demonstrating their dislike for Niels, the bodyguards released Alerio's arms and stepped away.

In a huff, befitting a four-year-old's temperament, Evzen Niels ran his sword into the scabbard with enough force to crack the guard. Then he turned his back and trudged towards his ship. Following behind, the ten-man infantry squad marched slowly as if fearing for their fate.

Izador raised a hand in the air, made a circle motion, and pointed a finger at Niels' warship. From the commander's vessel, an older officer traveled the ramp, crossed the beach, and took the ramp up to Niels' deck.

"Sometimes the young need mentoring," Izador mentioned. "My second in command will protect the crew."

"The young do need coaching, sir," Alerio agreed. "Does this mean I am not being detained?"

"Oh, Tribune Sisera, you are certainly under arrest," Izador promised. "And you will stand trial."

"In front of Chief Magistrate Niels?" Alerio questioned.

"Yes," Izador confirmed. "Take Sisera to the ship and tie him up. Anyone who is that competent a fighter, cannot be allowed the freedom to cause trouble."

"Commander Izador, can I remain free, if I give you my word that I will not cause trouble," Alerio asked, "or try to escape?"

"Is that supposed to mean something to me?" Izador scoffed. "Take him aboard and tie him up."

The hard grip of the bodyguards clamped onto Alerio's arms. Together, they guided him across the beach to the ramp.

"You'll need your gear," Abrax offered. He and two of his Hoplites grabbed Alerio's luggage and tossed the bundles to the deck of the Rhodian warship. The Hoplite NCO braced, saluted, and said. "It was good fighting with you, Tribune Sisera."

Alerio would have replied, but he was occupied with the coils of rope being twirled around his body.

'There is one good thing to come out of this,' he thought as his arms were pinned to his sides. 'I finally get a vessel going all the way to the city of Rhodes.'

Act 7

Chapter 23 – Challenge a Colossus

The Rhodian warships were far out to sea with only a line of land on the horizon. When the line faded, the trio curved around to the right and lined up on a single pole. But they were so far out, no one should be able to see a simple pole at that distance.

Commander Izador strolled to the mid mast and squatted beside Alerio.

"Can you see the marker from down there?" he asked. After checking, and seeing the prisoner could not, Izador untied Alerio from the mast and stood him up. "The pole is not a post."

"Is it a mast?" Alerio inquired about a single tall object on the horizon.

"What you are looking at is one hundred and five feet of iron and bronze statue," Izador described. "Dedicated to the Sun God Helios. He guards the entrance to our harbor."

"I'm not an expert but I know what one hundred feet is," Alerio boasted. "And your God looks taller. Unless the statue is on a hill."

"Very astute of you. The idol is mounted on a fifty-foot pedestal," the Commander of three warships added. "The statue shows the piety and intelligence of our city. And it is proof of our wealth and technology."

"If I'm supposed to be impressed," Alerio admitted. "Consider me mesmerized."

"Untie the Tribune. If he dives in, he will be eaten or drowned. In either case, he will not escape," Izador told a sailor. Once the ropes were gone, he instructed. "Walk with me to the fore deck, Sisera."

They strolled the sixty-five feet to the deck and Alerio looked back trying to see where one hundred and five feet would fall on the vessel. Then he tried to imagine the trihemiolia warship standing on an end, towering overhead.

"To you, oh Sun God, the people of Rhodes set up the bronze statue. Reaching to Olympus, when we had pacified the waves of war and crowned our city with the spoils taken from our enemy," Izador prayed in a loud voice while looking at the growing statue. "Not only over the seas but also on land did we kindle the lovely torch of freedom and independence. For to the descendants of Rhodian belongs dominion over the sea and the land."

Although Alerio mostly heard the commander, every oarsmen and sailor on the ship repeated the prayer to Helios. After reciting the invocation, Izador stepped down from the fore deck.

"The statue is more than an honor to the God Helios and a statement about the tenacity of the Rhodian people," the commander told Alerio. "If you live after your trial, I will tell you how the statue is a lesson in analytical thinking."

"I look forward to hearing the story," Alerio responded.

"Do you have a deity that watches over you?" Izador questioned. "If so, you might want to seek a temple or an image before the trial."

"There are no statues or likenesses of my Goddess," Alerio responded. "She is very personal with few followers.

Mostly, because her festivals are not festive, nor her feasts satisfying."

"I'd like to hear more about your Goddess," Izador remarked.

"After the trial," Alerio promised, "if I am condemned to death."

"Now that is intriguing," the Commander acknowledged.

The stature of Helios evolved as the ships neared the harbor of Rhodes. From a post on the skyline, the massive head and shoulders took shape, then the features grew taller and larger. Finally, the marble base itself cast a shadow over the waters of the harbor while the Sun God towered over the entrance.

Passing through the shadow gave Alerio a chill. And craning his neck back to look up at the bronze face of a God left him dizzy. Glancing around, he realized that everyone on the warship with a view of the sky was doing the same.

"Get a good look and get back to business," Izador warned. "It'll be a poor showing of respect to Helios if we crash into a pier or another ship."

The docks at Rome were busy but a lot of those boats were small coastal traders and barges. And the port at Ostia had large transports and military warship but neither compared to the harbor of Rhodes. Huge deep-water grain shippers were docked, sleek sea transports, like the snail trader rested at piers, and on the beaches, countless warships lounged as if sharks resting before a feeding frenzy.

"My bodyguards will escort you to the government center. Or to a temple first if you feel the need to pray," Izador mentioned. "Good luck to you Tribune Sisera."

"Aren't you coming to watch?" Alerio suggested. "You might find it morbidly entertaining."

"Is that supposed to mean something to me?" Izador questioned.

***

The streets of Rhodes radiated out from a central market. And it came as no surprise, the goods on display were as varied at the ships in the harbor. Alerio and the two guards strolled along the booths.

"Food?" Alerio mentioned. "I don't know about you, but I like a good meal before I am condemned to death."

"How many times have you been sentenced to die?" one of the Hoplites asked.

"I don't recall how many exactly," Alerio told them as he stopped at a stall selling fresh pork. "But I remember being hungry for a lot of them."

The pork came wrapped in leaves. As the three peeled back the wrapping and nibbled, they strolled through the marketplace.

"So, death," the other guard inquired, "it isn't scary for you?"

"How could it be?" Alerio replied. "I'm still alive."

As they walked, Alerio kept watch for a means of escape. Not simply getting away from the guards, that would be easy. He needed a way off the Isle of Rhodes. Before he thought of a route out, a commotion from the harbor side of the market drew his attention.

Evzen Niels and two other naval officers charged up the road.

"Bring him," he ordered the guards as he came from between the booths.

"What's the rush, Lieutenant?" one of Alerio's Hoplite guards asked.

"Another trio of warships just rowed in," he replied. "They signaled emergency. I want this man tried and sentenced before my father, ah, Chief Magistrate Niels, gets busy with another project."

The group pushed through the crowd heading for the government building.

"Too bad we were interrupted," Alerio notified the guards. "I was getting thirsty."

"Do you get thirsty when you are condemned?" one asked.

"No. In this case," Alerio advised, "the pork made me thirsty."

***

The government building had extensive walkways, wide doorways, and large rooms. Light and air flooded the building although the atmosphere was not the reason for the design. As a Democracy, the building needed to accommodate large crowds of adult male citizens when important issues needed to be discussed. There was nothing major on the day's agenda, so the office of the peoples' representative was mostly empty.

"Now look here Kolya," Pasi Vasil complained to the Chief Magistrate. "You know I swing a large block of votes. All I am asking is that you shave a few bronze coins off my taxes from shipments to Macedonia."

"Let's say, I ignore a few transports," Kolya Niels replied. "Can you help me build a new village in the country?"

"Say yes and I'll have the corner stones delivered tomorrow," Pasi promised.

"I think we can work out a fair..." Kolya Niels started but he was interrupted.

His son, and a crowd of officers, two Hoplites and a Latian piled through the doorway.

"I was just concluding an appointment," Niels scolded his son.

"This Latian put his hands on an officer of the Navy," Evzen Niels declared while ignoring his father's tone. "And he put a blade to the officer's throat. I was going to execute him on the spot, but Commander Izador stopped me."

"Pasi, excuse me for a moment," the Chief Magistrate explained to his visitor.

"Certainly Kolya, I believe we are done," Pasi Vasil stated. "I'll just step to the back of the room and watch you dispense justice."

"Thank you for your understanding, citizen," Kolya Niels said to Pasi. Then turning to his son, he asked. "Who was the assaulted officer? Have him step forward and I will hear the complaint."

"It was me," Evzen announced. "I brought witnesses. I want the Latian drowned. Today, if possible."

"Hold on," the Chief Magistrate ordered. Looking at Alerio, he asked. "Who are you?"

"Tribune Alerio Carvilius Sisera, military attaché from the Roman Republic," Alerio replied. He held up his orders and a note from Consul Calatinus. "I have letters of introduction."

One of the naval officers snatched the missives from Alerio's hand and walked them to the Chief Magistrate. While the Magistrate read the papers, the group shifted nervously. Mostly, it was in reaction to Evzen Niels pacing in front of his father.

"You attacked an officer of the Rhodian Navy?" Kolya Niels inquired. "And you held a blade against Lieutenant Niels' throat? Are these assertions true, Tribune Sisera?"

"I did not draw my weapon at the insult," Alerio described. "I drew it after the Lieutenant drew his sword and attempted to skew me."

"What insult?" the Magistrate inquired.

"Something about me puckering up and kissing cōleī," Alerio explained. "Again, I did not respond to the insult."

The Chief Magistrate turned on his son.

"You said that to a diplomatic representative?" he asked.

"He is just another scholar come to beg you for favors," Lieutenant Niels sneered. "Unimportant and arrogant. Sentence him, and let's all get on with our day."

Chief Magistrate Niels' face turned red and for everyone in the room his anger was noticeable.

"Magistrate, magistrate," another Navy Lieutenant called for attention while rushing through the doorway. "We need to send for Pasi Vasil."

"Hold on. This is the second time I have been interrupted," the Magistrate grumbled. "Let me finish one meeting before starting another. Now everyone be silent."

But the room didn't go quiet.

"What is it, Lieutenant?" Pasi Vasil asked as he rushed from the back of the room. "Why send for me?"

"Master Vasil. One of your transports was taken by Cilician pirates," the naval officer responded.

"Where? Which one?" Pasi demanded.

"Off the coast of Crete," the Lieutenant reported. "And sir, it was the Good Themis."

Pasi Vasil's knees failed him. Sobbing, the merchant sank to the floor.

"Pasi, what is the matter?" Chief Magistrate Niels asked.

"Symeon was on the transport," Pasi whined. "My Symeon. Oh, my Symeon."

Alerio leaned towards one of the guards.

"Who is Symeon?" he asked.

"Master Vasil's oldest son," the guard answered. "Pasi traveled on business for years, dedicating himself to commerce and didn't marry. When he did, it took years before he had a son."

"How old is the boy?" Alerio questioned.

"Symeon Vasil is twelve," the guard informed him.

"Oh, Hades," Alerio swore.

"Exactly," the guard replied.

"They took the youngest and strongest crewmen. The others they left on the beach," the naval officer who delivered the news described. "Luckily, my ship was patrolling the coast when we spotted the survivors. That was two days ago."

"We need to launch the fleet," Pasi Vasil suggested. "We can finally clean out that nest of vipers on Antikythera. But mostly, I want my son back."

"Send for the Admiral," the Chief Magistrate instructed. "And take Sisera to the cells. I'll get to his punishment when the crisis is over."

The guard gently shoved Alerio. Rather than going with the hint, the Legion officer shoved back.

"If you send in your fleet, your assault elements will get stalled at the wall. The boy will be killed along with the other prisoners," Alerio yelled as he pushed and broke away from the Hoplites. "And if you take too long to plan and organize, he will be shipped to Qart Hadasht territory and sold at the slave market."

At the mention of both fates, Pasi Vasil cried out for his son.

"And you have a better idea?" Magistrate Niels challenged.

"I do," Alerio replied. "Send me in to rescue the boy."

"Why would I do that?" the Magistrate inquired.

"Because I am an officer in the Republic's Legion, and I need to open negotiations with the Isle of Rhodes," Alerio explained. "What better way to endear myself. Plus, being on a mission is more desirable than rotting in a cell."

"No. No, I forbid it," Evzen Niels shouted. "You cannot…"

"Get him out of my office," the Chief Magistrate ordered. The two guards reached for Alerio. But the senior Niels redirected them. "No, not him. My son. Get Lieutenant Niels out of my office."

Bellowing and complaining the Magistrate's progeny was hauled from the government building. When things quieted down, Kolya Niels looked into Alerio's eyes.

"What do you need," he asked, "to rescue my friend's son?"

"A coastal trading vessel," Alerio responded, "and the use of Commander Izador and his warship."

"I can assign you an entire fleet," the Magistrate protested.

"This requires stealth, not a display of power," Alerio told him. "At least not until the display is needed."

***

Commander Izador thought it curious when Sisera, the Latian, came jogging towards the harbor. Behind him the two guards trotted but did not seem to be gaining on the Tribune. Thinking him an escaped prisoner, the Commander started to call to Lieutenant Perseus Archos, the First Officer of his second warship. Before he voiced his concerns, Sisera reached the end of the pavers and dropped onto the beach.

"Are you running from the sentencing?" Izador inquired from the deck of his warship. "If so, you've picked your path poorly."

"An interesting choice of wording, Commander," Alerio commented as he stopped and peered up at Izador. "I may have picked the wrong path for both of us. But at the time, it seemed like the right thing to do."

"You have my attention," Izador admitted. "What path are we taking?"

A messenger raced down the street, leaped to the sand, and sprinted to the warship. Scrambling aboard, he handed the Commander a note.

"A message from Chief Magistrate Niels," Izador described. After reading it, he waved the paper and asked. "What do you need Sisera?"

"A visit to the market, a dugout canoe, a coastal trader filled with grain, two brave men I can trust and who will follow orders," Alerio replied. "Plus, you and your three warships."

"The obvious question then," Izador queried, "is where do you want this tiny flotilla to gather?"

"Menies Beach," Alerio answered, "on the northwest arm of Crete."

Chapter 24 – Infiltrating Antikythera

Two trihemiolias rowed into the cove, maneuvered around, and back stroked for the beach. They aimed for either side of a third warship already high and dry on the narrow shoreline.

"I hope that meets your needs," Izador remarked.

The Commander indicated one of the warships. Tied to the top deck was a papyrus reed boat.

"No sail or mast?" Alerio questioned.

"For those features you need a fishing boat," Izador explained. "You wanted small. With small, you get a single rear oar. That type of boat rows up and down the Nile by the hundreds every day. And they are used as ceremonial boats for wealthy families."

"That is a river," Alerio pointed out. "This is the sea. And I don't plan on any type of ceremony."

"You can't sink a papyrus boat," Izador stated in defense of the choice. "The reeds float, although they will burn. Besides, at sea you don't have to worry about river crocodiles."

"Only sharks and other demons from the depths," Alerio responded.

A twenty-five-foot coastal trader rowed into the cove. One of the crewmen rowed with a pair of oars from midship while the other rocked a rear oar from side to side adding propulsion and guidance.

"Anything bad to say about the trader?" Izador inquired.

"No, it is the perfect boat," Alerio told him. "Maybe a little too clean for the mission."

"What now?" Izador questioned.

"I think if the crews from the warships clean their fish on the deck," Alerio told him. "It should be ready for tonight."

The trader slipped in between two warships and the men jumped into the water and pushed it ashore. With wet legs, they marched up the beach to Izador.

"Commander, the boat handles well, and the hull is solid," one reported.

"Tribune Sisera, this is Lieutenant Perseus Archos," Izador introduced the crew. "And the big man is Sergeant Teppo Petya."

"Good to meet you," Alerio added. "Now, go find older more distressed clothing."

"Commander Izador. Are we taking orders from a Latian?" Perseus asked.

"Yes, Lieutenant Archos, you are," Izador assured him. "But maybe the Tribune could explain before issuing statements as orders."

Alerio realized he was focused on himself. It wasn't wrong seeing as he was a long way from Legion support, comrades, or even friendly companionship. But he needed these men to perform and for that they needed a clearer picture of their part.

"We need to appear desperate," Alerio told them. "Desperate enough to row into a pirate settlement to trade goods which might have been stolen."

"We will appear to be minor brigands doing business with the only market open to us," Perseus Archos summed up the cover.

Alerio and Izador nodded their agreement.

"When do we leave, Tribune Sisera?" Sergeant Teppo Petya inquired.

"Just before sundown," Alerio answered. "We have thirty miles of open water to cross. I hope your navigation skills are up to the task, Lieutenant."

"I am an officer in the Rhodian Navy," Perseus boasted. "The sea and stars are as familiar to me as the face of my father."

***

In the moonlight, the sheer rocks rising from the water appeared black and blank as the mouth of a cave. But the low light allowed Alerio to guide the papyrus boat to a fissure with a slope in the back. Between the rocks, he used his hands to guide the boat.

Once at the back of the crevice, he climbed to shore and pulled the boat up out of the sea. Then he checked the location from several angles before slipping by the boat and dropping back into the water. The vessel constructed of papyrus remained behind.

"I don't understand," Lieutenant Archos complained when Alerio pulled himself into the coastal trader, "why you brought the boat only to leave it here."

"A lot depends on what we find in the settlement. The stashed boat might be our way off the island. Or something else," he replied. Then to the shadowy figure of Sergeant Petya, he advised. "Let's go play with the Cilicians."

Teppo and Alerio dipped oars and powered the boat around the knot of land. Not long after leaving the location of the papyrus boat, they entered a cove where embers from campfires glowed on the shoreline.

"Xiropotamos Beach," Alerio mentioned. "Remember, we have been here since sundown."

"But we are just arriving," Perseus advised. "Who is going to believe that we've been here all night?"

"Hopefully, enough people so everyone thinks we've been vetted," Alerio replied. "Stay with the plan. Now hush up and steer."

At first, the island of Antikythera loomed over them from one side. But as they rowed closer to Xiropotamos beach the stars were blocked from view on three sides by the land rising above the cove.

The coastal trader gently touched the rocky sand. Alerio and Teppo slid into the cove, spun the boat, and shoved it out of the water and onto the island. Then, quietly, they climbed back into the boat and stretched out on the deck.

A few light sleepers on other ships noted the disturbance. But, after deciding the newly arrived boat presented no threat, they rolled over and went back to sleep. Higher on the beach, the boat did not register with the men sprawled around the dying campfires. When the beach settled and snoring and coughing resumed, Alerio pulled a cape over his shoulders and placed a hat on his head then dropped from the boat. Slowly, so as not to wake the sleeping boat crews, he worked his way off the beach and up towards the town.

***

'This slope is a man killer,' Alerio thought while climbing. 'Cilician archers, spearmen, and slingers stationed at the top could drop rocks, arrows, and spears, as well as rolling barrels full of rock, down on arriving Rhodian transports. Before the invasion force could organize and begin the assault, injured infantrymen would litter the beach. Win or lose, blood, bones, and funerals were the cost to take Antikythera by force.'

At the top of the rise he stopped, and despite the morbid images he visualized while climbing, Alerio smiled. Fire pits glowed at a gateway marking the entrance through the defensive wall. But it wasn't the fires that thrilled the Legion staff officer.

Tribune Alerio Sisera strolled to the entrance and approached the sleeping sentry.

"Who is on guard duty?" he inquired while tapping the man's shoulder.

The sentry's eyes fluttered open.

"I am," he blustered. After taking in the expensive cape and hat, he added. "I wasn't sleeping, Captain, I swear."

"That's good. Because punishment for sleeping on watch is not pretty," Alerio warned. He added a shake of an accusing finger in the man's face. "Have you seen anything suspicious tonight?"

"No Captain," the guard assured him.

Alerio touched the brim of his petasos in salute and moved to the gateway. The market at Rhodes had a wide variety of goods. Although he overpaid for the beaver felt hat, and the rich cloak, the items had just paid for themselves. Unchallenged, Alerio ambled into the Cilician settlement as if he belonged there

***

Locating Symeon Vasil required four steps. The first three revolved around finding the crew who captured the transport, Good Themis. Although four days had elapsed, Alerio knew from experience any team coming off a successful mission celebrated, and the hardier pirates would still be bragging about taking a major merchant ship. And still be boasting about plans for their share when the captives were sold.

Having infiltrated the settlement, Alerio began the second step. For this phase, he let his ears do the searching. Strolling and listening, he remained attuned to the sounds of the pirate haven. In the middle of the night, the revelries should be identifiable by the level of noise they made. When he heard loud voices a few doors down, Alerio headed for the establishment.

The most difficult part of his search was about to begin. How to stay sober while pursuing information about the Vasil boy.

***

Inside the tavern, the bar was constructed of ship's planks stretched over pedestals of stacked stone. And as he's seen from the Gála as it sailed by the island, there was no roof. In this place the owner didn't even try. He counted on a beautiful display of stars for a ceiling.

"What will you have?" an old man asked.

"The last time I was in, I was disappointed with the beer," Alerio lied.

"Then you'll be having the mead," the bartender offered.

Alerio slid a bronze coin onto the planks, took a clay mug of the beverage, and went to an empty seat. At the next table, four men drank and talked.

"You would think they brought down a squadron of those Rhodian Navy warships," one man complained.

"But they are buying drinks," another offered.

"If you can stomach the bragging," a third stated.

Alerio's premise proved correct. Capturing a prized transport caused an extended celebration. After a few more sips, he spilled half of the mead on the ground behind his back.

"I'm going to bed," he told the bartender. "Late night guard duty is terrible for the nerves."

"You must be one of Captain Mirza's boys," the old tavern keeper suggested.

"I must be," Alerio replied.

He left the pub and began cruising. He now had a Captain's name and confidence that he could find the right crew.

***

The third pub he entered held six customers. All looking as if they hadn't bathed, eaten, or sobered up in the last four days. Then, Alerio heard golden words.

"I am going to buy a piece of land," a pirate exclaimed. "Once Captain Parviz sells the ship and the sailors, I'm taking my coins and buying land."

Not only was Alerio in the correct tavern, but he also had the name of the pirate Captain who took the boy.

"Wine," he ordered from the proprietor.

"I don't recognize you," the bartender remarked.

"I'm the new man on Mirza's crew," Alerio told him using the Captain's name he heard at the first pub, "and I just got off guard duty. If my coin isn't good here, I'll go where it's wanted."

A voice called from across the room, "You on Mirza's crew?"

"Yes," Alerio confirmed. He turned to face the man. "Is that a problem? The bar keeper has already kicked me out."

"Not yet he hasn't," the man declared. Then he invited Alerio. "Come drink with us."

"You sail with Captain Parviz?" Alerio guessed.

"You are new," another man proposed. "Everyone knows our crew and what we did."

Alerio arrived at the table and poured a mug of wine.

"Like I said," Alerio reminded, "I am new. Tell me what you did."

"What we did?" the six men roared. "We captured the Good Themis. And took eight crewmen and a boy captive."

"A boy," Alerio repeated. "He'll fetch a good price at the Qart Hadasht slave market."

"See that's what I've been saying," one slurred. "With my cut, I am going to buy a piece of land."

Alerio settled in for another difficult part of his search. Staying sober while keeping the pirates talking.

***

According to the six pirates, each of them vaulted onto the merchant vessel, fought hand-to-hand with the merchant crew, and singlehandedly captured the ship. Alerio listened to tales of heroism and personal sacrifice. It was all very thrilling and mostly lies.

"What did Captain Parviz do with the prisoners?" Alerio inquired while pouring another mug.

His offhanded question seemed innocent, but he listened intently for the answer.

"The Captain stowed them in the pen at the top of the hill," one replied.

Alerio waited for a little longer before excusing himself.

"I have early duty tomorrow," Alerio declared. Then he stood and announced. "Congratulations on the prize ship."

He left the tavern to hoots and hollers from the crew. Outside, Alerio breathed deeply to clear his head before heading uphill. He had three of the steps to saving Symeon Vasil completed. He had infiltrated the settlement, knew who held the boy, and a general idea of where Symeon Vasil was being held.

While walking to the next tier of the town, Alerio tried to remember the layout of the settlement. His quick glance in the daylight from out at sea didn't help. With stone walls on either side and the rough street under his feet, he moved upward looking for anything resembling a pen.

At an intersection, Alerio noticed three men coming from a side road. He paused and made exaggerated movements as if looking for something.

"You lost?" one of the men inquired.

"My Captain sent me to help Captain Parviz," he explained. "But I can't find the pens where the merchant crew is being held. I'm late."

"Your Captain doesn't like you very much does he," one of them teased.

"I don't know," Alerio admitted.

"At the top of this street, turn left, and follow your nose," another replied.

The three laughed as they walked away.

'Are they laughing at me,' Alerio pondered. 'Or at the directions, or the assignment?'

Taking advantage of the only clue he had, Alerio started uphill, sniffing as he climbed.

***

Alerio's nose alerted him, and he slid into the shelter of a stone wall and peered around the corner.

Rotting slop on a still summer night gave the air a unique fragrance. And explained why the hog pens were located high above the town. If placed at a lower elevation, the stink would hang in the air. However, allowing the wind to clear the aroma by blowing it over the crest of a hill did not justify the presence of two guards. The value of pork might have warranted a single sentry to prevent theft. But two meant they were guarding something more.

So far, nothing Alerio had done would anger the pirates. Sneaking, information gathering, and reconnaissance were benign practices. With the discovery of where Symeon Vasil was being held, the steps of infiltrating Antikythera ended.

Alerio could return to Rhodes, report that Symeon lived, but a rescue was too dangerous for both him and the boy. Or Tribune Sisera could go tactical and perform acts that would enrage the Cilician settlement. To that end, he left the hog pen area and moved across town heading northward.

Chapter 25 – Ceremonial Boat

The defensive wall on the North side of town lacked height. As Alerio scaled the barrier, he stored the fact away in case he got involved in an assault on the island. Once among the rocky landscape and low brush, he studied the terrain for recognizable features.

It took investigating four little inlets before locating the papyrus boat. When he found it, the Tribune lifted a lamp from the bottom of the vessel, broke the seal, and splashed oil around the inside. When the reeds dripped with excess oil, Alerio set the lamp in the bottom of the boat. Stretching reed fibers over the wick stopper to hold the lamp in place, Alerio struck flint and lit the wick. To keep from disturbing the lamp, he eased the boat into the water and gave it a gentle push. Then he ran for the wall, the town, and the boy.

***

There were two sentries for a pen of hogs and a pen of humans but nothing else. As undisciplined troops are likely to do, the pirates sat together for company. And they had their backs to the street. On one hand, keeping their eyes on the prisoners and the pork made sense.

On the other hand, Alerio came out of the dark unnoticed.

Requiring precision, the smaller blade needed to silence and pacify with a quick thrust. From the side, the knife punctured the guard's windpipe, silencing him. A snap of Alerio's wrist ripped the blade out through the front of the guard's throat. That prevented him from fighting back.

The gladius required less accuracy but more force. In a vertical chop, the blade cut the hair and skin on the back of the guard's neck. Passing easily through the muscles, the Noric steel hewed completely through the bones in the second guard's neck.

Alerio sheathed both weapons and squatted beside the bodies. Voices carried from a block away, but none sounded an alarm. After waiting for a few moments to be sure he wouldn't have company, Alerio relaxed. But he had two problems, hiding the bodies, and freeing the prisoners. Leaving the bodies at the pen was not an option. Anyone walking by could see the dead men and raise an alarm.

It might have been the lack of sleep, the wine, the weeks of traveling, or simply a blessing from Coalemus, the God of the Stupid. In any case, Alerio carried the bodies to the hog pen and dumped them over the rail. Then he rushed to the human pen, but too late, the commotion began.

For a farm boy, it was unforgivable. The sows and boars discovered the flesh and began an orgy of feeding. Complete with loud aggressive grunting and manic squealing, the swine announced an event at the pens.

"Symeon Vasil, are you here?" Alerio asked in a voice above conversational level. It was necessary to be heard over the noises coming from the pig pen.

"I am here, sir," a small, frightened voice replied.

"Give me your hand boy," Alerio instructed. "I'm taking you home to your father."

"He ain't going nowhere with you, pirate," a male voice in the corner of the human pen stated.

"We don't have time for a democratic debate," Alerio warned. "Or a vote. I've removed the guards and you are free to go. But if you fight me, I will leave you here bleeding and still take the boy."

The man, obviously a crewman or a ship's officer from the Good Themis, demanded, "What's his father's name?"

"Pasi Vasil spent his youth building his business," Alerio recited the litany the Hoplite guard told him. "Master Vasil married later in life and didn't have a son for years. Until Symeon came along. Can we go now?"

A shape much smaller than a grown man slipped from the back of the pen.

"Please, sir. I want to go home," Symeon begged.

"We will do that little man," Alerio assured him.

Eight men came forward from the pen.

"What about us?" the ship's officer inquired.

"I can only take the boy," Alerio informed him. "But I can tell you, the pirates will be launching their ships tonight, so stay away from the beaches. Gather food and hide until tomorrow night. Then steal a boat and row for Crete."

"The Cilicians will catch us before we can reach a town with a garrison," one of the crewmen complained. "They'll cut our bellies open and feed us to the sharks."

"You get to the shores of Crete," Alerio assured them, "and the Rhodian Navy will be there waiting to greet the Cilicians."

"Who are you?" the ship's officer asked. "Where are you from?"

"I am Tribune Alerio Sisera from Rome," Alerio answered. "Now go, before we have to fight our way through four thousand pirates."

The crewmen sprinted to the south in the direction of the beach. Alerio, with a hand on the boy's shoulder, stood still.

"Aren't we going with them?" Symeon inquired.

"Commander Izador promised me an example of analytical thinking," Alerio replied. "But the crewmen just demonstrated a lack of it. Didn't I warn them the pirates were going to launch their ships tonight?"

"You did, sir," the boy answered. "But it's very quiet. Perhaps the crew thought to escape before the pirates stirred."

"Or they didn't believe me. Or maybe they didn't listen and think about what I said," Alerio remarked. Rotating the boy until he faced north, Alerio dropped the felt petasos on Symeon's head and urged. "Walk slowly so we don't draw attention to ourselves."

Resembling an older brother out for a stroll with his younger sibling, they strolled northward. They were two blocks from the pens when shouts of alarm broke out. Running feet filled the streets as angry pirates searched for the escapees. Before the Cilicians reached Alerio, he hoisted Symeon to the top of the north wall.

"There is nothing here," the boy commented when they were both on the far side of the barrier. "Except a view of the sea."

"That is the point," Alerio confirmed.

He untied the dark cape and fluffed it overhead. As the billowing cloth settled, Alerio pulled the boy down beside him. Covered with the dark material, they could have been any rock on the island of Antikythera.

"How long will we stay here, sir?" Symeon asked.

"Until the pirates tell us it's time to move," Alerio replied.

"Why would they do that?" the boy gasped.

On the other side of the wall voices announced the arrival of search parties.

"See anything?"

"No and I don't expect to."

"Why?" a voice questioned from directly behind and overhead of Alerio and Symeon.

The pirate was leaning over the wall probably scanning the land outside the settlement.

261

"If I were them," the man on the wall replied, "I'd head for the beach and try to find a boat to steal."

"We have crews searching at both beaches," the second voice added.

This time his voice came in clear enough to show he had climbed onto the defensive wall as well. Symeon
Vasil shivered in fright. Alerio eased an arm up and over the boy's shoulder trying to comfort him.

"What is that?" the first voice insisted.

Symeon froze and his teeth chattered in fright.

"What?" the second asked.

"There, offshore," the first instructed. "It's a floating beacon. Must be a signal to a larger ship."

"Captain Parviz needs to know they are escaping by boat."

The sound of running feet faded as the search parties raced to the south, the beaches, and their boats.

"How did you know?" Symeon questioned.

Alerio opened the front of the cape. Out on the water, the papyrus boat blazed in the night. From high up, it did appear to be a signal fire on a boat escaping the island. But Alerio understood there were no other boats out on the water watching for the flame. And he knew the boat made of reeds was consuming itself and would eventually vanish. Hopefully, not before all the pirate boats from the beaches rowed out searching for the crew of the Good Themis.

"I didn't know," Alerio admitted, "But I had faith."

"Now what, Tribune?" the boy asked.

"We keep the faith," Alerio replied, "and head for the water."

***

The pirate stronghold at Xiropotamos beach provided an opportunity for brave traders. After all, what was the value of merchandise from a captured merchant ship in a settlement awash in stolen goods. The exchange rate on Antikythera proved too tempting to resist. And although potential victims of the brigands while at sea, traders rowed in and took advantage of other merchants' misfortunes.

A Cilician Captain arrived at the beach, kicked sleeping pirates awake, and hollered.

"Get up, get up," he insisted. "The merchant crewmen have escaped. Get up, find them, and claim your reward."

On the trading vessels that came to do business with the Cilicians, the crews rolled out from under their blankets.

"What's going on?" Perseus Archos asked.

The shadowy forms of two pirates approached the boat. They finished strolling to the coastal trader before answering.

"Captain Parviz's prisoners have escaped," one replied. He scaled the sideboards, reached the deck, and came to his feet. Then he said as if it was a challenge. "We've been ordered to hold all merchant boats on the beach after searching them."

"Help yourself," Perseus invited the man.

At the bow, Teppo Petya added wood to a brazier and blew the embers to life. From that flame, he lit the wick on a lamp.

"Here, this will help," he offered the light to the pirate.

"And two of Captain Mirza's crew are missing," the other pirate said while he climbed up. "But, more than likely, they are off getting drunk."

Of the six merchant ships on Xiropotamos beach, Perseus Archos' coastal trader was the smallest. With limited storage spaces to hide escaped prisoners, the search ended quickly.

"We have wine, bread, and cheese," Teppo Petya announced. "Stay and breakfast with us."

Neither Sergeant Petya nor Lieutenant Archos wanted to socialize with the Cilicians. But Tribune Sisera's instructions stated that once pirates were on board, the Rhodians were supposed to keep them on board.

Why, they didn't know. But both understood orders and as a result, Perseus held up a wineskin while Teppo unwrapped a large chunk of cheese.

"Yes, stay and breakfast with us," Perseus invited the pair. "We are all awake. And you must guard us, so why not eat?"

***

Perseus, Teppo, and the two pirates, Cas and Kaveh, sat on crates around a box holding the food.

"We arrived late yesterday but don't know anybody," Perseus complained while passing the wineskin to Kaveh. "Now we are stuck with a cargo hold full of grain."

"We can help you sell the load," Cas assured him.

From the beach came cries of, "The prisoners are in a boat. They have taken to the sea."

"That's interesting," Teppo commented. "I wonder how they got a boat."

His casual remark relayed more information to Perseus than to the pirates.

"I guess they will escape," Perseus added.

"No, they won't escape," Kaveh disagreed. "Once our ships-of-war are launched, they will be recaptured easily."

264

"I haven't seen any ships-of-war," Teppo noted.

"They are beached a quarter of a mile from here," Cas reported. "You haven't seen them yet because the crews need to be rounded up before they can launch the ships."

"Did the Captain earlier say there was a reward?" Perseus questioned.

"Sure, those prisoners are worth a lot to Captain Parviz and his crew," Kaveh exclaimed. "He'll pay handsomely for their return."

"And yet the unarmed prisoners are rowing away," Teppo reflected on the situation, "while you wait for the ships-of-war to launch."

"What are you suggesting?" Cas demanded.

"Nothing," Perseus stated. "Or maybe, we launch, find the prisoners, and collect the reward."

"Can we do that?" Teppo asked.

In the flickering light of the lamp, the Lieutenant and Sergeant peered into the faces of the pirates. Moments passed, then Cas stood.

"We can do this," he declared.

"We can?" Kaveh inquired. Then he remarked. "But the Captain said no merchant vessels were to leave the beach."

"This vessel is under our control," Cas explained. "Besides, I want the reward."

"We are under your command, Captain," Perseus confirmed. "Orders, sir?"

"Launch the boat," Cas commanded.

"Yes, sir," Teppo acknowledged.

He slipped over the side and shoved the boat into the cove. The launch of the coastal trader drew a few shouted questions.

"Don't you worry about it," Cas hollered a reply to the concerned pirates. "Kaveh and I are going for the reward."

With Perseus on the rear oar, Teppo and Kaveh on the main oars, and Cas on lookout at the bow, the coastal trader moved out of the cove and into the bay.

"You are too close to shore," Cas called back. "Angle us more to port and away from the rocks."

"Yes, Captain," Perseus acknowledged.

But the boat held its course and continued to row close to the black rocks.

"How is that?" Perseus called to the fore of the coastal trader.

"More, move us more," Cas replied. "No wonder the boat stinks. You are not a sailor."

"Now?" Perseus asked even though he hadn't steered the boat away from shore.

"No, no. More to port, more," Cas insisted.

***

They had traveled around a finger of land by inlets while continuing the loud exchanges. Fed up with the unresponsive nature of the merchant, Cas spun and faced aft.

"Did you not hear me?" he shouted. "Steer us away from the rocks. Never mind, I'll take control myself."

Stomping in frustration, he walked the length of the vessel, having to step over and around Teppo and Kaveh.

"Those rocks are dangerous, even for a coastal trader," he informed Perseus. "One submerged can sink…"

"Look. There," Perseus pointed out, "in the water."

Cas pivoted and bent forward to study the black sea. He noted waves before a man with something around his neck stroked into the open water from between the rocks.

"There is one of the prisoners…" Cas gasped as a dagger slid between his ribs.

Closely following the gasp, Teppo finished a stroke and while returning to the dip the oar blade, he yanked the oar inward. The end of the oak smacked Kaveh in the head. Barely conscious, the pirate tumbled overboard.

"Cas is down," Perseus announced.

A splash preceded Teppo's declaration, "Kaveh is gone, as well, sir."

Act 8

Chapter 26 - Tap-Tap-Tap-Tap

Symeon Vasil clung to Alerio's neck as the Tribune swam out from between the rocks. For long moments, the two had waited in waist deep water. Then as the voices of two men arguing reached them, Alerio swam out of the fissure.

"Tribune Sisera," Teppo acknowledged Alerio as he reached the boat. "You seem to have a snail on your back."

"This Sergeant Petya is Master Vasil," Alerio replied. "Kindly help him into the boat."

Teppo reached down, shoved a big hand under Symeon's arm, and lifted the boy into the boat. Alerio scissor kicked his legs, came partially out of the water, and grabbed the boat rail.

"Where do we stand with the ships-of-war?" Alerio questioned as he rolled onto the trader.

"According to Cas, one of our Cilician guides, the Captains were still gathering their crews," Perseus answered. "We should lower the sail and get away from here."

"Symeon, this is Lieutenant Archos of the Rhodian Navy," Alerio told the boy. "Until you get back to the city of Rhodes, you will stay by his side. No matter what happens, you become his shadow."

"What's going to happen, Tribune Sisera?" he asked.

"I wish I knew," Alerio admitted. Then to Teppo, he asked. "How strong are you?"

"I am as good as two men," the Sergeant boasted.

"We will not be using a sail," Alerio informed the two Rhodians. "The fabric catches moonlight, making us visible to the Cilicians."

"Then how are we going to avoid the ships-of-war?" Perseus inquired.

"Sergeant Teppo and I are going to row us away from Antikythera," Alerio explained as he took the oar left by Kaveh. "Keeping a low profile is the best chance we have. Sergeant Petya, man your station."

Sound traveled over water incredibly far. But as sound did in hilly terrain, the source's direction was hard to discern. Except the call in the early morning to run out oars could only come from the upper reaches of the bay.

"The ships-of-war will be along shortly," Perseus warned. "Stroke, stroke. Walk it together, stroke, stroke."

Teppo taking long strides forced Alerio to quick step. They had no natural rhythm in common. In a boat crew, a deck officer would have them separated. But they didn't have the luxury of other oarsman to balance their natural assets.

"Stroke, stroke, pull it together," Perseus encouraged. "Stroke, stroke."

But the Tribune and the NCO continued to struggle with combining their styles. Although the coastal trader moved, the boat lacked the rapid forward momentum necessary to clear the mouth of the bay. Or even to clear the point of land before the Cilician ships-of-war arrived.

A stick tapped the deck. Again, it rapped on the boards. When the stick knocked a third time, a young voice song out in the dark.

"Demetrius is knocking

Do not let him in
The Prince wants the children
To raise as yearlings
What can we do to save our kin
Remain behind the walls
Do not let them in
Remain behind the walls
Do not let Demetrius in."

And the stick kept time with a tap-tap-tap-tap.

Alerio and Teppo matched the rhyming and evened out their strokes.

"Demetrius is knocking
Ignore his tools of war
The Prince wants an open door
For our gold he rowed ashore
To do the deed its ram and bore
Siege engines pound
Ignore his tools of war
Remain behind the walls
Do not let Demetrius in."

And the stick kept time with a tap-tap-tap-tap.

The coastal trading boat rounded the arm of the bay. Halfway across a narrow strait between the island and a small crop of land in deeper water, Lieutenant Archos bent down and took the stick from Symeon.

"It's a schoolboy's song," Perseus complained. "This is a serious situation. There is no place for a melody from a playground. Besides, his voice will carry across the water."

"I kind of like it, Lieutenant," Teppo admitted. "It helps me slow down for the little guy."

Alerio glanced back to see if the Sergeant was referring to Symeon. But the big NCO was not talking about the boy.

"If over one hundred oarsmen are quiet enough to hear a boy singing, we are doomed anyway. Symeon Vasil, continue your song," Alerio encouraged. "It helps Sergeant Petya keep up with my strength."

The two oarsmen tighten their grips and flexed into the next stroke. Symeon felt the stick as it was thrust back into his hand. He tapped the deck and sang.

"Demetrius is knocking
Man the defenses
The Prince takes the offense
Making the year tense
In the horror he dispenses
Rhodes stands strong
Man the defenses
Remain behind the walls
Do not let Demetrius in."

And the stick kept time with a tap-tap-tap-tap.

While Alerio and Teppo sweated and dug their oar blades in the water, Perseus moved the rear oar and watched the dark mountain of the island slide by. But the Lieutenant's duties extended beyond keeping them off the rocks, steering, and adding a little propulsion.

Above his head the stars glistened but not for long. With the coming sunrise, the naval Lieutenant would lose the multi point navigation aids. Measuring the boat's direction by hands and finger's widths from the sun worked for long hauls. But Perseus needed to locate a slice of Crete just two and three quarters of a mile wide. The waning night required him to nose the boat into the proper course before daybreak. Guided by the stars, he eased the craft away from Antikythera.

With a break in his voice from exhaustion, Symeon Vasil continued to keep the beat while singing.

"Demetrius is knocking
Show him no pity
The Prince was very snippy
Against our walled city
Let him whine let him get snitty
From brave Rhodes he fled
Show him no pity
Remain behind the walls
Do not let Demetrius in."

And the stick kept time with a tap-tap-tap-tap.

***

Miles of hard rowing carried the boat out of sight of the island just before the land would have appeared in the sunlight of a new day. Thanks to Harpocrates hiding them in the dark, the God of Silence and Secrets helped them avoid the ships-of-war.

"Good singing," Alerio complimented Symeon. The Tribune rotated his shoulders in an attempt to work the knots from his muscles. Then he announced. "We are visible with or without a sail."

Alerio and Teppo put away the oars, pulled lines and unfurled the cloth. Symeon dropped the stick and collapsed to the deck. Perseus held a hand up beside the sun on his left while trying to decipher a southeast heading towards Crete.

"Lieutenant Archos, do you need help with steering?" Alerio inquired.

"Tribune Sisera, that would be most helpful," Perseus replied. He glanced at Teppo who had dropped to the deck beside the boy. "If you have the energy?"

"I haven't started honing my blades," Alerio responded.

"Is there a meaning behind that remark?" Perseus questioned. "Or am I too tired to figure it out?"

"In the Legion, we are taught to complete the mission before tending to our gear," Alerio said while walking to Perseus. As he took control of the rear oar, he explained. "And to rest only after repairing our gear. Give me a heading, Lieutenant Archos, this assignment is not over yet. There is no rest."

***

For all the speed the trading vessel caught from the wind, it was not in the same class as a bireme. With a huge sail pushing one hundred feet of vessel, the ship-of-war appeared off the starboard side moving passed them.

"What do you think, Lieutenant?" Teppo asked. He held the rear oar steady while Alerio rested. "Do we veer off and try to outrun her?"

In a thoughtful movement, Perseus lifted his face and peered at the mid-morning sky.

"The answer is not up there, Lieutenant," Alerio suggested as he stretched. He pulled his gladius and examined the Noric steel. "The answer is here in this blade."

"That's a two banked ship-of-war with one hundred and twenty oarsmen," Perseus cautioned. "We can't possibly fight them all."

"You are correct," Alerio agreed. "You, Symeon, and Teppo can't."

"Hold on, Tribune," Teppo scolded. "If you can fight, so can I."

"Not this engagement," Alerio replied. "You and Perseus are needed to sail this boat to Crete, find the Commander, and return young Vasil to his father."

"And while we are sailing into the sunset," Perseus asked, "where will you be?"

"On the bireme's steering deck," Alerio replied. "Hopefully disrupting their navigation."

"Sir, how do you plan to board the Cilician vessel?" Teppo inquired.

"It's a test," Alerio remarked, "of Lieutenant Archos boat handling skills."

"You believe you can fight one hundred and twenty oarsmen plus the ship's officers," Perseus challenged.

"I'm guessing they aren't sailing with a full crew," Alerio responded. "There shouldn't be more than eighty pirates on board."

"Eighty against one," Symeon Vasil remarked. "Why Tribune?"

"I'd like an answer to that as well," Perseus said. "Why?"

"In the future, the Republic hopes to have mutual defense treaties between Rhodes and Rome. I was sent to Rhodes as an attaché to contact your military," Alerio reported. "But a sword hangs over my head. If I fail, it will affect more than me. The failure will have consequences for my adopted father. Dying while saving Symeon clears me of any responsibility. There will be no adverse effect on my father and the act will set up the next attaché for success."

"You, Tribune Sisera, are as honorable as a Rhodian naval officer," Perseus complimented Alerio. "It has been an honor serving with you."

"Does this mean you can get me on the aft of that bireme," Alerio questioned, "while keeping the boat clear of grappling hooks?"

"I am a Lieutenant of the Rhodian Navy," Perseus boasted. "I was sailing before I could walk. There is no pirate who can throw far enough or accurate enough to trap us."

"Besides, if any get lucky," Teppo assured Alerio, "my blade will be there to cut the lines."

"Lieutenant Archos get me on that vessel," Alerio instructed.

He walked to the front of the boat for some privacy and looked out over the water with unfocused eyes. As the wind blew in his face, he tasted the salt air and prayed.

"Goddess Nenia, you have been with me through campaigns, skirmishes, scouting missions, ambushes, deceptions, and errands of revenge. When I fought in those situations, I expected you to take me at any moment," Alerio intoned to his deity. "During the coming action, I will finally meet you. Hopefully, as you spirit my soul to Hades, I can thank you in person for your guidance over the years. And I can apologize for doubting your value when I was on Sardinia. Until we meet, I ask one more thing. Allow me to send you enough dead pirates to delay the Cilician ship before you come for my soul."

Alerio's eyes refocused and he felt a little disappointment. No pressure on his back announced the presence of Nenia Dea looking over his shoulder. For the first time in a long time, Alerio Carvilius Sisera was going into battle alone.

***

All things were relative. A sprinting man appeared slow compared to a galloping horse, and both were slower than an arrow in flight. Yet the man had the ability to turn in a tight radius. The horse less so, and the arrow, not at all. Such was the difference between the long ship-of-war with its massive sail, and the coastal trader a quarter of the bireme's size.

Coming from the pirate's flank, Perseus worked the rear oar using the wind as well as Teppo's powerful muscles on the oars for speed. Grappling hooks arched through the sky and splashed into the sea. As the lines were recoiled, the trading boat sailed out of range and towards another section. Those hooks tumbled through the air and, just short of the coastal trading boat, they dropped into the water.

The Cilician Captain and his ship's officers ran down the center board shouting for their rowers to capture the boat. At the rear of the bireme, the boat cut inward and vanished behind the aft boards. The officers stopped, alerted the rowers near the rear to be ready to throw. They waited for the boat to come around from behind the ship-of-war. And they waited until, the pirate Captain noticed the small sail curving away in the other direction.

"Port side," he bellowed to the man on the steering platform. "Turn us to port."

He glared at the trader as the boat returned to its original track. Under sail and with one-man rowing, it headed towards the southeast.

"Can you believe that?" he laughed. "I've seventy of Cilicia's best oarsman and they have one rower. I have a massive square rig and they have a bed sheet. How far does he think he can get?"

Another thing that was relative. The power of a ship-of-war required harnessing. No matter how much wind filled the sail or how many oars dipped into the sea, without direction, the ship could not fulfill its purpose of pursuing an enemy.

The Captain noticed his ship had not turned to port. Irritated, he twisted to stare at his steering deck and his mouth fell open.

Tribune Alerio Sisera stood over the body of the navigator. After fitting a Cilician helmet over his head, and strapping on a shield, he saluted the Captain.

"Under the authority of Council/General Aulus Calatinus," Alerio shouted. "I claim this vessel as a trophy for the Roman Republic. You will submit or face the consequences."

His words had no real meaning and were said to give the pirates pause. They chuckled at one man demanding their surrender. The humor did the trick and they delayed before taking up weapons. In the gap between Alerio's arrival and the fight, two things happened.

The sail on the coastal trader reached the horizon. A moment later, Perseus, Teppo, and Symeon vanished. From then on, the pirates needed either luck or fate to find the boat.

And soon, the coastal trader would sail into the protection of a trio of Rhodian warships.

The other thing that happened was personal. When a big oarsman picked up a sharp and massive battle axe, Alerio felt a warmth on his shoulder blade. And his gladius rose as if guided by another presence to point at the oarsman.

"Come on big man," Alerio challenged the rower. "I have someone who you are dying to meet."

Chapter 27 – Battle at the Aft Deck

The ax gave a hint to the big guy's fighting style as did his massive shoulders. Straight on, overhead chop, designed over many fights to split a shield and segment the defender underneath it. Hoisting the ax as he ran, the big man got a foot on the platform.

Before he came fully up and could deliver the killing chop, a shield swiped his left side spinning him to the right. Caught unbalanced on the edge of the steering platform, he was stabbed with a gladius and kicked off the deck. The injured oarsman's body did not hurt anyone as he rotated and fell back into the crowd. But the big man's battle ax, tumbling from his hands, split another rower's forehead.

Alerio rapped his gladius on the shield. After each tap, the Noric steel rang as if the blade was singing. Hearing the music of battle, Alerio added his voice to the song.

"Demetrius is knocking
Show him no pity."

278

Two pirates rushed the steering platform. Shoulder to shoulder, they charged.

Alerio dropped to a knee and caught one on his shield. With a heave, he launched the man up and back. As his partner flew, the second one caught a length of steel in his groin. Pivoting on the knee, Alerio chopped the first one's neck.

"The Prince was very snippy
Against our walled city."

Two men bleeding out on the aft deck made the boards slippery.

Three men jumped to the platform and lost their footing. Alerio hammered one, stabbed another, and kicked the third. Then he repeated the assaults in different order until all three were dead.

"Let him whine let him get snitty
Against our walled city
From brave Rhodes he fled."

Bodies equaled barriers and the next pair had to step high over corpses while keeping their balance. Smacks from the shield put both down. And while a stab took out one, the second pirate scrambled back and off the platform to safety.

"Show him no pity
Remain behind the walls
Do not let Demetrius in."

Alerio sang then finished the verse with raps on the edge of the shield. "Tap. Tap. Tap. Tap."

***

The Cilician Captain could justify losing men while taking a prize ship. Or even in a fight with another pirate crew. But having his men see their companions and, in some, cases family members murdered by one man was undermining his authority.

"Demetrius is knocking
Do not let him in."

Alerio sang as he paced between bodies and glared at the shipload of rowers.

Then a ship's officer stepped forward and announced, "I am Captain Mirza."

"Captain, you need to coach your men on staying awake while on guard duty," Alerio told him. "Especially to be watchful when guarding prisoners."

"What do you mean?" Mirza demanded.

"Your two sentries at the pig pen," Alerio described. "They were sitting together which is bad form. And they both faced the prisoners and the hogs. It was easy to come up behind them and feed them to the pigs."

Alerio wanted the crew mad. Angry mobs killed their opponents and did it quickly. Vengeful men might decide to torture a murderer. Alerio did not like that idea.

A satisfying rumble of rage ran through the crew. Formalities out of the way, it was time to fight and die.

"Are you going to just stand there?" Alerio barked. He rapped on the edge of the shield with the gladius. "Or are you cowards going to punish me."

Tap. Tap. Tap. Tap.

***

They came for Alerio in a mob. Except, the center board on a bireme was not wide. Pushing, shoving, and trying to be the first to visit revenge on the man who killed their crew mates, caused dozens to fall off the boards. They landed hard on the rower benches. Adding to the chaos, some grabbed arms for balance taking more members of the rushing mob down with them.

Alerio braced, sang, and watched to see who would make it out of the stampede.

"The Prince wants the children
To raise as yearlings."

Three abreast was the limit of the boards when it reached the steering platform. If any made it to the deck, they would have the full ten feet, beam to beam, for maneuvering.

Alerio realized it and met the pirates at the end of the boards with bashing and stabbing. He held until the weight of several dead on his legs and the mass pushing against him forced a retreat.

"What can we do to save our kin
Remain behind the walls."

The pirates crowded around in a tightly packed formation. His endeavor to anger them worked too well.

Arms swung swords and knives, but they were restricted by the other pirates packed in beside them.

Alerio blocked the strikes with the shield. His back touched the steering brace for the rear oar, and he thought about ending the fight. He had two choices. Drop the shield, locate the longest sword, and jump on the blade. Or dive over the rail and feed the fish. Then a soft voice in his mind suggested, "Finish the song."

In times of high stress, some people see in slow motion. Arms and blades floated, making them easy to block. And decisions could be put off for pride and the opportunity to end a song.

"Do not let him in
Remain behind the walls
Do not let Demetrius in."

Because his shield and gladius were occupied, Alerio voiced the, *"Tap. Tap. Tap. Tap."*

***

The entire ship lifted from the water and men fell to the side in a mass of bodies. When the bireme settled, it listed to one side. Following the upheaval, a horrible wrenching and scraping of wood vibrated throughout the pirate ship.

"Get to your oars. Get to your oars," the ship's officers ordered. "We are under attack."

And as quickly as the mob crossed the steering deck and pinned Alerio, they withdrew and ran to their rowing stations.

On the side of the pirate's bireme, a Rhodian trihemiolia backstroked and extracted its ram from the Cilician's hull.

"Tribune, can you swim?" Commander Izador called across the divide between ships.

The Rhodian vessel backed away and did an impossible wiggle as oars in separate sections rocked the bow and stern in different directions.

"I need a bridge, sir," Alerio shouted back.

The trihemiolia leaped forward, swerved, and two oars at midship extended out. Alerio jumped to the rail and hopped onto the oar blades. Balancing on the impromptu bridge, he walked the oaken oars to the Rhodian vessel.

***

"We need to teach you how to swim," Izador remarked when Alerio climbed over the rail.

"All Legionaries can swim, Commander," Alerio told him. Holding up the Noric gladius, he exclaimed. "I did not want to leave this behind."

"Get us out of these waters," Izador instructed his ship's officers. "The Cilicians have six ships-of-war around here and I don't want to get tangled up in a sea battle."

"Yes, sir," the Captain of the warship acknowledged. Plus, he added. "Glad you made it, Tribune."

"Thank you," Alerio replied to the surprise congratulations. Then he asked. "Perseus, Petya, and Symeon, did you find them?"

"Symeon Vasil is on Lieutenant Niels' ship heading for Rhodes," the Commander replied. "Lieutenant Perseus and Sergeant Petya are telling everyone that you are a one-man army."

"That's a bit much, sir," Alerio commented. "They did a great job. Oh, I told the eight crewmen from the Good Themis that you would wait two days before leaving Crete."

"We can do that," Izador assured him. "I imagine Pasi Vasil will have a nice reward for you when we get back."

"I don't want a reward," Alerio insisted. "I rescued the boy to save my reputation. I need to make inroads with the Rhodian military."

"I understand that," he responded. "But wealthy men think everyone is either out to cheat them or looking for a payment of some kind."

"Can my success be shifted to credit with your military?" Alerio asked.

"Tribune Sisera, you are in excellent standing with our Navy," Izador informed him. "But we are a Democracy, placing the final decision about you with the citizenship."

"You mean Chief Magistrate Niels," Alerio guessed.

"He is the people's representative," Izador confirmed. "Your status is up to him."

"I don't think he likes me," Alerio complained.

"You are correct," Izador agreed. "You insulted his family. But that can wait for later. Right now, you need to get cleaned up and changed for the party."

"What party?" Alerio inquired.

"Perseus put it to a vote," Izador replied. "You are going to become an honorary Lieutenant in the Rhodian military."

"Well, that should solidify my position," Alerio stated.

"Not necessarily," Izador advised. "Your rank won't make Magistrate Niels like you anymore. Now go find a sailor with a rope and bucket and get cleaned up."

Chapter 28 – The City of Rhodes

Alerio climbed down from the carriage and marveled at the villa. Located three miles from the harbor, the main house sat on the side of a hill and offered a partial view of the sea from the driveway. He could only imagine the majestic scene from the rear.

"What do I owe you?" he asked the coachman.

"Nothing, Lieutenant Sisera," the driver replied. "Master Vasil has taken care of it."

Ever since Alerio returned from Crete, Pasi Vasil had organized an apartment, meals, entertainment, almost everything Alerio needed. Except for one thing. He would not or could not arrange a meeting with Chief Magistrate Kolya Niels. The invitation for a midday meal, Alerio hoped, was a step in that direction.

A house servant held the front door open.

"Right this way, sir," he invited Alerio. "Master Vasil awaits your pleasure on the veranda."

Open and airy, the house, as others on the Isle of Rhodes, was designed to allow breezes to blow through the rooms. On the back patio, Alerio found a table loaded with fruits, cured meats, raw vegetables, a selection of olives, and a pitcher of wine. At a second table, a man with ink-stained fingers, a stack of papyrus paper, and a bottle of ink nodded in greeting.

"Tribune Sisera, can you write?" the scribe inquired.

"Thanks to my mother, I can write in Latin," Alerio told him. "And from experience I am able to scribble legible notes in Etruscan and Umbrian. But those are the limits of my letters."

"Latin will be sufficient," the scribe declared.

"Sufficient for what?" Alerio demanded.

"To write a letter to Senator Maximus,"
Pasi Vasil answered.

The merchant came from a side door, walked directly to Alerio, and offered his hand. They clasped palms and Pasi waved Alerio to a chair.

"What does my adopted father have to do with anything?" Alerio asked.

"I propose a business venture," he explained. "I will send two of my largest transports to Rome with grain from Egypt and goods from Asia Minor. But it is a large investment."

"A considerable investment," Alerio confirmed. "And very trusting of you to send cargo blindly without an agreement in place."

"Very shrewd of you to recognize that," Pasi commented. "I, of course, expect goods and gold back from your father. But as you pointed out, I have no contract with Spurius Carvilius Maximus."

"You want me to write a letter of introduction," Alerio guessed, "and spell out some of the terms."

"That, yes, plus I need some sort of collateral," Pasi Vasil informed him.

"I don't have credit in Rhodes or that amount of coins," Alerio informed the merchant.

"I realize your problems, and I do not expect you to provide surety for your father," Pasi explained. "I expect you to be the guarantee. At least until the ships return."

"You want me to volunteer to be a hostage on Rhodes?" Alerio asked. He jumped to his feet and inhaled several times to cool his temper before speaking. "I am a Legion staff

286

officer. Not a merchant Prince free to spend months lounging around."

"Allow me to offer a different viewpoint," Pasi advised while holding out both hands to stop Alerio from leaving. "My navigators estimate the voyage will take one hundred and fifty days for the round trip. Now consider this. If Magistrate Niels denies your credentials as an emissary, he can order you out of Rhodian territory and thus end your mission. But with a contract binding you to Rhodes and me, he cannot banish you. You will have one hundred and fifty days to change his mind. Plus, I'll work on your behalf to get you recognized as a military attaché."

Alerio sat, put his head in his hands, and attempted to analyze the situation logically.

"Wine, Tribune Sisera?" Symeon Vasil inquired.

Looking between his fingers, Alerio studied the small frame and the bright eyes. They no longer displayed stress and exhaustion.

"You appear well," Alerio commented. He took the mug from the boy and saluted with it. "Master Vasil. You have an extraordinary young man here. During our escape, he acted as the coxswain, setting the stroke rate with a beat and a song. I was truly honored to be a part of his adventure. You, sir, have done an excellent job of raising him."

"That is an interesting remark," Pasi related. "I was thinking the same about you and your father. Honorable to a fault, is not a talent you are born with, it's a learned trait. Will you write the letter to your father and allow me to help you?"

***

Alerio's hobnailed boots echoed on the tile walkway. On his first visit to the government building, he wore traveling

clothing and was under arrest. For this trip he donned his
Tribune armor and had his staff officer's helmet stuffed under
his left arm.

"Good day, Chief Magistrate Niels," Alerio stated while
saluting. "May I present myself and my credentials."

"I have reviewed your letters and have had numerous
people swear to your character," Kolya Niels replied. His face
twisted displaying an internal struggle. Finally, he voiced his
thoughts. "You held a knife at my son's throat and for that I
should exile you. But there seems to be a business matter that
I cannot ignore."

"Thank you for your consideration," Alerio
acknowledged, hoping a little humility would sway the
Magistrate.

"I will not recognize you at this time," Niels declared.
"But as you are required to stay, I am issuing you a warrant
as an observer for Rhodian forces on Asia Minor. I will review
your behavior before the shipping contract is fulfilled."

"Thank you, Chief Magistrate," Alerio said.

Then he about faced and marched out of the building.
He didn't get what he wanted but the situation had triggered
a trading agreement. Despite the setback, he still had the
opportunity to complete his mission as a military attaché.
And all it required was for Alerio to stay out of trouble for
one hundred and fifty days. It couldn't be that difficult, could
it?

Chapter 29 – Lack of Analytical Thinking

Alerio and Commander Izador sat on a stone wall looking up at the giant statue of Helios in the harbor.

"Forty-eight years ago, the son of King Antigonus sailed to Rhodes and began a siege," Izador described. "He built enormous weapons to break our walls."

"Demetrius, right?" Alerio guessed. "But he never broke the walls of Rhodes."

"Correct. How did you know?" inquired the Commander.

"I heard the legend in lyrics while escaping from the pirates," Alerio replied. "I understand it's a schoolyard song."

Commander Izador smiled at the reference as if he remembered singing the song as a schoolboy. Then he continued.

"After a year, Demetrius sailed away, leaving behind all of the siege engines. To give you an idea of the size, one was a massive battering ram that required a thousand men to swing," Izador told Alerio. "After the King's son abandoned the machines, they were either melted down for metal or sold for coins. Then the citizens decided to build a statue to honor Helios, the Sun God, for delivering them from King Antigonus."

"And that's how Rhodes ended up with a one hundred and five-foot tall statue?" Alerio submitted.

"Not at first. The initial discussion and contract called for a fifty-foot figure," Izador corrected. "A native son of Rhodes, Chares of Lindos, was contacted for the sculpture. He quickly worked up an estimate for the iron, bronze, granite, and the labor required to complete the statue. Overjoyed at the prospect of building the project, he gave an aggressive estimate."

"It must have been a great honor to be associated with developing a task of that size," Alerio noted while scanning upward to the face of Helios. "Bidding low made sense."

"After reviewing the estimate, the citizens cheered Chares as a hero. His cost was so low they demanded to know how much to double the size of the statue," the Commander explained. "Chares, caught up in the heat of adoration, is reported to have said double the size, double the cost."

"It is a huge statue," Alerio remarked. "How did they get the head up there?"

"The engineers ramped up dirt as they built the statue and slid the head up the slope to mount it," Izador responded. "That was just one of the issues with doubling the size of Helios. Beyond the cost of the ramp, the iron and the bronze requirements increased by eighteen-fold. The additional charges bankrupted Chares which led to his suicide. A sculpture named Laches, with a new budget, completed the statue."

A sailor jogged up and saluted Izador.

"Commander. We are ready to launch when you are," he announced.

"Come, Tribune Sisera," Izador instructed while jumping down from the wall. "Your ride awaits."

"The Colossus of Rhodes," Alerio said admiring the statue of Helios. "It is a wonder for the ages. I can understand a builder getting carried away with excitement over it."

"But is it worth a man's life," Izador inquired, "to please the masses?"

Alerio leaped off the wall and they marched across the sand to the waiting warships.

The End

A note from J. Clifton Slater

You are amazing, and from the bottom of my heart, I thank you for joining me on this adventure. Book 14 in the Clay Warrior Stories has taken us from the battlefields of Sicily to the Colossus of Rhodes on the Isle of Rhodes.

Tullia Major's song is from Roman legend. As the oldest daughter of the 6th King of Rome, Tullia Major married Lucius Tarquinius Superbus. But her sister, the Minor, wanted to be queen. Minor seduced Superbus and convinced him to murder Minor's husband and the King, while Minor poisoned Tullia Major. Thus, Superbus became the 7th King and Tullia Minor became the Queen of Rome.

In the Clay Warrior Stories books, I attempt to use quotes from famous Generals and philosophers who lived in times before the date of the story. In keeping with that theme, all the Consuls of the Republic mentioned in the series were Consuls / Generals in history. On Sicily, I introduced Tribune Marcus Calpurnius Flamma, a real hero.

Tribune Flamma, in 258 B.C., did take 300 Legionaries and draw the Carthaginian forces to a fight on a hill. By the sacrifice of the infantrymen, the Tribune allowed the trapped Legion of Consul/General Aulus Calatinus to escape an ambush.

History does not tell us much about the staff officer except he was awarded the Grass Crown by the grateful Legion. I took advantage of the gap in history to fill in details that helped the story of Rome's Tribune.

Did the Spartans at the Battle of Thermopylae influence Flamma? I have no idea. But he got the idea for 300 Legionaries from somewhere, so why not the famous Spartan battle of 480 B.C.? For readers who look up ancient battlefields be careful of the Battle of Thermopylae. Search for the monument built to honor the 300 Spartans and the shrine dedicated to the 700 Thespians' Hoplites who also died there. The ground has silted in, and the sea levels have changed over the last twenty-five hundred years. Today, the cliffs and the narrow battle site are located far inland from the Gulf of Malian in Greece and buried under yards of silt.

History reports that Archimedes did call out Eureka, Greek for 'I found it'. His exclamation resulted from an observation of the water displaced when he got into a bath. From a bath, Archimedes Phidias of Syracuse, the serial inventor, and creative mathematician, created many equations still used today.

During Alerio's travels, he encountered the sea snail trade. A cash crop in antiquity, Murex sea snails from one location were harvested and used to color indigo dye. And from the islands of Kithira and Crete, those sea snails created dye for Tyrian purple. Once a growing industry, snail traders are long gone from the world of modern business. With other chemicals available to use in dyes, the process of harvesting snails to color cloth is mostly a lost art.

The Aegean Sea and the eastern Mediterranean were terrorized by pirates in antiquity. They were commonly known as Cilicians because the islands and nation of Cilicia on the coast of Asia Minor produced so many of the organized pirate bands. They thrived between the rise and fall of various navies in the region until the Roman General Pompey crushed the organizations in 67-66 B.C.

On the Isle of Rhodes, Alerio experienced the Colossus of Rhodes and learned the size and the builder's story behind the statue. The Colossus stood from 280 B.C. until it was destroyed by an earthquake in 226 B.C. Lucky for me, the statue honoring Helios, the Sun God, existed during the time of Rome's Tribune.

I am J. Clifton Slater and I write military adventure both future and ancient. Because I do extensive research and most of it does not make it into the books, I do blogs about ancient topics. You can find them on my website as well as a sign-up form for my newsletter that will start in 2021.

As always, I enjoy getting your emails and reading your comments. If you enjoyed Rome's Tribune, please leave a written review on Amazon. Every review helps other readers find the stories.

If you have comments, please e-mail me.

E-mail: GalacticCouncilRealm@gmail.com

To get the latest information about my books, visit my website. There you can sign up for the newsletter and read blogs about ancient history.

Website: www.JCliftonSlater.com

Facebook: Galactic Council Real and Clay Warrior Stories

Until we travel together again, Alerio and I salute you and wish you good health and vigor. Rah!

I write military adventure both future and ancient.
Books by J. Clifton Slater

Historical Adventure – *Clay Warrior Stories series*
#1 Clay Legionary   #2 Spilled Blood
#3 Bloody Water   #4 Reluctant Siege
#5 Brutal Diplomacy   #6 Fortune Reigns
#7 Fatal Obligation   #8 Infinite Courage
#9 Deceptive Valor   #10 Neptune's Fury
#11 Unjust Sacrifice   #12 Muted Implications
#13 Death Caller   #14 Rome's Tribune
#15 Deranged Sovereignty
#16 Uncertain Honor   #17 Tribune's Oath
#18 Savage Birthright #19 Abject Authority

Novels of the 2nd Punic War – *A Legion Archer series*
#1 Journey from Exile   #2 Pity the Rebellious
#3 Heritage of Threat   #4 A Legion legacy

Military Science Fiction – *Call Sign Warlock series*
#1 Op File Revenge   #2 Op File Treason
#3 Op File Sanction

Military Science Fiction – *Galactic Council Realm series*
#1 On Station   #2 On Duty
#3 On Guard   #4 On Point

Printed in Great Britain
by Amazon

42714365R00165